R
Force
by

Hurricane Reese

"I'm still in book hangover heaven."
—Love Bytes

"Excellent book and there is so much to learn about both of these characters. Never assume you know a person just as they appear to be on the outside."
—Diverse Reader

"How do I even begin to explain the love I have for this book? It was unexpected, surprising, and incredibly emotional...."
—OptimuMM

Typhoon Toby

"With a strong plot, an expertly crafted cast of supporting characters, and deep empathy, Merrill's novel will keep readers hooked."
—Publisher's Weekly

"This was definitely a book that I'm thrilled to have read and I'm excited to see the next story in this series"
—Gay Book Reviews

By R.L. MERRILL

FORCES OF NATURE
Hurricane Reese
Typhoon Toby

SUMMER OF HUSH
Summer of Hush

Published by DREAMSPINNER PRESS
www.dreamspinnerpress.com

R.L. MERRILL
SUMMER OF *Hush*

Published by
DREAMSPINNER PRESS

5032 Capital Circle SW, Suite 2, PMB# 279,
Tallahassee, FL 32305-7886 USA
www.dreamspinnerpress.com

This is a work of fiction. Names, characters, places, and incidents either are the product of author imagination or are used fictitiously, and any resemblance to actual persons, living or dead, business establishments, events, or locales is entirely coincidental.

Summer of Hush
© 2019, 2020 R.L. Merrill

Cover Art
© 2019, 2020 Kanaxa
Cover content is for illustrative purposes only and any person depicted on the cover is a model.

All rights reserved. This book is licensed to the original purchaser only. Duplication or distribution via any means is illegal and a violation of international copyright law, subject to criminal prosecution and upon conviction, fines, and/or imprisonment. Any eBook format cannot be legally loaned or given to others. No part of this book may be reproduced or transmitted in any form or by any means, electronic or mechanical, including photocopying, recording, or by any information storage and retrieval system, without the written permission of the Publisher, except where permitted by law. To request permission and all other inquiries, contact Dreamspinner Press, 5032 Capital Circle SW, Suite 2, PMB# 279, Tallahassee, FL 32305-7886, USA, or www.dreamspinnerpress.com.

Mass Market Paperback ISBN: 978-1-64108-186-3
Trade Paperback ISBN: 978-1-64405-434-5
Digital ISBN: 978-1-64405-433-8
Library of Congress Control Number: 2019903601
Mass Market Paperback published January 2020
v. 1.0

Printed in the United States of America
∞
This paper meets the requirements of
ANSI/NISO Z39.48-1992 (Permanence of Paper).

To my daughter—I'm grateful you introduced me to Warped Tour. You gave me a whole new way of experiencing the music I love. Thank you for some of my best concert memories.

To my son, who makes the music that warms my heart, thank you for sharing your talent with the world. You're a rock star.

You both make my world go round.

Acknowledgments

I AM grateful to the team at Dreamspinner Press for believing in my stories and sharing them with the world. Special thanks to Sue Brown-Moore for your initial feedback on this story. Someday I really will write that category romance. To Liz, thank you for continuing to help me hone my stories into something special. And thank you to Lynn and Elizabeth for all of your support.

My fellow Dreamspinner authors, many thanks for the hours of entertainment you've given me reading your books. I'm thrilled to be a part of the team.

Special thanks to my beta readers, Marcy and Wendy, for always being there to handle my crazy. To my members of Ro's Roadies of Romance and my Goddesses who have been with me since Haunted, I think you'll love Hush. You guys rock.

My dream team—Ellay, Kimberlie, Kerrigan, and Cynthia. You are always there when I need you, and your feedback has been invaluable on this journey. I love the community we've formed and will treasure your friendship always.

The members of the San Francisco Area and Silicon Valley chapters of RWA are some of the most brilliant and generous writers in the industry today. I love our meetings and the sense of creative collaboration and determination you inspire in me. I've learned so much from all of you, and I hope that I have been able to support you as well. I'm also grateful for the online camaraderie of the Rainbow Romance Writers, and I'm proud to be a member.

My Camp NaNo cabin from last year, thank you so much for keeping the momentum going. This was my April 2018 project, and though it's grown and blossomed since then, its roots are firmly in the Bay Area Sexy S'mores. #getshitwrit

And I save the most important for last—my husband, my children, my family. I love you and appreciate all you do to encourage and motivate me. Someday the patio room will have a visible floor.

Stay Tuned for more Rock 'n' Romance....

Chapter One

ORGANIZERS HAVE announced that this will be the last-ever summer-long Warped Tour, and I'm torn. The industry is moving forward and times are changing, but the youth of America has found their tribe year after year at this beloved festival. Despite a few instances of bad behavior, the positivity spread by concert goers, nonprofits, and the musicians has never been replicated. I will be checking out a few dates on this last hurrah, and I hope to capture the magic.

"Did you see this?"

Los held up his phone and displayed it like Vanna White in all her glory.

"New Guru?" Silas asked, his heart rate making the jump to lightspeed.

"'The Last Warped Hurrah.' He's coming. You'll for sure get to meet him." Los wiggled his eyebrows at Silas, who tried to play the whole thing off as though he wasn't ready to start jumping on the couch and doing back flips.

"That's cool," he said, hiding his excitement. *The possibilities....* He'd had his hopes up that he might meet him two years ago when they played Warped, but the Guru never said what show he attended. Silas had analyzed his posts to see if he could get any idea where it might have been. Ridiculous. Tons of dates, a blur of venues, and thousands of screaming fans in the hot sun—it was hopeless. The guy didn't answer private messages either. Because he'd tried that.

"Says here he'll be posting about the shows," Los said, still reading through the blog while waiting for his hair dye to set. Jordan volunteered to be their hair maintenance person because he'd gone through barber school before he became a rock 'n' roller.

"Dude, stop moving," Jordan scolded Los. He was trying to avoid getting black dye on his red T-shirt, but Los kept moving around.

"Sorry."

"Man, it's definitely time to touch up these roots. Must be tough being a blond Mexican and keeping your hair dyed black. How does that happen anyway?"

"When your Mexican dad marries a chick from the Netherlands," Los said. "I fucking speak Spanish and Dutch. And I smoke excellent weed whenever I am visiting family."

"No weed on the bus, Los. You promised," Silas reminded him.

"I know. I didn't bring any." Los went back to reading.

Silas checked the tour schedule hanging at the front of the bus. "There are thirty-eight dates on this tour. He could be at any of them. It's not like anyone knows what he looks like. All of his videos are animated."

"Maybe he'll post about the different shows, like who he sees. And Brains is doing his workshops. Dude—"

"Dude, why are you guys being so loud?" Billy Brains climbed from his bunk on the tour bus and stretched his lanky body in the narrow hallway. The band had held its final run-through last night at their rehearsal space in Oakland and was headed to Pomona for the opening date of the show that weekend.

"Because, bruh, Silas might finally get to meet his crush."

Silas threw a rag, but Los dodged it and was reprimanded by Jordan for moving again. It could have had anything on it, but they were just getting started on their tour, so the likelihood it had already been tarnished with some sort of bodily fluid was low. By the third or fourth leg of the tour, you never knew what kind of funk it could be contaminated with.

"Just let it go, Los."

"Why?" Los asked. "You've been sprung on this guy since…."

Silas knew it was hard for all of them to talk about it and they still tended to trail off whenever the topic was brought up.

"He did a beautiful piece about Gavin," Brains said softly as he slid into the booth next to Silas and rubbed at the stubble on Silas's freshly shaved head. "Unlike the rest of the press. If I never have to talk to another reporter…."

Silas dropped his head on Brains's shoulder. "You won't have to." Brains was right. The press had crucified the band after Gavin's death, and they'd all agreed only Silas would give interviews from then on. There were several news sources that were *persona non grata* with them. Brains was their drummer and truly their rock. Without his determination, songwriting talent, and experience in the business, there was no way they would have made it through the last two years. "Sorry we woke you up. It's Los's fault."

"It's all right. I wasn't sleeping. I was watching one of Chris Motionless's makeup videos. I fucking love how he does his eyes."

Brains loved makeup and had a huge obsession with shows on horror- and fantasy-inspired art. He'd brought his kit with him to the table to experiment. Silas often let him practice on him. His stage makeup creations were badass.

Los threw the rag back and Silas caught it. "He's got to meet him," he insisted. "It's the last Warped!"

"How do we make this happen?" Brains asked. "Oh, I know. Let's hit the socials. Spread the word out that we want the Guru to come to my TEI workshop. We'll send him a free ticket if he'll come."

"Yeah, put it on your Snapchat story, Silas," Los said. "You have an assload of followers. Someone is bound to see it."

"And what do I say, huh? 'Gee whiz, Guru. Pretty please, come to my drummer's workshop for a meet-cute'? That's lame."

"Wait, isn't he always claiming that no one can beat him at *Mortal Kombat*? Challenge him to a duel on our tour bus or something," Jordan chimed in. He finished Los's roots and took his utensils to the sink to clean up.

"No one knows who he is for a reason," Silas said. "Just forget it."

Silas didn't want to get his hopes up. Again. He needed positivity. This tour was going to be hard enough. It was his first time touring without Gavin, and while he was confident the album was a great showcase for their new guitarist, Jordan Barrett, and held enough of Gavin's spirit to be a hit, he was on edge. They needed this summer to be huge, or else it was time to wrap up Hush and move forward in his life without his true loves—music and his best friend.

"If it's meant for you guys to meet, it's gonna happen," Brains said as he looked in his lighted mirror and smeared foundation on his face. He did a powder overlay and then pulled out his liquid eyeliner. The dude was smooth. Chicks everywhere envied his application techniques.

"I don't know. You really believe in that kind of fate shit?"

Silas wanted to. *Oh*, how he wanted to. But the next part of that wish was that the Guru was just as incredible in person as he was in his writing, and that was probably pushing his luck.

"You know I believe it," Brains said, finishing his eyeliner. He used some dark eyeshadow in midnight blue and deep bruise purple and then lined his eyes with a glitter liner that looked stunning. "Fate has always kept me going. It's what brought us together, right?"

True, the formation of their band had been a sort of kismet. Brains, Los, Gavin, and Silas had all been in the same place in their lives with all the magical elements that made their music stand out among their metalcore brethren. If Brains wanted to chalk it up to some mystical force, Silas could buy that.

"Fate is a powerful thing," Jordan said as he wandered back over with a beer. "You never know when it's your time, am I right? I never thought I'd end up with you guys, and here we are."

Los fist-bumped him. "Damn right and a-fucking-men for that."

Brains and Silas joined in the fist bumps, which turned into some weird, obscure Wonder Twins Power references, and pretty soon they were all cracking up.

Yeah, Fate had been fickle with Silas and his band. She'd given them the world on a platter, then yanked it away. Everything had crashed and broken into pieces, but she was slowly putting them back together. Would she continue to grace them this summer?

Chapter Two

KRISH'S FINGER hovered over the Play button.
What if it's not enough?

Krish sat in his bedroom. His last final was this morning, meaning he'd unceremoniously finished college. He came straight home from school to start his new adventure. But before the insanity started, he had something very important to listen to—an album he'd been waiting two whole years to hear. The band was Hush. The album, *Sunrise*, was their fifth studio album since their founding in 2008.

It would break his heart to give a negative review to his favorite band. His alter ego, the Guru, was known for his brutally honest metal reviews. He had a million subscribers on his YouTube channel, where he posted weekly animated shows, five hundred thousand Twitter users who followed his musical and political rants, and his blog posts were often mentioned on such popular sites as Metal Hammer, Loudwire, and even HuffPost. He owed his readers an accurate review, even if he was conflicted.

What if losing their guitarist meant the end of Hush? He'd loved them since his brother introduced him to music—specifically metalcore—and though he loved them best, he tried to be impartial to all of the bands he reviewed, from live performances and new albums to whatever he felt the need to riff on.

And then there were his posts about social issues, namely mental health and the LGBTQ community. Those tended to get really personal, and after Gavin West committed suicide, his love of music and his personal life intersected. The blog he wrote about Gavin's death was his most viewed ever and the one he almost didn't post.

"Krish, darling, did you want anything to eat? You didn't have lunch, sweetheart. I am worried about you."

Krish's mom stuck her head in his room and found him in the same position—earbuds in, finger over the button, and holding his breath.

"Is it the new album from Hush?"

Krish nodded.

"How is it?"

"I'm afraid to play it."

His mom patted him on the shoulder. She knew how devastated he had been by the death of one of his favorite musicians nearly two years prior. She'd cried alongside him, just as she had a year before that when they lost his brother.

"Whatever they've done, it will be beautiful. They're talented boys."

Krish smiled up at his mom. How he managed to land the coolest Indian mom on the planet was a mystery he'd yet to solve. She indulged his every passion, from music to politics to books and his guilty pleasure, video games. Her own childhood had not been so free, so she was determined her boys would be able to do whatever they wanted with their lives. For Vivaan, that meant joining the Marines after college. For Krish, it meant a career in music journalism, and now that he'd finished his degrees, he was anxious to get started.

"Have you finished packing?" she asked him.

Krish swallowed hard. *Warped Tour.* The other benefit of his blog was that he'd caught the attention of *Alt-Scene* magazine. Their assistant to the editor in chief had arranged for Krish to join the tour. He'd remain anonymous and only the tour office manager would know who he was and why he was there. To everyone else he was just her intern. He'd post his blog as usual but also work on a piece for the magazine. If the magazine liked how he covered the tour, there was a full-time position waiting for him at the end of it.

"Mostly. Jake's not picking me up until Friday morning. That means I have one more day to stress over what I can and can't fit into the one duffel bag I'm allowed to bring on the bus."

She smiled at him and tugged on his shaggy curls. "A whole summer on a bus. I hope you made room for air freshener and hand sanitizer."

"There will be women on the bus. I'm sure between them they'll have something that smells nice."

"It's been wonderful having you home," she said, her voice softer. "I'm going to miss you."

"I'll miss you too, but it's only two months," he answered. Krish had moved home when they received the devastating news about his brother, and he'd commuted to UC San Diego for the remainder of his time there, needing to be near his parents as they all worked through their grief. Now that he'd graduated, it was time to start the next chapter in his life, and he'd been given the opportunity of a lifetime.

"The first two months of the rest of your life. This is an exciting time for you."

He heard the tears behind her voice. He couldn't look at her or he'd be lost.

"I wish he were here," Krish said quietly. His brother should be having his own adventures while cheering on his little Guru. But Krish was on his own now, and it was time to think about not only starting a career and leaving the nest, but standing on his own without his biggest supporter.

"I'll come down in a second." Krish hugged her waist and exhaled a shaky breath.

"I'll heat up some dinner."

"Is there any of that tandoori chicken left?" he called to her.

"I'll heat some up for you. Don't get lost up here. Just push Play."

She totally understood him. "Thanks, Mom."

She closed the door behind her, and Krish resumed his position. In less than two days, he'd be surrounded by the music he loved. He'd have his first shot at real journalism, reporting on the tour with one of alternative music's biggest magazines, and he'd get to see his favorite band live almost daily.

I'll love the album no matter what.

I owe it to them to listen objectively, and not just because of Gavin.

I'll do it for you, Vivaan.

I miss you.

He hit Play and held his breath the millisecond it took for the first song to load.

Chapter Three

SILAS TOOK the Left Foot stage on the Pomona Fairplex with the bravest smile he could manage. He strolled out to the center with his arms open wide, as though he wished to hug the entire crowd of nearly ten thousand fans who had braved the ninety-degree Southern California weather to rock out with Hush and fifty other bands today.

They greeted him with thunderous applause that went on and on for what felt like forever. He didn't bother to hide the tears that spilled from his eyes as he gestured to Gavin's spot on the stage. Thank goodness for Brains's waterproof makeup.

"Thank you, Pomona! I'm feeling the love. Gavin is feeling your love right now." He pointed up to the sky and squeezed his eyes shut to gain some composure. He purposely avoided looking to the spot on his left where Gavin's mic stand would have been, the pole lined with his trademark hot pink picks. He'd stroll out onstage, and they'd face each other seriously. Then at the appointed moment, they'd break out into their crazy jumps and head-whipping frenzies. Gavin's long black dreadlocks would dangle around his face like his heroes, Munky and Head from Korn, and during his solos, he'd flick them about. The only time the audience would get a clear shot of his gorgeous mug was when he was screaming his vocal parts to complement Silas's leads. They were a team. Well, they'd *been* a team for a long fucking time.

Silas squeezed his eyes shut once more and then let out his breath.

Today is about new beginnings and giving Jordan a phenomenal debut.

Brains started the kick drum rhythm for the opener, "Faceless," which they'd been playing for the past two tours. It had become their signature. Silas waited anxiously for the single sustained note of the guitar to begin and prayed the crowd's response would be favorable. This was Jordan's first live performance with the band. A lot was weighing on this show.

The clear, strong note began, and Jordan walked onstage with confidence, his left middle finger on the fretboard moving just enough to keep the sound steady, and his right hand hanging at his side as though he were enough of a virtuoso that he could play it all one-handed. His long black hair, cut stylishly like the scene kids wore theirs, covered one eye. The other was lined with thick black liner. The stage lighting reflected off his spider bite piercings as he moved forward with a grin on his face. *Cocky bastard.*

"Ladies and gentlemen, may I introduce Jordan Barrett!"

They didn't give the audience too much time to react as Jordan and Los ripped into a harmony that sounded so pure it surpassed Silas's expectations. He was so affected by the moment that he almost forgot to pick up the bassline until Los stood next to him and nudged him.

Then it was on. Silas sang with a power he hadn't thought he'd ever have again. He sang as though his life—the band's life—depended on it. And he was happy. He felt on top of the world, as a twenty-eight-year-old guy with two gold and two platinum records and a string of hit singles behind him should feel.

They blazed through "Faceless," "Morbid Curiosity," and "Fanatic" before playing two of the songs from *Sunrise*, their new release, which had dropped the day before. Radio had picked up the title track a couple months before, and the response from fans had been ecstatic. Silas prayed they'd receive that response today.

And sure enough, the mosh pit was one of the biggest they'd had and even the fans along the side pogoed up and down with him and the band on their closer, "Goodbye is Not Forever." It was a fucking brilliant performance. Silas felt it all the way down into the pit of doubt that had taken up residence in his gut.

The band huddled backstage in a group hug for several long moments after their set, panting and laughing together, relieved their first show was a success. They'd all been nervous about this for their own reasons. Brains was the self-appointed caretaker of the band since he was the oldest and most experienced. He was always up in his head about the start of a new tour and hadn't totally recovered from losing Gavin. Los had been anxious about having a new partner to play off of, but Jordan's skills were on par with Gavin's. And Jordan, even with his chops, was stepping into the shoes of a beloved musician. It was intimidating no matter how good you were.

And Silas felt like he'd been missing a limb. He'd had faith they could make it work once they decided to move forward, but he hadn't been sure until Jordan hit that opening note.

"I love you guys," he said as they sweated all over each other. "I love you, Gavin."

"We miss you, Gavin," Los and Brains said.

"I'm just happy I didn't fuck up," Jordan said, and the hug broke apart on a laugh. They pounded each other's backs as they walked back to their bus with their arms around each other—the three musketeers and their new recruit.

Back on the bus, Silas took several minutes to just sit with this hopeful feeling. The other guys seemed a bit stunned as well. If they could keep this up for thirty-seven more stops, they'd be in great shape. Silas prayed it wasn't a fluke.

Los tossed Silas a Gatorade from the fridge and flopped down next to him on the couch. "Let's hope we still get that response after they've all heard the new album."

Silas squeezed his thigh. "I want more."

"Los, make sure you watch me for the changes on 'Sunrise,'" Brains said as he stormed past them to the bunk area and started to strip. "It felt a little choppy."

"Bésame culo, cabrón," Los said and blew him a kiss.

Brains paused with his shorts around his knees. "Translation, please?"

"Do you seriously go commando while you're onstage?" Jordan had just joined them on the bus in time to get an eyeful of Brains's dick.

"I need freedom from constricting clothing when I perform." He shrugged and stepped out of his shorts. "I'm going to hose off before my workshop. Silas, don't let me be late."

"Ten-four, good buddy."

Jordan still stood frozen. Silas stuck out a foot and nudged the back of Jordan's knee, sparking the reflex that would make it bend.

"Jordan, let me clue you in. Brains has a reason for everything he does. Sometimes his answers are fascinating, sometimes you'll wish you never asked him the question. You'll get used to his peculiar ways soon enough."

Los belched loudly. "It's either get used to it or suffer debilitating nightmares for years to come."

Jordan shook his head and then looked down at Los. "You have nightmares?"

"Oh, absolutely," Los said as he pulled off his sweaty muscle tee and used it to wipe his face and armpits, thankfully in that order. "It took me months to overcome my fear of waking up in the morning to Brains's naked ballsack hanging in my face."

"You pulled the shortest straw," Silas said. He took a long pull on his Gatorade, realizing he'd been dangerously close to dehydration from the heat. "Shortest straw used to get the bunk under his every time. Now we leave it open for storage…and ventilation."

Jordan chuckled, and Los groaned. Silas felt his heart swell. He'd be spending the next couple of months sharing everything with these fuckers. He'd miss Gavin every day, but being on tour again and having his close friends would make it all a little less painful.

THE GUYS all went to Brains's workshop on drum technique—for moral support, and truthfully, to heckle the guy. Silas wondered if the Guru might show up, but he'd have no idea who he was anyway. How the blogger managed to remain anonymous in today's interconnected world was astonishing. His blog had no pictures, and the YouTube videos were all animated. Frustrating how you couldn't even find him in a Google Images search!

Everything went as planned at the workshop. Brains gave a talk full of complicated music theory, paired with a demonstration of techniques and some geekery about his favorite video games. He even fanboyed on his favorite drummers. No one hopped up and said, "I am the Guru," but there were plenty of adoring faces with eager questions for Brains. Some of the kids were even wearing shirts from Brains's first band, Sullen. If Brains hadn't come into Silas's life when he did, he and Gavin would likely have remained broke, unknown, and hustling on the street for gas money to get from gig to gig in their shitty VW bus that literally ran on a rubber band.

Silas watched Brains for a while, but when nothing out of the ordinary happened, he wandered on to hear some of the other presenters. Roxanne from Just Like Love, a band they'd toured with before, was talking about developing your brand with confidence. And farther down the row of tents set up backstage, guitarist Burke Dickens from the band Backdrop Silhouette was discussing guitar riffs. He was really a whiz, and Silas thought it might be worth the ass kicking he'd get from Los if he suggested his guitarist check it out.

Later that night the band caught the blistering set by Motionless in White that closed out the show. Then Silas and his bandmates had a private celebration with their crew and toasted Jordan, who was initiated by being sprayed with several cans of Cheez Whiz until he was a gooey, sticky mess, and not in a good way. At the end of the night, the guys all piled onto the bus with Lester, their driver. Their manager, Jessica, merch girl Mischa, and roadies Theo and Logan followed behind the band in a small RV. The band often took turns cooking breakfast for their crew, and Silas had volunteered to cook the next morning. He was just making up his special dipping sauce for french toast when the bathroom door slammed open. Brains stood there, naked once more, his expression intense.

"Uh, Silas?" He'd gone in to take a shower, but by the odor wafting out, he'd decided to unload his unholy bowels before cleansing. He was always the one to break the cardinal rule—bus johns were for pissing and emergency shits only.

"Dude," Los said from the table where he was restringing his guitar. He'd been so into his performance that he'd broken two strings on one of his guitars and one on the other. "What crawled up in you and died?"

"Shut up, dick. I have irritable bowel syndrome and stress exacerbates my condition. I'd say today was a pretty fucking stressful day. It's important that I listen to my body, and my body said it was time to purge all the toxic waste built up in my colon. Perhaps if you'd read that book I bought you—"

"Lord, not with the self-help literature." Los sighed as Silas joined him at the booth. "Sometimes I regret joining a band with a genius."

"No you don't." Silas kicked him under the table.

"No, I really don't. But I do regret not riding in the RV now that Sir Shits-A-Lot has debased the throne."

"Normal bowel movements are healthy. Just because you get stopped up. Your colon is like a drain begging for Liquid-Plumr—"

"My bowels are just fine, assmunch. At least the john doesn't require a ritual cleansing after I use it."

"Guys," Silas begged, his stomach turning at all the scatological references. "What was so important that you had to break the seal on that door and bring us all into your misery?"

"Well, before I was so *rudely* interrupted," he said, glaring at Los, "the Guru posted. He listened to the album."

Silas scrambled for his laptop and pulled up the link he knew by heart. The familiar splash appeared, and he held his breath.

Hush have reawakened, and it's about to get loud.

No one could predict whether metalcore darlings Hush would rise from the ashes of such a terrible loss, but I had a good feeling they would. Silas Franklin, Billy Brains, and Los Morales were not through making music, and the arrival of wunderkind guitarist Jordan Barrett seems to be the limb they needed to make themselves whole again. The new album, Sunrise, *illuminates the metalcore stage like never before. Franklin sounds pure, heartfelt, and determined on tracks "Goodbye is Not Forever," "Never Step Back," and "New Day." Franklin and Brains stepped up in their songwriting prowess, proving that Gavin West was not the only lead-quality talent in their outfit. The power combo of Morales and Barrett scorches the hits, and the tender piano bit on the cover of Alice Cooper's "How You Gonna See Me Now" shows Franklin shining in a new light. There's no doubt in the Guru's mind that Hush will dominate this last Warped Tour, and I intend to see for myself that all is well in their camp.*

"What did he say?" Los asked, trying to look over his shoulder. "Did he like it?"

Silas's lip twitched as he tried not to beam in victory.

He liked it.
He said I shined.

"Silas is in loooove—"

"Shut up." Silas threw an elbow into Los's shoulder. He knew Los was just fucking around, but it was still aggravating.

"You guys talking about the Guru?" Jordan asked as he leaned out of his bunk.

"He had nice things to say about you as well, Sir Shreds-A-Lot," Los said as he snatched the computer away from Silas and carried it over to Jordan.

"Hey, how come he gets a cool knight name?" Brains complained.

Jordan read over the review and nodded. "Right on. Hey, my brother's coming tomorrow to San Diego. You think we can get him and his friend passes to come hang out with us?" he asked.

"Is he cute?" Brains asked.

"What does he look like?" Los asked. "I think Silas needs to get laid."

"My brother is square as hell, but he's hilarious when you get him drunk. As for cute? Y'all better keep your filthy hands off him."

"Is his *friend* cute?" Brains asked.

"I don't know. What I do know is the last thing my brother needs is to get hooked up with another fucking musician."

"Sounds like there's history there," Brains said.

Jordan muttered something under his breath and went back behind the curtain of his bunk.

"He probably just wants to be left alone to watch the show," Silas said, wishing the guys would drop it. Silas wasn't sure he had the bandwidth to meet someone new… well, unless it was the Guru. He certainly would like someone to lean on when life with the band got to him, but it had to be someone who could handle the maelstrom that was his life. He would have to be a very tolerant, special, patient person.

Los threw his arm over Silas's shoulder. "Better off without 'em, that's what I think."

Silas looked at his brothers-in-music and sighed. He really had the best friends a guy could ask for. Even Jordan, who had been an acquaintance up until a year ago, had become someone he totally trusted with the band, their music, and his life. He had a mature manner of handling their grieving mess. It was as though Gavin—or God himself—had placed Jordan in their path. He'd been an easy fit from the start.

Silas stood and went to the back of the bus to change clothes in the small lounge. He needed to crawl into his bunk and sleep, but he was restless. He listened to the guys planning how they could fuck with Jordan's brother, and Jordan shared some of their more epic battles, but Silas's thoughts were a little heavier.

"You guys hatch whatever insanity you want," he called as he climbed into his bunk. "I'm going to get some sleep."

"Good night, sweetheart," Brains said.

"Sweet dreams," Jordan said.

"Don't let the bedbugs bite your dick off."

"Fuck you, Los. Good night guys." Silas shook his head and smiled to himself.

Too much emotional back-and-forth. He needed rest if he was going to make it through the next day, but all he could think of when his head hit the pillow was the possibility of meeting the Guru this summer.

Even if he did, a crush based on some guy's internet rants didn't necessarily form the basis of a strong, healthy relationship. Nor did it guarantee any sort of attraction to anything other than the guy's brain, which at this point in his life, Silas would almost prefer.

Pretty faces were plentiful on tour. He'd partaken of them for years, but finding a smart dude who could challenge him as much out of bed as in bed would be heaven. If he was going to hook up with anyone, it needed to be someone he could have the heavy conversations with. After two years without his best friend, he needed someone to fill that role in his life.

Chapter Four

JAKE BARRETT was an even bigger nerd than Krish, and that was saying something. You'd never know his brother was a metal guitar virtuoso. Krish glanced at the guy's wardrobe choice for the day—pastel plaid Bermuda shorts, Teva sandals, a mint-green polo shirt that only sort of blended with his shorts, and a maroon Vans windbreaker, his only acknowledgment that they were headed to the music festival the brand sponsored. His blond hair was barbered into a clean-cut fade with a bit of flair at the front. His brown eyes were friendly and his rosy cheeks showed off his enthusiasm about everything in life to varying degrees, but his smile truly set him apart. It contained enough wattage to power half the UC San Diego campus, where they'd met five years ago.

"I can't wait to see my brother. I know he's so excited to be touring. After his last band broke up, he was worried he'd never play again, much less the Warped Tour." Jake had greeted him at his door with a big hug and without a hello after their four-month separation. Before Krish opened the door, he was further into the conversation than Krish's brain could catch up with.

"Good to see you, man. You hit much traffic?"

Jake had driven down early that morning from the Inland Empire. He'd moved on to graduate school there after December, when he finished his bachelor's degree. Krish had needed one more semester. Now Jake was interested in earning his MBA and making money, while Krish wanted to write about music, social justice, and video games. Despite their divergent career paths, they remained the best of friends.

"None, if you can believe it, but then I left at five, just to be sure."

"Such the eager beaver." Krish had been awake that long, lying in bed, staring at the ceiling. He was finally experiencing the cliché, "Today is the first day of the rest of your life." Everything was going to change for him… and this was the day he might finally meet Silas Franklin. That thought had his palms sweaty and his mouth dry.

"I'm glad you're here," Krish said, giving him another hug and trying to collect himself. He really had missed Jake, and his enthusiasm would make it easier to loosen up. He was so damn tense. "Thanks for driving me. I can't believe I'm doing this."

Jake raised his eyebrows. "Can't believe you're *doing* this? You're about to spend the summer surrounded by music and hot guys. I can't believe you'd consider *not* doing it. It just sucks that your finals schedule meant missing the first day."

"I know. As it is, my parents are pissed I'm not walking at graduation. But I told them they had better things to do than sit in the baking-hot sun for hours waiting for the two point eight seconds I'd be onstage getting my diploma."

"They'd do it, though. They did it for Viv."

Krish's smile passed from excited and nervous to sad as he remembered when the three of them attended Vivaan's college and boot camp graduations. Krish had been in such awe of his brother, especially his physical transformation from skinny cross-country and track star to beefcake Marine. He'd given him shit about it for a long time.

"That all you can take? Gawd. I'd never be able to live out of a duffel bag for two whole months."

Krish grabbed his bag and closed and locked the door behind him. Both of his parents had to work today, so they'd said their goodbyes earlier. His mom had hugged him about fifty times between the kitchen and the doorway, making him promise to text her every day and call at least once a week, as though he were going to summer camp. He kind of was, but it was his job, and he probably shouldn't be sad about kissing his mommy goodbye. But they hadn't been apart for any length of time since Vivaan....

"You can just toss that in the back of the Bro Van," Jake said, tearing Krish from his melancholy thoughts.

Krish laughed as he remembered the night they named Jake's inherited minivan. They'd been bonding over "bros before beaus" after Krish's date dumped him. They christened the van with what was left of a bottle of peppermint schnapps, which had made them both sick as dogs by the end of the night. Served them right for attempting to go to a frat party. Neither of them fit in there, and they'd had more fun hanging out with the band than the frat brothers.

"I made a whole playlist of bands I want to see today." Jake was a music enthusiast like Krish, but his tastes ran more toward the indie/folksy side of alternative rock. Krish liked his music harder, faster, and louder, but they did find common ground with bands like Hush and a few others. They could always agree on Asking Alexandria, Black Veil Brides, and Escape the Fate.

"Sure, man. Whatever." Of course, if Krish were driving himself, he'd be blasting Hush's new album. He'd been listening nonstop to every breath Silas took between lyrics. He knew the words by heart and would likely start teaching himself the guitar parts when he got home from the tour. He was going to miss his guitar.

Krish looked up to find that Jake was staring at him.

"What?"

"What? I'm just shocked. You never let me have control of the tunes. You feeling okay?"

Krish barked out a laugh. "Yeah, sure. Just anxious, a little."

They climbed into the Bro Van and buckled up for safety. Before he started the engine, Jake grinned. "Are you actually going to talk to him this time?"

Krish had come close to meeting Silas once before. He'd been at a show in LA with Jake and they'd gone to the afterparty at a nearby club. He'd watched Silas from afar as he danced with everyone, took off his shirt, did several rounds of shots, and led the bar in a metalcore rendition of "Happy Birthday" to Gavin. Back then it had been enough to watch. Now he wanted a chance to see if his fantasy could be a reality.

Krish focused his eyes on the dashboard. "I don't know, man. What if he's, like, disappointed? Or what if he hates me because of what I've written about the band? I probably won't even get to talk to him."

"Well, I've taken steps to ensure that you do. First," he said, pulling out a folded-up piece of paper, "I got us passes to Brains's workshop. Silas may or may not be there, but it's a start. Second, I texted my brother that I was coming—"

"Did you tell him about me?"

"Calm down. No, I didn't. I know you want to keep your Guru secret. Geez, Krish, what's gotten into you?"

Krish rubbed his hands on his cargo shorts. "I'm just nervous."

Jake put a hand on his shoulder. "Look. I've never met him, but he seems like a cool guy. Maybe he'll be a total dweeb in person and you'll finally get over your crush."

Krish shot him a look of complete disbelief.

Jake sighed. "Yeah. I know. Impossible."

They pulled off the freeway exit near the festival grounds, and Krish's heart pounded out of control. It was now or never.

"Look, it's not like he's going to know it's you, right?"

He's right. I can just be Krish, and he won't know the truth.

"You won't tell Jordan, will you?"

Jake waved off his concerns. "I won't tell him. He's got a big mouth. But have you come up with a cover story?"

"Yeah. When I spoke to Kevin Lyman's personal assistant, Chantal, she suggested I just tell people I'm Krish the intern, and that I report to her. She'll give me some tasks to do so I look legit, but I'm on my own the rest of the time."

"But won't they figure it out when your blogs are published?"

Krish shrugged. "My blogs are going to be my general impressions of the tour. I won't be doing official interviews or anything, and if I decide to write anything specific, I'll set them up after the tour and notify the people involved. As for using the Guru if I get hired at *Alt-Scene* permanently, they said we could discuss that. I'm not sure I want to bring that part of me along on the next phase of my journey. A lot of what I wrote was really personal. I want to write for *Alt-Scene*, but down the road? Sky's the limit. If Krishnan Guruvayoor becomes synonymous with the Guru? I'm not sure that's the best move."

Jake nodded. "I see. But will it be the best move with Silas Franklin? Ohmygod, he's fucking beautiful, Krish."

Krish barked out a laugh. "I can't believe I might actually meet him… talk to him." But Krish was torn. Part of the reason he was attracted to Silas was how much they had in common, how much he thought Silas might get him. If he got to know him, how could he continue to write about Hush? It would be a conflict of interest.

Being a blogger was much different from being a journalist, something he was still getting used to. He wondered if he had the skill to actually take himself out of the equation the way traditional journalists needed to. He'd always seen himself as more like his hero, Jon Krakauer. Reading *Into the Wild* as a high schooler had inspired him to write about the things he was passionate about. Krakauer took his own life experiences and commingled them with important events. He did intensive research and wrote in a metacognitive style that really appealed to Krish. That was the approach he'd taken with his blog, and it had been successful. Could he wear a different hat this summer?

Without being too stalker-ish, Krish had read quite a lot about Silas, who loved to give interviews and had been incredibly open with the press about his band, their music, and their shenanigans… until Gavin died. The press had been brutal in their coverage, claiming everything from drugs to undiagnosed mental illness, even horrific statements about Gavin being gay as the reason for all his troubles. Krish's heart went out to Silas and the band. They didn't deserve that kind of shit. *Alt-Scene* had stuck to the facts, and that was one of the main reasons Krish wanted to write for them.

But given what he'd seen and read, Krish couldn't know how all of those sound bites would play out in person. He had a hunch they'd get along famously, but he had no way of knowing until he actually got up the courage to strike up a conversation.

"It'll be fine, Krish. I promise," Jake said as though he overheard Krish's internal monologue.

"I hope you're right."

IT WAS *not* fine. Krish's stomach was so off by the time they got through the lines to get in that he ran for the first bathroom, just in case. Thankfully the restroom trip wasn't necessary, and he didn't embarrass himself. Jake had texted Jordan to connect with him, and they agreed to a meeting place. Krish had an appointment to meet Lyman's assistant at 11:15 a.m. to get his credentials, and then he would meet up with his bus mates to drop off his things. He and Jake would hang out, and then he was on duty. His task? Take in all aspects of the tour, share posts online, and then share his impressions and thoughts with the *Alt-Scene* assistant editor, Monique. If she liked what she saw, his work would potentially become a feature piece for *Alt-Scene*. If they liked it, the permanent job was his. The Guru would still post periodically, but Krish Guruvayoor would be the journalist. It could work. In a perfect world.

Krish went to the main security office. He showed them the email from Kevin Lyman's assistant, Chantal Jackson, and they let him in. One of the security guards walked him back to the makeshift office for the tour staff and attempted small talk along the way that Krish was too nervous to recall. Then he left Krish outside the door to the trailer.

He knocked and heard someone yell for him to come in. Inside the trailer were several desks occupied by people chatting on walkie talkies and cell phones. He stood for several moments until a young woman hung up and looked in his direction.

"Are you Krish?"

He smiled and stepped forward, trying not to knock things off the surfaces with his duffel bag. As he approached, he stuck out his hand to shake.

"Chantal?"

"In the flesh. Nice to meet you. Is that all you brought?"

He looked down at his bag. "Well, your email said—"

"Yes!" Chantal pulled her fist down in victory. "Someone finally listened. Hey, we had a little bit of a snafu this morning. Do you mind if I just take you over to the bus? You can drop off your stuff, and then we can meet tomorrow? You can just hang out and take it all in today."

"Yeah, sure. I don't want to be in your way."

She waved a hand at him and scrunched up her nose. "Not even. I just have to deal with this mess. I'll have more time and you'll have more of my focus later on. Cool? Cool. Oh, here you go."

Chantal held up a lanyard with a badge on it.

Office Intern
All Access

Krish reached for it with shaky hands, grasped it reverently, and gazed at it for a long moment, until he realized he was being a dork.

"Your first time with an all-access pass?"

His cheeks hurt from smiling so hard. "Yeah. I've been to a lot of shows, and I've met some bands, but this is… different."

Chantal grabbed a sweater from the back of her chair and gestured for him to follow her. "Sweet. You're about to have quite an adventure. You're actually going to be staying in the bus with the office staff and two photographers. We could have put you with a band or a crew, but we thought you'd be more comfortable with us, especially if you're trying to work. It'll be easier to keep up the intern story."

"Thank you," he said. "I appreciate your help."

She led him through the venue and out to an adjacent parking lot. Rows of buses greeted them, and he wondered how he'd be able to find the right one—

"You won't lose us, that's for sure."

He laughed when she pointed out the black bus with the pink fuzzy dice hanging from the rearview mirror, the row of solar dancing creatures on the dashboard, and the full-size skeleton wearing a bus driver's hat in the driver's seat.

"That's Clarence. He's our mascot. He tends to end up in a lot of post-show party pictures."

She led him to the bus and knocked on the door with three short raps, a pause, and then two more.

"Secret knock?"

She laughed. "Just a warning. Hate to catch anyone with their pants down." She winked and opened the door. "On this bus, besides yours truly, are Margeaux and Timmy. They both work in the management office with me. Then we also have Casey and Vinh, the photographers. Our driver is Butch, and we clean up after ourselves. You can have the top bunk on the left side, and there are cabinets in the back for your things. Did I mention we clean up after ourselves?"

Krish chuckled. "Loud and clear."

"All right. I'm going to leave you here. You can get yourself back inside? With that badge you can go anywhere, although I wouldn't go wandering around the buses or where the bands are setting up, at least not without talking to band management."

"Understood," Krish said, looking around. The bus was a utilitarian older model but neat and clean. Taped all over the place were pictures that featured all the different bands Krish knew were on the tour. There were neatly marked piles of food on the counter. Somebody was obviously a fan of label makers, because all the cabinets, drawers, and areas of the counter were marked. An empty spot even had his name.

"Lunch and dinner are catered, and we grab our own breakfasts. It doesn't look like you brought much?"

He shook his head. "Kinda didn't think about much more than protein bars."

Chantal looked him up and down. "I can see that. Don't worry. Butch can stop at a Target on our way to the next date, and we can run in and grab some supplies."

"That would be great."

Chantal was tall, maybe five-foot-nine, with natural hair pulled back into two puffs, and a bright smile. She wore a septum piercing, dangly silver earrings, a white Warped T-shirt, and green camo leggings. Krish didn't think she was much older than him, but it was difficult to tell. She carried herself with confidence, yet she seemed approachable. Krish hoped she'd be a good resource and potentially even a friend.

"It's good to have you, Krish. Sorry to rush out. Here, give me your phone. I'll add my number in case you need anything."

Krish handed her his phone, and she punched in her number.

"Have fun, be safe, and I'll see you tonight?" She waved as she headed toward the door.

"Yeah. Thank you."

And with the click of the door, he was alone.

The job had been a dream come true… until now. Now it was reality. Could he even do it? Could he deliver?

Relax. You're here to watch the bands. Get lost in the music. Stop freaking out. You were born to write. Stop whining.

It was too late for whining. It was time to get to work.

HE MANAGED to make his way alone back inside the venue and found Jake talking to Jordan near the fenced-off area next to the lot. He saw them hugging and laughing. Krish hung back, his stomach still uneasy.

"Krish!"

Jake waved him over. He stood with his arm around his brother, who was just the slightest bit shorter than him. Jordan wore ripped black pants that hugged his slim legs all the way down to his black motorcycle boots, a Misfits T-shirt with the sleeves cut off, and a denim vest with the sleeves cut off as well—typical metalcore dress code. His long dark hair hung below his shoulders and covered one eye. Tattoos curved up the opposite side of his neck and around his face. The brothers couldn't look any more unrelated… until they smiled. Their smiles were identical.

"Krish, meet Jordan."

Jordan stuck out a tattooed hand. Krish wiped his sweaty palm off on his shorts and accepted it.

"Good to meet you," Jordan said, holding on to his hand a little longer.

"Krish is a friend from college."

Jordan smirked. "Like, your special friend?"

Jake punched him in the arm.

"Ow, fucker," Jordan said, and the two grown-ass manchildren began duking it out. Krish was too shocked to say anything until they started to get looks from security.

"Guys," he stage-whispered.

Jordan threw his arm around Jake in a headlock. "Sorry, man. I don't get to see my brother enough." He showed his affection by scrubbing his knuckles over Jake's carefully coiffed hair while Jake struggled to get free. The security guard, a big burly black dude, frowned, yelled at them to knock it off, and then turned to watch the beer booth.

When Krish looked back at the brothers, they were laughing and hugging each other again. His breath hitched in his chest. Something was missing. Had he lost something? He had his bag, his phone and wallet…. *He was missing Vivaan.* Watching the Barrett brothers felt like a punch to the chest, like all the air had been knocked out of him. He recovered quickly, but it hurt.

"You guys are a mess," Krish laughed, relieved that nothing worse had happened.

"Yeah, your guyliner is smudged," Jake said to Jordan. He licked his thumb and said, "Here, let me get it."

Jordan slapped his hand away so hard the sound echoed off the building next to them and caught the security guard's attention again.

"You guys better get out of here before they throw your asses out," Jordan said, snickering and fingering his band badge. "I'll try to get you a couple of these for after the show. You're sticking around, right? I want to get wasted with my little brother. It's been too long."

Jake pushed him into the fence as he laughed, and Jordan flipped him off. "Krish doesn't need one. He's working on the tour."

Jordan squinted at his badge and smirked. "Intern, huh? Cool."

"I'll see you later," Jake said.

Jordan pointed both hands at them in fake guns, shooting the triggers as he winked. He laughed and waved as he turned toward the rows of tour buses and tents.

Krish exhaled harshly.

"You okay? You look like you've seen a ghost," Jake said laughing.

"Yeah. Just… maybe a little overwhelmed?"

Jake grew serious for a minute and placed a hand on his arm. "You going to be okay? This is big for you."

Krish exhaled and shook his head. "Yeah. Wow. Crazy. But the woman who showed me the bus was cool, and I'll be staying with people who are there working, so hopefully…."

Yeah, he was going to be fine. He'd just have to keep telling himself that.

"Come on, let's go get some food," Jake said. "The gates are opening in a few minutes, and I'm already starving. I wonder what type of vegetarian items they'll have?"

Krish rolled his eyes at Jake. "Come on, man. I need some protein or I'm going to keel over."

Jake couldn't accept the fact that Krish wasn't a vegetarian. Jake had been a stalwart PETA supporter all through college and continued to be that one friend who constantly lectured his friends on their lifestyle choices. Luckily, he had enough redeeming qualities to make up for it.

They ended up with rice bowls from a food truck—Krish's with teriyaki chicken and Jake's with tofu and veggies. Both came away satisfied and ready to face the day.

"Our workshop with Brains isn't until three, so we actually have time to go see some bands first. Hush plays after Brains's workshop."

Krish pulled out the schedule they'd picked up from the front gates and saw that, yes, Hush was on the main stage in the early evening. Warped was an unusual festival, a bit more egalitarian. Though bands were slated on stages based on their album sales and status, headliners played throughout the day, starting as soon as the gates opened, and the schedule changed from stop to stop.

Krish and Jake had agreed on most of the bands they wanted to see, but there were a couple of indie bands Krish had no interest in seeing, and Jake certainly wasn't up for the more metal acts, like The Amity Affliction and Motionless in White, so they split up for a while. Krish was content wandering the festival grounds alone and enjoying the bands whose music made his spirits soar.

The music brought such vivid memories of Vivaan it was almost as though he were standing next to Krish. Music had been the brothers' common language. Vivaan taught Krish all he knew and took him to shows as soon as their mother agreed they were old enough to go alone. Warped had been their favorite, and standing at the rear of the crowd watching the new generation of Warped fans screaming and ready to mosh reminded Krish of how it had felt all those years ago with his brother.

As The Amity Affliction ripped into their song "Pittsburgh," Krish was taken back to the last show he and Vivaan went to before Viv was sent overseas. He ignored the tear that slipped down his cheek and recalled how he played the song over and over during his initial grieving period. His blog had just begun to take off, and many of his readers related to his posts about losing his brother and continued to follow him over the years despite what direction he took the blog. It was always music, but he wrote about grief, he wrote about being an LGBTQ man who happened to be a person of color, and he wrote about the responsibility all Americans had to preserve the rights of others.

And he wanted to keep writing. This summer he needed to produce his best writing yet to prove he was ready for the job. That should have been enough to ground him. But as the afternoon crept closer to Brains's workshop, Krish became even more anxious about the possibility of meeting Silas than he was about the job. At least with the job he knew what to expect. The magazine liked his writing and appreciated his viewpoint and perspective. In contrast, he had no clue how Silas felt about what he wrote.

Jake found him lingering around the TWLOHA tent dictating a blog post. He held up a finger to Jake so he could finish his thought.

"I've always been moved by To Write Love On Her Arms, an organization dedicated to sharing alternatives to self-harm for teens. I've known too many kids, in high school and in college, who were in so much pain that they saw no other alternative than to cut, burn, or scar themselves. TWLOHA is one of many organizations doing important work here on Warped Tour, and I'm grateful for that, but it also leads me to moments of sheer rage about the lack of available resources, even for kids with insurance. Nonprofits are wonderful and they do terrific work, but just imagine if the outrageous amounts people pay for healthcare actually took care of them? Or if our government took the needs of those with mental health issues seriously? Imagine a world where there wasn't so much pain." He stopped the recording. "Ugh, that's a topic I get too angry about."

"Yeah, but just think of what you'll be able to do when you join *Alt-Scene*. You could hopefully publish articles in their social justice department."

Krish loved Jake's optimism. "If and when they hire me."

"Whatever. Hey, you ready for this?" Jake held up their passes and wiggled his eyebrows.

Krish swallowed hard. "Sure. Let me just grab some water, okay?"

"Already got us bottles. No more stalling. It's time for you to meet your man."

Krish elbowed him as they walked toward the tent where they'd meet up with their group and be led to Billy "Brains" Brennan's workshop on drum techniques. No big deal.

Krish didn't play drums, but he knew enough about music to be in awe of all that Brains had accomplished, not only with Hush but with his previous band. He also had equipment deals with companies like Zildjian and Ludwig. Krish had watched his YouTube videos and admired how Brains applied music theory and even different philosophies to metal. It was easy to see where his nickname came from. Krish's double major in music and journalism had given him an excellent background for his future, but self-taught people like Brains inspired him.

Krish and Jake lined up with the other ten people who'd bought tickets for Brains's workshop and they gaped at the long lines for Andy Biersack's and Roxanne's workshops going on at the same time. Krish had been to one of Roxanne's workshops before, and he wrote up a nice piece about how the lead singer of Just Like Love was able to assert her feminism into her music and her career in a male-dominated industry. Being a female lead of an all-male band meant she'd often had to work harder than her male counterparts, but she held no grudges and was determined to be a positive influence in her genre.

The guide from TEI, the organization who sponsored the workshop, led them back through the gates and over to a row of tents where Brains was waiting for them behind a scaled-down drum kit. Brains wore a black muscle shirt that fit his slim frame snugly and a pair of roomy black board shorts. His black hair was styled into a faux hawk with glittery product in it, and he'd done his makeup dramatically, with expert-level eyes, lips, and brows. He was playing lightly and concentrating on what he was doing, so he was almost startled when he looked up and saw his pupils sitting on the tarp in front of him.

"Oh, hey," he said, smiling. "I'm Billy. Welcome to my drumming-technique workshop. How many of you guys play?"

Four teenaged boys in front of Krish and Jake raised their hands along with a sole young woman who could have been anywhere from late teens to early twenties. An older kid—maybe early twenties—sat behind Krish, and Jake and held up a single finger as though he didn't want any attention called to himself. Jake had fixed his eyes on the guy's legs, which were heavily tattooed and on display in a pair of cargo shorts, and Krish had to elbow him to get his attention back on Brains.

"Cool. Okay. I've been told I tend to talk fast. I'm not really sure why they asked me back again, but here we are. Um. Okay. So—"

Brains talked about foot placement on the pedals and how he preferred thicker sticks that were double butted, which got a lot of giggles from a group of girls off to Krish's right. They were obviously just there to ogle Brains. Then one of the huge groups walked by, chatting excitedly about meeting Andy, and Brains stopped speaking until they were past.

"Wow," Brains finally said. "That guy sure pulls them in. Thanks for not leaving me sitting here alone. I know I'm not as cool as Andy—"

The kids in the front row cut him off.

"I love your makeup, Brains," one young lady said.

Brains blushed. "Thank you."

"You should do a tutorial video," her friend said.

"You think? Wow."

"Yeah. My friend has a whole wall of pictures of your different looks."

Brains blinked and appeared to be truly touched. The girls asked him what products he used, and the conversation derailed a bit more before he held up a hand.

"Thank you, guys. Seriously. I know you could have picked Andy—"

They begged him to keep talking, saying Andy's workshop was just a bunch of girls staring at him.

"And dudes," the young woman said, rolling her eyes. "I know just as many dudes who would love to get with Andy, so…."

Brains looked between them and shrugged. "Anyway, so what I was saying—"

Another large group came by on their way to sit in front of Roxanne. Her tent was between Brains's and Andy's, and her group was large but not quite as giggly.

"Really, guys. Thank you for not leaving me alone with them."

The group laughed as Brains jumped back into his talk, demonstrating things as he went. He talked about the placement he used for his toms to achieve his signature sound and why he preferred a Ludwig kit and how he tended to go through a lot of drum heads because of the power he used. The young woman asked him a couple of questions about his training, and the talk veered off into influences, of which Brains cited a wide variety, from Neil Peart to Ginger Baker and then Joey Jordison to Dave Grohl.

Krish paid as close attention as he could with the noise coming from the tents next door. He brought out his phone a couple of times to jot down notes he would include in his blog and tried not to be disrespectful. Jake elbowed him at one point, so he showed him what he was doing, and Jake smiled.

"Are there any particular songs you guys want me to break down for you?" Brains asked after a bit.

The guy behind Krish raised his hand.

"Yeah?"

He cleared his throat. "Could you show how you make the transitions on 'Faceless'?"

Brains's face lit up a bit, and he launched into a very technical discussion that Krish was soon lost in. He watched Brains play some very complicated parts without his usual power, but even so, some of the folks from the other group looked over wide-eyed.

"And you can both go fuck yourselves," Brains said, and Krish nearly jumped out of his skin. Who was he talking to?

The group all turned their heads to see Silas and Los standing behind them and doing a two-man wave. Silas laughed and elbowed Los. "Sorry, Mr. Brains. We didn't mean to interrupt you."

Silas may have sounded contrite, but he appeared to be full of mischief. Krish couldn't look away. That smile was even more powerful up close. Not because it was a handsome smile, but because it seemed to hover on that line between sweet and unhinged. Krish had always loved watching Silas's performances, both live and on their music videos, for that very reason. Silas would start out with his eyes flashing and a grin on his face that would eventually morph into something like an insane person's expression. On anyone else it would have been comical, but on Silas it let Krish and everyone else know that he wasn't just a pretty face or a talented singer, he was a deep feeler and thinker and didn't take shit from anyone. His smile embodied all the things Krish loved about him.

Well, *love* might be a strong word. And how silly to be in love with a rock star who'd never even notice you? Except for the blog. The blog might catch his attention, but Krish wasn't sure that would be a good thing. And he was still staring. Brains had moved forward with his discussion, and everyone else had turned around except Krish. And now Silas was smiling at him.

Krish turned around in a panic. He'd been caught. Jake eyed him and failed to keep his laughter quiet.

"Busted," Jake whispered.

Krish couldn't respond and was afraid if he elbowed him to shut up he'd call even more attention to himself.

Maybe Silas hadn't noticed just how long he'd been staring. Krish looked toward Roxanne's group and tried to be sly as he peered over his shoulder.

Silas was still smiling at him, and Krish couldn't tear his eyes away. The guy was stunning. He'd shaved his head recently, and the stubble was his natural dark color rather than the multicolored hues he'd had for a few years. He already had his stage makeup on, it seemed, as his bluish-green eyes were lined in black and he wore black lipstick. He'd added a nose ring to his piercings since the last time Krish had seen pictures of him, and the gauges in his ears were wider than he remembered, about the size of nickels now. His wiry frame was drenched in black from his tight black pants to the black Judas Priest shirt he wore with the sleeves cut way low so his muscular torso could be seen beneath. He was stunning. His porcelain skin, marked heavily with colorful tattoos from the neck down, was smooth and hairless, and his teeth were so white they nearly blinded Krish. Because he was still smiling at Krish.

Krish's lips turned up at the corners out of embarrassment, but also excitement. Silas was here. And he'd noticed him.

"And that's all I've got. Anyone have any other questions?"

The kids in the front row began to clap, and Brains stood up and flipped off his bandmates, who cheered the loudest.

"You're our hero," Los shouted in a voice cracking like a pubescent teen.

"You know, someday they're going to ask you to do one of these talks, and I'm going to heckle the crap out of you."

The band's manager appeared at his side and gave him a hug.

"Everyone meet Jessica, our mom—ouch!"

"I'm not old enough or crazy enough to be your mom," she said as she pinched his side. "Okay, everyone, if you'll all turn around and get together, we're going to take a group picture. And then you can line up if you want individual pictures with Brains."

Krish allowed Jake to lead him to where they needed to be for the pictures, because he was still kind of stunned and had to concentrate hard on not giving himself whiplash trying to see where Silas went.

"Everyone, on the count of three, say 'Brains.' Here we go. One… two…."

A body crashed into Krish from behind.

"Three."

"Brains," Silas growled like a zombie as he shoved his face between Krish's and Jake's. For a smaller guy, he sure was strong. Krish had to steady himself so they didn't all fall forward under Silas's weight. Krish turned to look down at Silas and got an up-close-and-personal view of his gorgeous smile. Silas winked at him and then ran over to jump on Los's back.

As the group moved into a single line to take pictures with Brains, Krish hung back. Silas and Los took turns photobombing each of the individual pictures, each trying to outdo each other while Brains tried to be professional... well, as professional as he could be with Silas's tongue in his ear.

His long, pierced tongue.

Krish couldn't help but laugh at his antics. It was good to see them having so much fun together after all the hardships they'd been through.

When it was Jake's turn, Los and Silas crowded each side of him, and a shout from behind them caused their heads to turn.

"Quit mauling my brother, you pervs."

This led to a bunch of handshakes and more fighting between Jordan and Jake. Silas looked in Krish's direction and then whispered something to Jake.

The moment of truth. Could Jake play this off?

"Hey, didn't you want a picture with them?"

Jessica, the tour manager, stood next to Krish, her eyebrows raised in expectation.

"No, thank you. I'm fine." That was the last thing he needed. More pictures circulating around social media. He'd kept the Guru anonymous. He just had to trust that Jake would keep his secret.

"So that's Jordan's brother, huh? He's so—"

"Square? Yeah."

Jessica laughed, clapped a hand over her mouth, and lifted it to say, "He really is. I can't believe they're brothers. Does he even like metal?"

"Some. He likes Hush. But mostly he came to see The Maine."

Jessica snorted. "I can't say anything. They're cute. So, who were you looking forward to seeing?"

Silas. And more Silas. And Silas.

"Kind of everything, I guess. These guys. The Amity Affliction and Motionless in White. It sucks this is the last year."

Jessica sighed. "Yeah. We'll just have to make something of our own. The guys have made some good connections and some of the other managers and I have been talking. We've got some ideas."

Krish perked up. That would be something else. It wouldn't be the same as Warped. Nothing ever could compare to the mix of music genres and personalities and the causes represented there, but on a smaller scale? Perhaps. Before he could actually contemplate the awesomeness that would be a metalcore festival, Jake gestured for Krish to come over. To join him. With Hush.

Jessica glanced down at his badge. "Intern, huh?"

He looked as well, forgetting he had it already. "Yeah. I'm working in the tour office with Chantal."

"That's cool. She's awesome." Jessica's attention strayed back to the spectacle in front of them. "Oh hey, your friend is calling you." Jessica grabbed Krish's arm and led him over to where the band stood with Jake. He hoped it didn't look as though he was dragging his feet or reluctant. He just couldn't get his body to move in a normal fashion. He felt like Edward Scissorhands—totally out of his element and awkward.

"Guys, this is Krish. Krish, this is the guys." Jake smiled reassuringly at him and put an arm around him. "He's a writer."

Krish wanted to smack Jake. *A writer?* Why not just out him? Instead he gave a closed-lipped grin and waited for their response.

The band looked at each other as though there was some inside joke he was missing. Silas was the first to reach out a hand.

"Welcome to Warped, Krish."

Chapter Five

SILAS HELD on to his hand probably longer than what was socially acceptable, but he couldn't let go. Not yet.

It wasn't as though he thought he'd get some sort of psychic message when he touched the guy that would let him know if this was the Guru, the man who wrote such poignant words about the band's music, about the death of Silas's best friend, and about the issues most dear to his heart. Okay, maybe he did hope for that. There was definitely a tingle. Yeah, a tingle. Krish, Jordan's brother's friend, was fucking gorgeous, with his deep sepia-toned skin and dark, curly hair. His big brown eyes were super intense, and Silas was drawn in like some poor sucker on a diet standing outside the cupcake shop. Salivating.

"It's nice to meet you," Krish said to him. He licked his lips, and when he smiled, deep dimples cut into his cheeks. He was about six inches taller than Silas, which wasn't unusual. At five-foot-six, Silas was used to everyone being taller than him, and he'd worked hard to be able to compensate for his height. His big attitude and bigger voice had done wonders for his confidence.

Brains cleared his throat, and it was enough to break the magic spell. They let go of each other's hands, but not their eye contact.

"Jake said you're quite the gamer," Jordan said. "We might have to battle sometime this summer."

Silas blinked. A gamer. Huh. Not that most guys in their twenties didn't play, but still. Jordan and Los waggled their eyebrows at each other, and Krish's eyes went wide, as though he'd just gotten caught cheating.

"I play some. I, uh, just finished college, so I haven't had a whole lot of time to play."

"Can we get a badge for Jordan's little bro tonight?" Los gave Jessica his most innocent smile.

"Yeah, please, Mom? I want to party with my little bro. He's fucking hilarious when you get him drunk," Jordan said.

Jessica raised an eyebrow at him. "Not if you ever call me Mom again. Ever."

Los rested his chin on her shoulder and hugged her. "But we miss our moms."

"I will beat you like your moms should have. I am no one's mom, so knock it off unless you want to sleep underneath Brains."

"No. You promised we'd keep that a storage bunk! I can't do it, dude. I slept under him last time." Los was pleading. No one wanted to sleep under

Brains. At least once or twice a week, the dude had noxious gas that about knocked them all out of their bunks. They finally decided to give him the back lounge when that happened, so he wouldn't kill them all. He locked himself in with the windows open and a little fan. It helped, but there was definitely seepage and residual funk.

"Then don't mess with me," she said with a vicious smile. Even Silas was afraid. He knew better than to fuck with Jessica.

"How about the pass, Your Majesty?"

"Now that's better," she answered and allowed Silas to take her hand and reverently kiss the back of it. He knew how to charm the lady. He'd even do her laundry at their next stop if it meant he could potentially spend more time with the gorgeous specimen before him. It didn't matter to Silas if he was the Guru or not. Silas intended to find out if he was still this hot after some socializing.

"Guys, it's time to get ready," Brains said. "Hey, thanks for coming to my workshop," he said, shaking Jake's hand and then Krish's and taking a moment to look him over—a moment too long. Brains never really went for guys while on tour. He barely spoke to anyone outside the band save a few of their friends from other bands, but every once in a while, Brains found someone to hook up with. *Well, it isn't going to be this guy.* Silas had plans for him.

"Intern, huh?"

"Yeah. I'm, uh… working in the tour office for the summer."

The guys all raised their eyebrows and looked at Silas. He shrugged and turned toward Krish, and their arms brushed, causing the hair to stand up on his skin. Goose bumps were an excellent sign. "I'll see you after the show." Silas smiled up at Krish. He had so many questions, but there'd be time for that later. For now he needed to get psyched up for their set.

He grabbed Jordan by the scruff of his shirt and dragged him away from the pounding he was giving his brother. Those two were a trip. Jordan had been mostly quiet on the tour so far, but with his brother, he'd let loose. They definitely needed time together. It was just an added perk that his brother came with a beautiful friend.

Silas spent a little time in the tour bus doing his vocal warm-ups and drinking his honey-and-lemon tea. Then he joined the rest of the guys. They always stretched together, determined to avoid injuries at all cost on the tour. Hush couldn't afford any more setbacks.

"What if that's him?" Los whispered to Jordan. "The Guru?"

Jordan frowned and shook his head. "Nah. He's just a friend of Jake's from college."

"But maybe he is? Would your brother keep that from you?"

"Doubt it. They're just friends. I think he said the guy teaches music lessons or something. I don't know."

"Maybe you guys should stop trying to be the Scooby gang and warm up so you don't pull a damn hammy."

Silas tried to squash their speculations, but he continued to observe Jordan closely to see if he was withholding the truth. Maybe he was just looking for something that wasn't there. Hell, maybe they all were. It would be awesome if his literary hero was wrapped up in a package so fucking delicious that Silas couldn't wait to sink his teeth in. But regardless of who he was, he'd like to do some teeth-sinking with Krish later on. Just thinking about him had Silas pumped and ready to let loose onstage.

Their first show in Pomona had been great, but today in San Diego they were just a little smoother, a little more into the groove. Jordan meshed seamlessly with Los, Brains was on fire, and Silas felt stronger than ever. Their new material required him to stretch his voice even more than he had previously, and he relished the challenge. He felt so alive.

He might have been a little distracted onstage looking for Krish in the crowd. But when he fumbled over a lyric on their new song, "Forever Sounds," he buckled down and regained his focus. No one noticed but him, of course. Silas was a perfectionist, and he held himself to higher standards than the rest of the guys.

Los had stepped up big-time with the loss of Gavin. Silas watched him closely, noticing that he took to the mic with much more confidence, and he even played cleaner this tour than he had in the past. Los had always been Silas's vocal counterpart on clean vocals, backing him up during live performances, and Gavin's scream was a trademark part of their sound. Silas did his fair share of screaming, but their sound required a second, deeper growl to really pack that punch. Jordan had been apologetic when he'd admitted he could sing, but he couldn't scream.

"Dude, I sound like a girl. It's all bad."

He was right, sadly. Los had said he'd give it a try, and *damn*. Why hadn't they used him before? His scream sounded very different than Gavin's, but in a good way, and it was powerful. And now there they were, next to each other, so close they had to concentrate on not banging their guitars together. They shared a mic and screamed their hearts out. Silas shivered, feeling giddy over how good they sounded, and for the millionth time since losing Gavin, Silas was grateful for his band. He couldn't have survived such an awful tragedy without them. As they finished the chorus on "New Day," he leaned in and kissed Los on the cheek. He got a scrunched-up face in return, followed by a middle-finger salute. Silas flicked his tongue at him, and Los cracked up.

And then their set was done. Too soon, as far as Silas was concerned. The one drawback to Warped Tour was the shorter sets. Silas often felt as though he'd only just begun the buildup by the time they had to wrap. It was like rushing an orgasm. At least he had something… or someone… to look forward to.

Offstage they group hugged and laughed together. Los playfully pushed Silas and said, "What was that kiss for? I thought I made it perfectly clear that your big dick doesn't tempt me in the least. Neither does that tongue of yours. You're just not my type, babe."

Silas rolled his eyes. Los had always made jokes about their different ends of the sexual spectrum. He was unapologetically heterosexual and happy to remind Silas and Brains, but he never gave them shit about who they chased after. He'd certainly been encouraging Silas to find the Guru.

Being out in the metalcore community had sort of been like having a huge zit on your face. Most people were cool about it. They didn't say anything, or if they did, it was because they knew the struggle was real. Then some would try so hard not to stare that they'd nearly hurt themselves trying not to look. They had no clue how to act. Then there were the ones who turned into middle school bullies once again. They made fun, threw beer bottles, wrote nasty notes, and other such atrocities. None of it bothered Silas. Gavin, however, hadn't been able to cope. He wanted to be out, to live his life in the open, but the cost was too high for him.

Fuck. Not the time to think about Gavin.

"I need to go get showered," Silas said, hoping to avoid the ration of shit he knew he was going to get from the others. No such luck.

"Yeah, you should do that," Los said, sniffing at him. "You don't want to smell bad for your date."

The guys laughed, but Brains frowned at him. "Do you think it's him?" he asked.

They all looked at each other. "It's not like I want to ask him," Silas said. "Let's just pretend he's not and go from there."

Jordan had gone ahead with Logan, their guitar tech. Apparently he'd had some issue with his setup and wanted Logan to help him fix it. Los and Brains watched him walk off and then turned to Silas.

"I don't know," Los said. "Whoever he is, just be careful."

Silas frowned at him. "What's that supposed to mean?"

Los crossed his arms, serious for once. "It means if he is the Guru, be careful. If he's not, still be careful. I don't want you to get hurt, you know. The last guy you hooked up with—"

"I thought we weren't going to talk about that anymore." Silas didn't need a lecture. Yeah, he'd dated a reporter once from *Mass Emo Online*, and the guy had printed a bunch of shit about the band that wasn't even true. And the last guy he met on tour and hooked up with had sticky fingers on his way out of their shared house in Oakland. A laptop, some beer money, and a bunch of their clothes were missing the next day, and Los had really laid into Silas. It wasn't as though it was the first time one of them had brought trouble into their world, but losing Gavin had brought all past wounds to the surface and forgiveness was a little harder to come by.

"Sorry, dude, but you know—"

"Yeah. Point taken," Silas said and stomped off toward the bus. Why Los had to be a buzzkill right now, he had no clue. One minute he was encouraging Silas to meet the Guru and get laid, and the next he was telling him to be careful, as though Silas was so fucking stupid he'd fall in love with the first guy to come along. Well, he was quite a bit more emotionally mature than Los, and he knew how to handle himself, dammit. Silas was going to have a good time tonight whether the sourpuss liked it or not.

He ran up the steps to the bus and paused at the entrance to the lounge area.

Good God, his bandmates were pigs.

They'd only been on the road for a couple of days, and there was already shit everywhere—mostly Los's. Brains had left out his breakfast dishes, and Jordan's makeup was still spread all over the table. He had half a mind to chuck all their stuff in the garbage, but instead he did what he always did and cleaned it all up, bitching the whole time. It took him forty-five minutes and then another forty-five minutes to shower, shave, and get dressed. He missed the rest of the festival, and he hated that he didn't see Falling in Reverse, because Ronnie always did something outrageous to keep Silas entertained.

Silas threw on a pair of Dickies board shorts, a white tank, and some Vans and left the bus. He headed over to the central gathering spot, where a bunch of the other bands were hanging out around a bonfire someone had lit in a garbage can. Probably that wasn't a good idea, but what could it hurt? A bunch of drunk young folks around an open fire. Perfectly safe.

"Hey, dude. What took you so long? The guys from Incorrigible are already killing it at horseshoes."

Los threw an arm around Silas's neck and dragged him over to the food.

"And Brains is building a huge sculpture out of solo cups. It's kind of brilliant, actually. He's cut them into shapes, and he's gluing them together with that Gorilla Glue stuff. It's in the shape of a chariot with a Greek god."

"That's awesome. Remember the time he made models of KISS out of duct tape?"

Silas laughed about that until he spotted Jordan's brother, Jake, and the object of Silas's thoughts all afternoon.

Krish—tall, dark, and sexy as fuck. He had that innocently adorable thing going on, even now. He didn't know Silas was watching him, but he was looking around like he was trying to find someone. He smiled every once in a while at something Jordan or his brother said, and he sipped at a bottle of water. Silas sighed as Krish tipped his bottle back and drained it, his prominent Adam's apple bobbing as he swallowed. Oh, what he wanted to do to that throat.

"Before you go doing any more than ogling, do I have to remind you that it's a bad idea fooling around with someone who has the potential to do harm to the band?"

Silas glanced over his shoulder at Jessica. She smiled at him sympathetically, but her job was to make sure the band members didn't do anything to fuck with the band's name, their brand, and their clout in the industry. There had been a lot of questions about whether they should be on tour after the events of the past couple of years. Jessica was hired because she was known for keeping self-destructive musicians in line and safe from themselves and anyone who wished them ill.

"Why do you say that?"

"He's an intern with the tour. And what if he *is* the Guru? Jake said he's a writer. If he's a journalist, you know how your brothers feel about that. Giving him behind-the-scenes access, or behind-closed-doors even, could be a bad idea."

Silas shrugged. "I'll be careful. I don't even know if he's potentially anything other than someone to talk to. If he is, well, I'll be careful."

Jessica raised her eyebrow but couldn't hold back a laugh when Silas gave her his innocent look.

"That bullshit doesn't work on me, Silas James Franklin."

"Ooooo, the full name treatment." He laughed and gave her a hug, which she reciprocated.

"Just be careful, got it?"

He clicked his heels together and gave her a salute. "I'll even use a condom."

Her eyes bugged out, and he laughed as he skipped away. "Yep," he called over his shoulder. "That guy handing out condoms at the show is my new best friend."

"Silas!"

He waved at her and blew her a kiss. Then he joined the guys.

"Hey," Jordan said. He stood behind a makeshift bar serving up cocktails to those in their camp. "I've got Shipwrecks going, or there's your lightweight beer in the cooler."

"Sapporo isn't lightweight. Just because you don't have to chew it," he said, rolling his eyes. They landed on Krish, whose intense gaze was so wide Silas thought he might hurt himself. Silas walked over and sat on the bench next to him. "I'll take one of your Shipwrecks, though." He turned to Krish and asked, "Can I get you one?"

Krish shook his head. "Thanks, but I better watch out for that guy," he said gesturing at Jake, who was laughing hysterically at something Roxanne was saying. Jake gestured wildly with his red cup and sloshed some of his drink out, prompting more laughs from the group he was with.

Silas accepted a drink from Jordan and held his cup to what Silas noted was Krish's second water bottle. The guy was either fighting some dehydration after the heat of the festival or he was nervous.

"Here's to a good show," Silas said.

Krish tapped Silas's cup with his bottle and smiled. "You guys sounded great. Things have really come together with Jordan, huh?"

"That sounded a bit like a professional question," Silas said with a smirk. "Do you have a professional interest in the band?"

Krish frowned at him and licked his lips. "I just meant he sounds great with the band, that's all. What do you mean professional?"

"Nothing. Sorry. Just…." Damn. How honest did he want to be? "I'm just, you know. I have to be careful." He glanced down at Krish's intern badge. It really was taking a risk to get involved with anyone on tour, but Silas knew how to be smart. Mostly. Usually. Sort of. Something about Krish compelled Silas to get in a little deeper, and he was ready to damn the consequences.

Krish gave him a look like maybe Silas wasn't right in the head. "I'm not a reporter, no."

Silas breathed a sigh of relief. "Good. Okay. I'm sorry. I just had to check. We've had problems in the past is all. You're not a thief, are you?"

Krish barked out a laugh. "A thief? Wow," he said, shaking his head. "I've never been accused of stealing during a first conversation."

Silas placed a hand on his arm. "I'm sorry. I just had to ask. I know it sounds stupid, but yeah."

"You hang out with liars and thieves a lot?" Krish asked, only sort of joking.

Silas shrugged and finished his first drink, already feeling the tingles around his upper lip. "Let's just say that some of my guests in the past have caused issues for the band, and the guys don't always trust my judgment."

Krish turned to face him and placed his arm on the back of the bench, his fingers grazing Silas's shoulder. "Is that what I am? Your guest?"

Silas felt a jolt through his gut. He most certainly had read the situation right. "I'd like you to be," he said. "After the workshop, I kinda thought maybe you might want that too." He looked away for a moment and gestured to Jordan that he wanted a refill. "Was I right?"

Moment of truth.

Krish cleared his throat. "I might have hoped I'd meet you today," he said, turning back to face front and wiping his hands on his shorts. He glanced in Silas's direction and then looked down at his hands, suddenly very interested in them. "I know you probably get that a lot."

Silas shrugged and leaned back against the bench. He put his arm over the back and let his fingers graze Krish's shoulder, hoping for a reaction.

Krish sucked in a breath and looked at Silas from under his heavy bangs. The guy had shaggy, curly hair that hung across his forehead, curled around his prominent cheek bones, and touched the collar of his white The Amity Affliction T-shirt. The color contrasted nicely with his brown skin.

"You don't strike me as the usual fanboy," Silas said as he ran a finger along the back of Krish's neck.

Krish's eyes closed a beat longer than a blink, and Silas smiled. If this guy wasn't into him, he'd have gotten up and moved after the first touch. Now he just wanted to see if there was more here than just a mutual attraction.

"You sure I can't get you a drink?" Silas asked him, thinking maybe he needed just a little loosening up. "Something a little stronger than water?"

Krish smirked at him. "You trying to get me drunk?"

Silas moved a little closer and let his finger dip below the collar of Krish's T-shirt.

"You could hang out with me a little longer."

Jordan came over with two cups and handed one to Krish. "You look like you could use this, dude."

Krish laughed, accepted the cup, and took a couple of deep pulls on the drink. He sputtered and coughed from the strong drink. Silas pounded on his back a little until Krish coughed out a thank-you.

"What's in that?" he asked, coughing some more.

Jordan smiled. "It's a little concoction I picked up on tour in Iowa. Pretty much the kitchen sink of fruit juices, rum, tequila, and whatever shit I find behind the bar. Good, huh?"

Krish took another swallow and nodded. "It's sweet. Takes a second for it to hit you."

Silas laughed and finished his second cup. "Yeah, but when it does, *woo*! Watch out."

They sat side by side, thighs touching, watching the goings-on around them for several minutes without talking. Silas loved observing. There was so much to learn from watching people's interactions. He liked to think of himself as an observer of human nature. He was confident he had a good grasp on what motivated people, made them tick. But that didn't always translate to men he wanted to seduce. He still wasn't sure if he was reading Krish correctly.

"Is this what you guys do every night after the show?"

Silas shrugged. "Mostly. Not always. We're close with some of the bands, so sometimes we act like a bunch of wild animals, sometimes we jam, sometimes we even write together, if we're feeling the magic."

Krish grinned. "I bet that would be epic. A bunch of you guys playing together? I often wondered why there weren't more collaborations at Warped, you know, with everyone in one place. A lot of you guys have been guests on each other's music. Makes sense to do it here live. No?"

Silas realized that no, Krish wasn't just your average fanboy. He'd put a lot of thought into it, and it wasn't as if he was asking a question, really. *Was* he the Guru?

"I've seen it a couple times, but honestly the sets are so short and the schedule so crazy…. I don't know, though." He laughed. "Maybe I should talk to Ryan. He and I go way back."

"That's right. And he and Gavin wrote together, didn't they? Oh…. Shit, I'm sorry."

Silas internally winced. He was so used to Gavin being the unspoken topic. Frankly, he was tired of it. "No, you're right. Ryan and Gavin did write a lot of music together. Most of it never went anywhere, but there are a couple of Backdrop Silhouette songs that Gavin is credited on. They had a serious bond, that's for sure. Did you know that they recorded a whole album together? Their labels threw a conniption and wouldn't let them put it out because they couldn't agree on a deal. It's just sitting in a vault somewhere."

"That's… that's tragic. I bet it's something else."

Silas grinned. It was mind-blowing. He was a little jealous when he first heard it, if he were being honest. Why hadn't *he* and Gavin come up with that? Had Gavin worked better with Ryan? What if… but that was a stupid road to go down. Nothing would ever have come between him and Gavin. Except death. Even if the album had come out, Silas would have supported them to the ends of the earth. "Man, I need to catch up with Ryan."

"Did you need to go?" Krish asked.

Shit. Silas hadn't realized he'd spoken out loud. "No, no no. I was just thinking I need to spend some time with Ryan. As hard as it is for us, Ryan and Gavin spent a helluva lot of time together during Warped. And now that Ryan is sober… I just don't want him spending all of his time alone."

Silas leaned back against the bench, suddenly feeling incredibly raw. He hadn't been able to talk like this in a long time. He gazed at Krish for a long time, into those fathomless dark eyes that seemed to be staring right into Silas's soul. Normally, at this point, he'd feel compelled to make some stupid crack to ease the tension. But as much as he kept waiting for that feeling to arrive, it hadn't.

"Sometimes it's easier to be alone when you're grieving. You avoid people in order to avoid thinking and feeling until you realize you haven't had a face-to-face interaction with any of your friends for a month and you gotta force yourself to take a shower, get dressed, and phone a friend." Krish smiled but it faded so quickly Silas thought maybe he'd imagined it.

"You speak like you have experience."

Krish leaned back and exhaled. Now their shoulders, hips, and thighs were pressed together on the bench. Silas's breath hitched as Krish shifted and their calves brushed together. He felt that contact shoot straight to his chest and then spread warmth through his body. He'd thought the guy was hot before they spoke. His brain was starting to get turned on, which was always important for him when he chose someone to be intimate with. If he could kiss? Silas might win the jackpot.

Krish must have realized how close they were sitting. He started to move over a little, but Silas stopped him with a hand to his knee.

"You're easy to talk to, you know?"

Krish looked at Silas's hand on him and he chuckled. "Thanks. I just…."

Their eyes met, and they were quiet for a few beats before shouts and loud singing started up.

Jake and Jordan were worse than drunken pirates trying to sing the Disney pirate song. Krish turned to watch as Jake hit a particularly high note and everyone clapped.

"Barrett junior has got quite a voice," Silas said, impressed.

"He's such a mess," Krish said.

"And he's gotten my guitar player wasted."

Krish snorted. "Pretty sure it was the other way around. Those Shipwrecks would knock anyone on their ass after two or more. My upper lip is already tingling and I haven't even finished my drink."

Silas mentally groaned. *Why did he have to talk about tingling? I'm fucking vibrating just sitting next to him.*

"We don't get wasted every night anymore. We're getting a little old for that. We spend a lot of time battling each other on Xbox on our bus."

"Yeah? Ha! Because that's so mature," Krish said with a belly laugh. "What's your game?"

"You're right." Silas laughed. "I should never intimate that we're mature in any way, shape, or form. We've been playing a lot of *Friday the 13th*. We picked that up before the tour, and *Outcast*. Always *Call of Duty*, but I'm also a sucker for *Mortal Kombat*."

Silas couldn't help dropping that little tidbit, knowing full well that the Guru considered himself an expert on *Mortal Kombat*. He claimed he had moves that were undefeatable. *One last hint, and then I'll drop it.*

"I've heard *Friday the 13th* is cool, but I haven't had a chance to play it yet."

Damn. It probably would be safer to just assume this guy wasn't the Guru. Silas shook his head and scolded himself. He didn't need to eat his cake and have it too. The cake was nice....

"So," he said, nudging Krish with his knee. "How about a game?"

Krish looked around. "Now? Here?"

Silas laughed and stood up. "Yeah. We've got a sweet setup on the tour bus. Come on. We've got snacks too." He wiggled his eyebrows, and Krish laughed.

"Snacks sound good. Uh, let me just tell Jake."

"You do that."

Chapter Six

KRISH'S HANDS shook as he walked across the parking lot to where Jake and his brother hung on each other, singing at the top of their lungs. They actually sounded quite nice. While Jake looked totally out of place in his preppy clothes, he sure could hold his own in the vocal department.

"Heyyyyyyy, Krish! Meet my friend Krish, everyone."

Krish recognized several of the members of Backdrop Silhouette, including a very sullen Burke Dickens, who Krish happened to know Jake had history with. He held up a hand in greeting and then turned back to Jake and spoke directly in his ear.

"Silas just asked me to go back to the bus to play video games."

Jake turned toward Krish and laughed, spraying Krish in the face with a fine mist of beer and spit. The dude was wasted.

"That's awesome, Gee!"

Krish grabbed his arm and pulled him closer. "Are you all right? Should I stay?"

"I'm fiiiiiine," Jake whispered. "Sorry, man. Really. But back to the bus? Are you ready for all that? Freaky shit happens on these tour buses, you know?" He shot a nasty look at Burke. "And if you play too good, he'll know you're…." His whisper turned into a burst of laughter that called a little bit too much attention to them.

Krish sighed. He couldn't hope to remain faceless forever, especially if the job came through. But tonight was not the night for a big reveal.

Wow. He'd gone several hours without thinking about his potential new career, which was kind of a miracle. Even though last week's initial interview had gone well and they seemed to have faith in him covering the tour, he was still new to all of this. He couldn't afford to mess up—

Not going to think about it. The potential job might be a dream come true, but Silas is my fantasy come to life, and he's waiting for me.

"Don't do anything I wouldn't do," Jake said and went back to hanging on his brother.

"Where's the fun in that?" Krish asked himself as he walked back toward Silas. Something much larger than butterflies had taken up residence in his stomach. Perhaps it was an alien chestburster and a creature was going to come flying out of his rib cage any minute, skitter across the ground, slap onto

Silas's face…. Wait, no, that was the face huggers. They impregnated their victims with chestbursters.

How could he be expected to keep his *Alien* monster lore straight when Silas had him so tied up in knots?

Silas had asked a couple of weird questions, and Krish wondered if Silas was probing him, like maybe he had suspicions about Krish being the Guru. But why would he care? He doubted Silas gave more than a passing thought to the Guru and his blog.

But then there was the touching. Silas was definitely flirting with him, and Krish barely knew how to handle it. How was he supposed to play video games with his crush sitting next to him on a bus with no one else around when the guy was so gorgeous and potentially interested?

"You okay? You look like you ate something bad," Silas said with a mischievous smile.

"No. No, not at all. I was just thinking about *Aliens*."

"*Aliens*? The game or the movie?"

"Either. Both. You a fan?"

"Absolutely. *Aliens* was my first horror film." Silas had a pleased smile on his face.

"The first of many?" Krish asked him, digging where the conversation was going.

"Yeah. I've been a horror junkie since I was seven years old. I used to stay up and watch with my dad. Until he left. Then it was just me. *Whoa*. Overshare. You ready to go get beat?"

That was random. Krish thought maybe Silas was just as nervous as he was. Maybe he just hid it better because he was used to being on display. Krish lived his life anonymously and made it a point to not call attention to himself. He wasn't sure who had it worse.

Silas linked arms with Krish and led him toward the buses. "You staying on one of these?"

"Yeah," Krish said, having to concentrate on forming words almost as much as walking. "I'm riding with some of the office staff and some photographers."

"Vinh Hoang one of them? He's hella cool."

"Yeah, uh, I haven't met everyone yet, but—"

"Ah, then I know which bus you're on. Casey's cool too. Just watch yourself. She's a prankster from what I hear. There are several of those around."

"I'll keep that in mind."

"Have you ever had the pleasure of visiting one of the band coaches? We've got a pretty sweet one this year."

Krish laughed. "Once. My brother knew the guys from Avenged Sevenfold back in the day, and he brought me to see them when they were in San Diego. We hung out before the show for a bit. That was a while ago. I was still in high school, like the beginning of high school even, and he was in college at the time. I just remember it being really messy and smelly."

"The smell goes with the territory. No matter how much incense gets burned or how many Arm & Hammer boxes we use, it never covers the stench completely. But I try to pick up after these assholes. It's not perfect, but it's home, and fortunately for you, we're only just barely out on the road, so the smell hasn't permeated everything yet."

"I'll consider myself lucky, then."

There was a lot of movement on the grounds as the crews packed up the bands' equipment and tore down the tents. Krish couldn't believe how quickly they worked. He knew from the schedule that they were playing tomorrow up north and figured it wouldn't be long before the buses started to leave. He wasn't ready to be done with the night, done spending time alone with Silas.

He looked down at Silas as they walked, amazed at how much larger he seemed while onstage. Krish hadn't realized there would be such a height difference between them, but then all of his prior musings had been more about Silas the lyricist, Silas the performer, and Silas the spokesman for Hush. He was enjoying getting to know Silas the flirt.

Silas led Krish to the same row of black-and-gray tour buses where his own was located and stopped at the third one. "Home sweet home," he said as he opened the door. "We have to hit the road in a bit, but we have time to get a few rounds in."

"Are you sure? I don't want to keep you from anything if you have stuff to do."

Silas paused on the first step. He turned around and laughed when he realized he was taller than Krish in that position.

"I have nothing more important to do than spending some time with you."

Krish felt that alien crawling around inside him again. It had been a long time since he'd made a connection with another guy. His last boyfriend broke up with him shortly after his brother died, and since then he'd been too busy writing and teaching music lessons to date a whole lot. He wanted something deeper than he'd had with guys he met online or through an app. He'd been crushing on Silas for years, but crush-Silas was nothing like this man in front of him.

"Come on." Silas gestured with his hand. "Let's play."

Once inside, Silas gave Krish the quick tour and led him to the back lounge, where they had their gaming consoles set up. Krish noticed they had a shelf full of titles he was familiar with, including *Mortal Kombat*, but it would be a dead giveaway if he asked to play that. He was incapable of losing, no matter the version, and he'd boasted about that on his blog.

"As you can see, we're huge nerds. We haven't actually had much time to play yet, but when we have a day or two on break, watch out. It gets ugly back here. You want something to drink?"

Krish sat down on the couch Silas gestured to. "Water, I guess?"

Silas grinned. "Two waters, coming right up."

He was back in a second and handed a cold bottle to Krish.

"So which game do you want to lose first?"

Krish laughed. "Competitive much?"

Silas shrugged. "Not as much as Los or Brains. They come to blows over this shit sometimes. I just let them rage and then I beat them when they get out of control."

"You pick," Krish said. "Let's see if you're as good as you say you are."

Silas raised an eyebrow and rested his hands on his hips. "Do you doubt me?"

Not in the least. You've already got me a mess over here and you haven't even handed me a controller.

Silas was dressed more laid-back than when he was onstage, and his makeup was gone. He was gorgeous with or without it, but tonight, in the dim light of the bus, he looked softer, a little more vulnerable, even with his feisty stance.

"We'll see." Krish couldn't help but smile.

They started with a little zombie killing on *Call of Duty* and then moved on to *Friday the 13th*. Krish laughed as Silas narrated what he was doing the entire time and his whole body reacted whenever Jason showed up.

"Oh, fuck me sideways. That scared the crap out of me."

"You keep going after him. What do you expect? He's Jason. He's going to kill you."

"Yeah, but I've beat him before," Silas complained. "I swear, we just got this one. I haven't mastered all the techniques yet."

"Mm-hmm," Krish said, pressing his lips together to keep from laughing. "Keep telling yourself that."

Silas elbowed him just as he got killed again. He flopped back against the couch and sighed.

"I think it's because I'm distracted."

Krish let Jason hack him to pieces with a machete and then leaned back next to Silas. "What's distracting you?"

"You," Silas said, and turned to face him, "and the fact that we have to leave soon and I haven't even begun to have fun with you."

There was the problem. They'd be on the road together the next couple of months, but who knew if they'd be able to spend time together like this? Alone? Their paths would likely cross again, but he was here now. Something about that made him feel brave.

"Then I hope you don't mind if I do this."

Krish leaned over and pressed a tentative kiss to Silas's lips. When he pulled back, he found a blissful smile on Silas's lips.

"I'll only mind if you don't do it again."

Krish leaned down again and placed his left hand onto the couch next to Silas's thigh to brace himself. He couldn't believe he was actually here, but he wasn't going to let that stop him. This time when he kissed Silas, there was nothing tentative about it. He dragged his lips against Silas's like he'd imagined on nights alone in his room, dreaming he'd meet him in person someday. He let himself try all the moves, taking the chance that he was doing it right, *praying* that he was doing it right.

Silas groaned as they came up for air. "You are a really fucking good kisser."

Krish smiled against Silas's lips and went in again, this time letting his tongue explore Silas's lips insistently enough that Silas opened for him. As Krish's tongue brushed Silas's and he felt the silver ball, Krish shuddered. He lost all composure and kissed Silas so deeply that he pressed him back into the couch. Silas slid his hand under Krish's shirt and up his back, his nails scoring Krish's skin, causing him to groan.

"I don't know how long we have until they come back," Silas whispered as he moved his kisses lower, to Krish's jaw and then his neck. "But I don't want you to go."

Krish's head was spinning. *God*, the feel of that ball as Silas licked up the column of his throat. "I don't want to stop kissing you," Krish admitted. The alien in his belly had settled, but his pulse was racing. He thought he might never take a deep breath again, and he didn't much care. He placed his hands on either side of Silas's head and brought his lips away from his neck and back to his mouth.

Don't let this end. I want to kiss you forever.

"Really fucking good kisser," Silas breathed. Then he dove back in and teased Krish relentlessly with his tongue and the piercing that had Krish so turned on he couldn't breathe.

The bus doors opened and loud partygoers burst into the front of the bus. Silas had opened the bathroom door enough that they couldn't see directly into the back, which gave them a moment to sit up and at least pretend they were still trying to defeat Jason.

"You guys decent back there?" a female voice asked.

"Yes, boss lady," Silas called out, giggling.

"Barely," Krish whispered. "Another few seconds and I would have had you out of those pants."

Silas laughed and ran a hand over the bulge in Krish's pants. "I would have had you stripped first."

Krish put a hand over Silas's and pressed it against himself. His eyes rolled back in his head and he groaned.

"Why don't we have more time?" Silas sat up, his green eyes wide. "Ride with us. Up to Mountain View. Please? Stay with me? I'm not done playing with you."

Krish laughed and sat back. He ran his hands through his hair and finally took a deep breath. "Stay? On the bus? But you need to sleep. You have to play tomorrow."

"And I will. With you. Right here." Silas grabbed Krish's hands, and his smile took on that crazy look that made Krish whimper and want to say yes to anything. "Do you have to go?"

"I don't know. I should probably check on Jake—"

The door closed to the bathroom and retching sounds could be heard through the thin walls.

"Jake is wasted," Jordan said, leaning against the doorjamb. "I win. I told him he'd get sick first. Dude, he's gonna need to stay here tonight. I had Theo drive his car out to the street where it won't get fucking towed. As soon as he's back, we're taking off." Jordan looked at their hands intertwined and laughed. "I'm giving him your bunk, since it looks like you won't need it."

"If he pukes, you're cleaning it and doing all the laundry," Silas said with a laugh. He turned back to Krish and squeezed his hand. "Darn it. I guess you're stuck back here in the lounge with me." Then his smile slipped. "Unless you have someone…?"

"Yeah. I do, but I can text her."

Silas let go of his hand and moved to get up. "Her?"

"You should see your face right now," Krish said, laughing. "Yeah, 'her.' My mom. I told her I would text her tonight." Still feeling brave, he grabbed Silas by the waist and guided him back down onto his lap. "I live with my mom. At twenty-five. I know that's hot, but there're reasons."

Silas linked his arms around Krish's neck. "It's sexy as fuck. Guys who are good to their moms are fucking hot." He bent down and captured Krish's lips again, sucking the bottom one into his mouth and flicking the ball against it. "Last chance. I can walk you back to your bus."

"I want to spend the night with you." Krish gazed up into Silas's eyes and loved the emotions he saw there—joy, arousal, excitement. He never expected Silas to be attracted to him. He wasn't sure what to expect when he came back to the bus. Did Silas just want to hook up and send Krish on his way? Did he just want someone to blow off some steam with on the gaming console? Or was it possible he felt like Krish did? Like maybe, just maybe, he was looking for a real connection?

"Good. I'll be right back."

Silas disentangled himself from Krish's lap and went up front, leaving Krish a moment to try to catch his breath. He pulled out his phone and sent a text to his mom.

Day One was great. We're staying on the bus with Jake's brother's band. With Hush. We go to Mountain View in the Bay Area tomorrow. I'll have my phone on me. Love you.

It was after eleven, but she texted back.

Oh Lord, be safe on those buses, Krishnan Guruvayoor! Use a condom and wear a seat belt. You know I'm afraid of those horrible bus crashes! You better come back to me in one piece. Say hello to Jake for me. XOXO

Krish snorted a laugh and shook his head.

Thanks, Mom.

Krish's phone buzzed.

We're heading out. Are you lost?

Chantal. *Shit.* He hadn't even thought someone might be looking for him.

Not lost. Sorry. I should have checked in. I'm on the bus with Hush. My friend's brother is Jordan Barrett, and they invited us to stay.

What else was he supposed to say? Was he breaking some rule? Had he fucked up already?

No problem. We just always check in so no one gets left behind. Have fun. Vinh said don't let Silas beat you at Mortal Kombat.

Krish's smile dropped. Why would Vinh have said that? Of all the games, *Mortal Kombat*? What if—
"You texting your mom?"
Krish started to answer Silas, but he froze.

Silas had changed into a pair of black pajama pants with rainbow unicorns on them, and he wasn't wearing a shirt. He wasn't wearing anything underneath the pants either. They rode low on his hips and accentuated his V. He was hairless, his nipples were pierced, and he was incredibly well-toned. Krish had seen pictures of Silas shirtless before and knew the entire front of his torso was covered in colorful tattoos—skulls, horror creatures, anatomically correct hearts, black cats, classic muscle cars. They all flowed together to create a living mural that Krish could spend forever admiring.

Krish's jaw hung open in awe.

Silas had a toothbrush in his mouth and a wicked grin on his face.

"Everything okay?" Silas asked, chuckling. He ran a hand over his flat stomach and hooked his thumb over the waistband of his pants. Just that gesture alone made Krish's mouth water.

"Yeah, um, you—"

"I have an extra toothbrush, but I think my extra lounge pants will be too short for you."

"That's okay. Um, shouldn't you sleep in your bunk, though? I mean, you have to perform tomorrow. You need your rest."

Silas turned and went into the bathroom to spit into the sink. Krish heard him gargle, and then the water came on. He came back into the room and handed Krish a toothbrush. "I'll be fine. You'll be my pillow."

Krish took the toothbrush from him and stood. Silas was so close to him he could smell his minty-fresh mouth and feel his breath on his face.

"Hurry up." Silas went back out front while Krish used the bathroom. He was so hard it took him several minutes to talk himself down. He felt like an idiot taking such a long time.

But then the creature in his gut started churning again. *What are you doing, Krish? How can you spend the night with him when he doesn't know who you are for real?* He felt like he was being dishonest. But how was he supposed to know he was going to get invited onto the bus? By Silas? That he would be *kissing* Silas freakin' Franklin?

Krish's knees wobbled a little, and he steadied himself on the sink. When he looked at himself in the mirror, he chuckled. His lips were swollen from their impromptu makeout session. Silas's face had been red from Krish's beard, and that made Krish's grin a little bigger.

Chances are Silas didn't even read the Guru's blog, right? He had much better things to do with his time. *Yeah.* And this was probably the one and only time Krish would get to live the dream, so *carpe diem*?

That thought sobered him. He needed to remember who he was, who he was with, and that he couldn't afford to do anything that would mess up his opportunity at Warped Tour. He sucked in a breath and let it out slowly. *I hope you know what you're doing, Krish.*

When he came back out, Silas had set out pillows and blankets for them on the couch in the back. The narrow couch.

"Uh, do these, like, pull out into a bed?"

Silas laughed. "I tried. If they do, I can't figure it out. I don't have a degree in engineering, nor am I brainy like Billy."

"Yeah, and I don't think a music major will be much help."

"Music, huh? You play?"

Silas lay down on his side with his back against the cushions. He rested his head in the palm of his hand and patted the narrow spot next to him. And didn't that spot look like the best damn place to be?

"Yeah."

Should he take off his shirt?

Should he take off *more*?

Krish certainly wasn't a blushing virgin or anything, but he had a feeling his experience was probably virginal compared to Silas's.

"Come lie down, Krish. I don't fuck on tour, if that's what you're worried about."

"I'm not worried." But he didn't sound very confident.

"Good. Then come here."

"Good. Sure."

Krish pulled his shirt off from the back collar and laid it on the opposite couch. He wasn't exactly embarrassed about his body, but it was nothing compared to the beauty that was Silas. Krish was... nondescript—a little on the thin side but not skinny. He wasn't weak, but he didn't lift weights or anything, so he didn't have that toned look that a lot of men preferred in their partners. And he was fairly hairy. He'd tried waxing once, but it was a miserable experience he never cared to repeat. At least he had it where hair was expected to be—his chest, stomach, and lower arms and legs. His cargo shorts were a little large on him, so he'd worn a belt, which he slipped off and set down with his shirt. He might be facing an uncomfortable night's sleep, but it would be miserable with a belt on. The top of his Calvin Klein briefs showed over his shorts without the belt, but by the look on Silas's face, he didn't mind one bit.

"You don't fuck on tour," Krish repeated as he lay down facing Silas. He kept some space between them, afraid of what would happen if he pressed up against all that gorgeous colorful skin.

"No. Fool around, yes. But no fucking on tour. For many reasons."

"I can understand that. For many reasons. You have to be careful."

"And not just the physical ones. For me, fucking comes with a whole other level of intimacy that I'm not willing to give away to someone I might only spend one night with. Does that make sense? I don't know. It might sound weird—"

"It makes perfect sense. That level of intimacy also makes people expect certain things too, right? And not to mention the ones who want the attention and want to spread stories."

"Exactly." Silas frowned. "Hey…. This is cool, right? Like, do I need to worry about this? I don't need any hassle."

Krish swallowed hard. "Yeah. Look. I know you just met me, but I'm not… I don't…. That's not what's going on here."

Silas visibly relaxed, which made Krish feel both relieved and irritated. Had someone done that to him before? Slept with him and then told everyone about it? Gone to the media? Did he make a habit of sleeping with reporters? Did it matter?

"I'm sorry. I just need to ask. Gavin never seemed to mind what was printed about him. I think that's why he used to get shit from people—the hate mail, more than anything. Discretion was never his strong suit, and he had a few messy situations go public. I never judged him or anything. I just think he made his life more complicated than it needed to be sometimes."

Silas rested his head on the pillow and closed his eyes, finally looking tired. He must have had a long couple of days. Krish slid down a bit and rested his head on the pillow next to Silas, using his right hand to drag his nails across Silas's stubble, still wondering if he had the right to touch him. Silas moaned happily, snuggled a little closer, and threw an arm over Krish's side. Guess that was his answer.

"How are you holding up without him?" Krish asked quietly. He didn't know if it was his place to ask, but Silas seemed comfortable enough with him that he figured it was a safe question.

"I have my moments. Jordan's been awesome. It's different, but once we got onstage for the first show, I knew we were going to be okay." He slid his hand farther up Krish's spine and goose bumps followed in the wake. "I miss him."

"I can imagine. It's not just your friend and companion but your creative partner that you lost. That leaves a much larger hole."

Silas smirked but didn't open his eyes. "You sound like the Guru."

Krish stopped his hand briefly and prayed Silas didn't notice him freeze.

"The Guru? How?"

"Just sounds like something he'd say. You ever read his blog?"

Krish swallowed hard, grateful Silas's eyes were closed, because he knew his expression would give him away. "Yeah, sometimes." *Fuck. Now you're a liar, Krish.* And this confirmed that Silas had read his blog.

"He wrote the most beautiful piece about Gavin after he died. I'd been really pissed at Gavin, but after reading the Guru's eulogy, I couldn't be mad anymore. It led to reaching that last step in those five stages of grief, you know?"

"I do," Krish whispered. He couldn't pull away, didn't want to. Silas had been through hell. He'd lost his best friend. Krish knew that pain intimately. Instead of coming clean, however, he slid his left arm under Silas's head and pulled him closer. Their chests brushed together, and Silas sighed.

"I'm a cuddler, just in case you were wondering," Silas slurred, his cheek smushed against Krish's shoulder. It was astounding how he'd gone from the psycho showman, to the flirty sex god, to a cuddle buddy in the space of a few hours.

"I am pleased by this development." So much so Krish couldn't stop smiling. His cheeks were getting sore.

Silas's breathing grew deeper, and Krish was amazed the guy could sleep in such a cramped position. But then he'd probably spent countless nights in a tour-bus bunk, and those were pretty small.

Krish turned a little more onto his back. Silas came with and sprawled on top of him. Krish smiled blissfully and wrapped both arms around his cuddle buddy. He wondered what the morning would bring. He'd let his eyes drift closed and was nearing sleep when the voices outside their pocket door got louder.

The door slid open with a quiet hush. Jordan and Jake and Los all stuck their heads in, eyes wide. Krish blinked. After a moment, they burst out laughing and then shushed each other when Silas stirred. He shot an arm out behind him and flipped them off.

"Fuck off, you guys. Go to sleep." His cheek was stuck to Krish's chest and his words came out in a higher pitch than his usual voice. He lifted his head and smoothed Krish's chest hair down. "Tickles," he mumbled. Then he placed a kiss on Krish's chest and lay back down with a loud sigh.

"You need anything?" Jordan asked.

Krish shook his head. "Thanks."

Jake blew him a kiss and then hiccupped as Jordan dragged him out of the room.

Los frowned as he closed the door. Whether it was at the drunkard's behavior or Krish cuddled up with his bandmate, he wasn't sure.

Krish looked down at Silas's body intertwined with his and felt as though he were holding a valuable piece of art—fragile, priceless, and vulnerable yet strong. Silas was fierce and capable of completely turning Krish's world upside down. Cuddling was almost more intense than kissing Silas. It implied a level of trust Krish was shocked someone like Silas had to have in order to sleep so soundly.

Silas stirred and a little snore escaped.

Adorable.

And sexy.

And so far out of Krish's realm of comprehension.... Why had Silas chosen him? And why hadn't he just come clean? Perhaps it would have been fine, they would have shared some laughs and stories. But now he had a secret on top of a secret, and the person he admired so much would likely be hurt at his omission of the truth.

How was it possible that the best thing ever to happen to you was also the worst thing you've ever done?

DESPITE BEING unable to stretch out, Krish slept surprisingly well, at least once he'd stopped beating himself up. He'd deal with the consequences of his actions in the morning. He woke up a few times when the bus hit some vicious potholes and once when they came to a stop, probably at a rest area on I-5, but each time he smiled at Silas still stretched out on top of him. Around six in the morning, Silas groaned. Krish tried to give him some room to move, and when Silas rolled onto his back, Krish sucked in a breath.

The head of Silas's dick poked out from the opening in his pajama pants. He was pierced there too.

"Oh God." Krish clapped a hand over his mouth. He hadn't meant to speak out loud, but fucking hell, if he thought Silas was irresistible before....

"I gotta piss," Silas groaned again. He rubbed his hands over his face and sat up. "Oh, hello there," he said, looking down at his lap. He covered himself and then grinned at Krish. "I'll be right back."

He climbed carefully from on top of Krish and hit the button for the door. It slid open.

Krish was awake. Fully. By the time Silas returned, Krish had already imagined several thousand ways he wanted to show his appreciation for Silas, starting with—

"Good morning, gorgeous. You got room for me?"

Krish lay back and spread his legs, planting one foot on the floor. "Come here."

Silas pushed the button, and the door slid closed. He twisted the lock this time and then climbed back onto the bench and pressed his pelvis into Krish's, grinding their very awake cocks together.

Krish slid his hands down to grip Silas's ass and pulled him even tighter just as Silas bent down to kiss him deeply. Their tongues glided together in a slow build that set Krish's senses alight. Screw morning breath. Silas was apparently going for it, and Krish was helpless… and loving it.

"Is this the fooling around part?" Krish asked. He nibbled along Silas's collarbone and felt Silas shiver above him.

"There's nothing fooling about this. You feel good, Krish. Can I touch you? I want to touch you."

"Yeah. Touch me." Krish immediately wondered if he was dreaming. In what other scenario would Silas Franklin be here, asking to pleasure him?

Silas backed onto his knees and made quick work of unfastening Krish's shorts. He pulled them down enough to free Krish's erection. A wicked smile lit up Silas's face, and then he bent and licked up Krish's shaft.

Krish sucked in a breath and Silas laughed.

"You're perfect," Silas said and licked him again. He sucked Krish into his mouth and Krish moaned.

"Shhhh," Silas whispered, chuckling. "You'll have the whole bus listening at the door."

"I'm sorry," Krish whispered, "but that ball is going to make me insane."

Silas sat up and hooked his fingers into the waistband of his pajama pants. "Good." He slid them slowly down over his hips to reveal the longest, most gorgeous cock Krish had ever seen. The silver barbell passed through his glans and left a round ball above and below his ridge.

"That's magnificent," Krish said, his fingers itching to touch Silas. "May I?"

Silas smirked as he stroked his long shaft.

Krish sat up and placed his hands on Silas's hips. He ran his lips along the glans and loved the feel of the metal there.

Silas slid his fingers into Krish's hair and tilted his head back. "I fucking love seeing you like this."

Krish didn't break eye contact as he ran his tongue from the base of Silas's cock to the tip and then down again. When Silas tightened his grip on Krish's hair, Krish took him in his mouth and sucked hard, causing them both to groan and then giggle at their attempts to be quiet.

"So good," Silas whispered. "God, that's so good."

Krish could go down on this guy for the rest of his life and be the happiest man on the planet. There was something incredibly pleasing about how he tasted and smelled, as well as how his sensitive skin felt sliding along Krish's tongue and lips. And those metal balls were so fucking sexy.

Silas tugged on his hair. "Lie back."

Krish did as he asked. His cock throbbed as he watched Silas lick his own palm thoroughly. Then he lay down on top of Krish and wrapped his hand around both of them.

"I want to kiss you some more." He thrust his tongue into Krish's mouth as Krish thrust against his hand. Krish wanted to be even closer, but his shorts were in the way.

Silas laughed when he saw his predicament and he momentarily let go to help free one of Krish's legs. They fell back together in a tangle of limbs, and Silas once again took over stroking them both as they thrust together. Krish wrapped his long legs around Silas's hips, attempting to bring him even closer, and he groaned when Silas added more saliva to his hand. Krish dragged his fingers through their precum and clasped his hand over Silas's. He squeezed tight.

"I'm going to come so hard," Silas moaned against Krish's mouth. "Come with me, Krish. I want to feel you all over me. Come for me, baby."

One more thrust of Silas's tongue and his cock against Krish's and Krish exploded, his orgasm nearly turning him inside out. He kept coming and coming, and Silas stroked him until he thought he might pass out.

"That's it. God, you're so fucking hot, Krish." One more thrust and Silas's back arched as his whole body tensed. He came in a rush, his face red and splotchy. Krish loved how dark red Silas's lips were, and he couldn't help taking little nibbles at them. He tasted so good.

Silas sat up and reached for a box of tissue on the shelf above them. Then he sat back and just stared smugly at Krish's chest.

"I like me all over you," he said as he smeared his finger through their mess. "I want to do that again. A lot. More."

He took his time cleaning Krish up the best he could with the tissues and a little water from a bottle, and he giggled as he made Krish jump everywhere.

"Sorry. Quit squirming," Silas said. "I'll make sure you get a shower."

"Thanks," Krish said. And then they both fell quiet as Krish put on his clothes and Silas began pulling clothes out of a drawer for his performance—a subtle reminder that their night was over and it was back to business. Krish cleared his throat.

"I'll be out of your hair as soon as we get to the venue."

Silas turned around and frowned. "Hey," he said, taking a seat next to Krish. "What's this about? Didn't you have fun last night? This morning?"

"Of course I did," Krish said, running his hands through his hair. "I'm just trying to give you an out, you know?"

"Why the fuck would I want an out? Did I not make myself clear to you? I want you here. Can I at least tell you what I had in mind for today before you go running off?"

Krish sat back, a little stunned at the anger in Silas's voice. Silas cursed and appeared to make a concerted effort to soften the tone of this voice.

"I will find out this morning what time we play and what our other obligations are. The rest of the time, I was hoping we could hang out, watch some bands. Sometimes I can sneak around without getting mobbed, but I don't fucking care if I get noticed. I'm not done with you, all right? Now, unless you have a problem with that—"

Krish put his hands on Silas's arms. "No, not at all. Not at all. Last night and this morning were sublime, Silas. I just don't want to overstep my bounds. Okay?"

Silas grabbed his chin and forced Krish to look him in the eyes. "Let me be the judge of that. Right now, while I would love to have some more fun with you, I need to fix breakfast for those damn heathens out there and meet with Jessica about the day's schedule. I'd love for you to join me, meet the rest of the guys. Just be prepared. They're very protective of me, and they might ask you fifty million questions. Otherwise, they're my family, and I love them. Just don't be surprised if someone asks to, like, see ID or asks if you have a criminal record or something. You don't, do you?"

Krish barked out a laugh. "No. No record. And thank you."

"Thank me? No, babe. Thank you. That was fucking amazing. You are fucking amazing."

"No, you're the amazing one. I don't ever *not* want to have your cock in my mouth." Okay, wow. Had he just really said that out loud? Krish was in way over his head.

Silas burst out laughing and pulled Krish into an embrace. "You're fun. Thank you. Now why don't you go take that shower before everyone else gets up? I'll stick a towel in there for you. Fuck, why you have to cover up at all is beyond me, though. You're so hot."

"Stop it," Krish said with a laugh as Silas reached for him again. Just the brush of his fingers made Krish shudder.

It took them another ten minutes to leave the back lounge. Krish squeezed himself into the tiny shower stall. The setup was that you closed both pocket doors in the hallway and opened the toilet and shower doors to give you the bathroom and shower open together, or you just stayed behind one door for the shower. It was an interesting concept. Thankfully Krish was thin, but his height made the shower a challenge. He hoped it was okay to use whatever products were in there, avoiding the Axe products in favor of some Herbal Essences shampoo and Trader Joe's body wash. He hated not being able to shave. His beard grew in fast and thick and would probably look like a week's growth by tonight, but that couldn't be helped. Borrowing a razor was not an option.

Krish was in a daze as he tried to be quick with his shower. He'd awakened on Hush's tour bus this morning. In the arms of Silas Franklin. Who he was going to spend the day with. Shit like this just didn't happen to Krish. Yeah, he'd met some extraordinary musicians in the past, but as a fan. As Vivaan's brother, Krish. Not as the Guru. Not as Silas's guest.

"What do you think, brother?" he asked the heavens. "Am I living the dream or headed for a nightmare?"

Vivaan didn't answer. He hadn't for three years.

Krish stepped out of the shower room in the towel Silas had given him and was about to return to the back lounge to dress when he heard a moan.

"Please, baby Jesus, let this be a nightmare. Let me open my eyes to find myself back in my own bed."

Jake. His blond head hung out of the bunk in the middle row.

"Did you maybe have a little too much fun last night?" Krish asked him.

The head wobbled around and looked up at Krish, and Krish couldn't help but bark out a laugh.

"Dude. Your face right now."

Someone had gone wild with a black eyeliner pencil on Jake's face. Probably his brother. Whoever it was couldn't spell.

Jake pulled back behind the curtain and cursed loudly.

"'Can't hold his lick her'? Who the fuck is headed for the spelling bee? *Lick her*? Really? You hold the fucking bottles enough, you'd think the spelling would be ingrained in your memory by now, you Neanderthal. And Jordan, I know this is your writing."

The laughter from the front lounge was loud and rowdy. The pocket door at the other end of the bunks was closed, so Krish couldn't tell who all was out there, but it seemed like an awful lot of voices.

"I'm going to go get dressed," he said quietly, hoping he would be able to duck back inside without Jake's notice.

"Krishnan Gu—"

"Shut it," Krish said, dashing to Jake's bunk so quickly he nearly dropped his towel. "Come on, man."

"I'm sorry," Jake said, and thankfully he covered his mouth, since he had vomit breath.

Jake's eyes went wide as he took in Krish's state of undress.

"Holy balls, Krish," he whisper-exclaimed. "Did you get laid last night?"

"Shhhh," Krish warned him. "Shut up, Jake. It's not like that."

Jake laughed. "Oh really. What's it like, then? You lose your clothes somewhere?"

Krish dropped his head back and rested his hands on his hips. Jake still sounded drunk, so he'd be forgiven unless he continued to carry on.

"I just showered, okay? I'm going to go get dressed now, if you're finished."

He started to walk away, and his towel suddenly slipped. He frantically grabbed for it and turned to see Jake had hold of the end of it and was laughing hysterically.

"You've always had such a nice ass." More laughing.

Krish escaped into the back lounge and blew out a breath. Jake was normally a really together guy, if a little extroverted. But drunk? He was a disaster. He must have had quite a bit to still be drunk.

He tried to collect himself as he put on his clothes from the previous night, but the idea of meeting the band after they'd all seen him and Silas together had him all kinds of uncomfortable.

One foot in front of the other. Time for the walk of possible shame. He slid the pocket door open at the end of the sleeping area.

"I'm so glad we play earlier today, dude," one of the guys said. "I'm coming back here to nap after the fucking meet and greet."

Krish stepped out into the front lounge and all heads turned his way. Curious and amused grins met him. Brains and Los sat on one side of the booth, and Jordan and Jake sat on the other. Jessica stood with Silas next to the kitchenette where he was working a skillet.

"Let me get these fuckers fed, and then I'll make some for you," he said as Krish approached him. Silas pushed up on his toes and kissed him. All the guys groaned at their display.

"Not fair, Silas. I want someone to kiss good morning. All I've got is my drunk-ass brother."

Jake punched Jordan in the thigh, which set off a round of them trying to see who could give the other one a worse charley horse. Brains threw his hands out.

"Dudes. Jordan, leave your brother alone. Jake, we can't afford to have a broken guitar player today. Ease up."

Silas served plates of french toast and what looked like microwaved bacon to Jordan and Jake. Brains and Los were already working on theirs.

"Oh, thank you, Silas, but I'm a vegetarian," Jake said with an apologetic expression.

Jordan reached over and grabbed his bacon. "More for me."

Jake slapped his hand. "Maybe someone else wants it, pig. You already had some."

"Guys, there's enough to go around," Silas said. He turned to Krish and rolled his eyes. "You can sit on the couch over there. I'll be done in a minute or two."

"Thanks," Krish said.

"I think if you're going to walk around, you should take security, Silas. That's all I'm saying."

"I'll be fine, Jessica," Silas said. "I don't need a fucking babysitter."

Krish frowned. Maybe she was right. Silas could get hurt if the fans went nuts.

"It's okay, Silas. You don't—"

"I can take care of myself."

Silas's tone silenced everyone on the bus.

Chapter Seven

"I CAN fucking walk around the festival if I want to."

Silas glanced at Krish in time to see him wince and sit down on the couch with a glass of juice Jessica had handed him.

Here we go again. Silas was sick and tired of the fuss made over him. So what if he was smaller than the other guys? Yeah, he had a fucking temper, but could anyone blame him? He'd been messed with his whole life, either for being short, being a musician, being gay… whatever. He was sick of it. He hated having this conversation in front of Krish. And now he'd gone and upset him. *Awesome.*

Jessica took a step back and looked at the ground. "Look, I'm sorry, Silas," she said in a low voice once the others started talking again. "I'm not trying to babysit you. I'm here to serve the best interest of the band, and you getting arrested for fighting or—"

"That was one time," he said. "I wasn't going to sit back and let a couple of drunk homophobic douchebags ruin my night."

Silas dipped another piece of Texas toast into his mixture for french toast and slid the finished pieces onto a plate. He sprinkled powdered sugar on them, added a to-go pack of syrup, and handed it to Krish.

Krish smiled up at him in thanks as he took the plate, and Silas could breathe again. He dipped his finger into the powdered sugar and touched Krish's lips with it. Krish slyly licked it away, and Silas was reminded of how good the guy was with his tongue. He could really get used to having this gorgeous man around.

"Hey, loverboy. You got any more of that toast?" Los was moping this morning and Silas sensed he wasn't too pleased with him for having Krish stay. *Too fucking bad.* Los had brought plenty of girls on past tours. Shit, there'd been nights when they'd all had overnight guests at one point, which made for an interesting experience. Gavin would usually be the one to say "Screw the bunks" and get busy out in the open.

"Yeah, coming up."

Silas finished another round of french toast for everyone, and it was gobbled up along with the bacon. Then the bus arrived at the venue in Mountain View, and it was time to hustle. Jessica gave him one last look of warning and then left to go meet with the roadies. The rest of the band went to get cleaned up, dressed, whatever they needed to do. Have a morning wank. Jake moved from the table to the couch across from Krish and sprawled out. He was seriously hung over.

"Saw you had a piece of history hanging around last night," Krish said to Jake. "Awkward much?"

"And yeah, he probably wanted to hook up. I laughed in his face. No way I'm going back to that piece of shit."

"Which piece of shit?" Silas asked as he sat down next to Krish and kicked his legs over onto Krish's lap. Krish immediately started rubbing Silas's sock-covered feet, which felt fabulous after the past couple of days. He moved as though it were second nature, and that thought warmed Silas. It was one of those gestures that let you know the person cared for you….

"Burke Dickens from Backdrop Silhouette."

Silas's eyes bugged out. "Burke Dickens? What do you mean 'back to that'?"

"That piece of shit better stay away from you," Jordan called out from the hallway between the bunks. "He lays a hand on you and I'll break his fucking fingers."

Jake rolled his eyes. "We had a fling a long time ago. Trust me, I have no desire to spend any more time than I have to with him and his giant ego."

"We might be touring with them in the fall. Jessica's working out the details."

Krish squeezed a particularly tender spot, and Silas gasped.

"Sorry," he said. "Does that mean you'll go straight from Warped into another tour?"

"We'll take a couple weeks off to recover, I'm sure. But yeah. We need to do a major tour if we want to show that we're back in the game."

Krish nodded and went back to rubbing his feet, paying close attention to what he was doing. Silas loved watching his hands.

"Anyway," Jake said, as though trying to smooth over the conversation. "I'll be steering clear of him, brother dear. You don't have to worry. I am a big kid now, you know."

Jordan rolled his eyes. "Twenty-five doesn't necessarily mean you're a big kid. You're still going to school. Technically you're not an adult until you're supporting yourself."

"Oh, like you? Whatever. I'm heading into my last year of graduate school, and by this time next year, I'll have a better-paying job than you, so you can kiss my ass."

Silas rolled his eyes at the brotherly bickering and let them settle on Krish. He remained completely focused on the foot rub. If Silas were a betting man, he'd bet Krish was feeling uncomfortable, and he hated that. At the same time, he wanted Krish's hands on him however he could get them.

"That feels heavenly," he said. "It's a shame I have to get up and walk on those things now."

Krish patted them and smiled at Silas. "Happy to do it."

"Listen, let me go have a huddle with the band and Jessica. Then we can go hang out for a bit, see a couple of the bands. We don't go on until this afternoon. Then after our set, we can…."

Krish smiled, but it wasn't quite that blissed-out smile he'd had earlier. "As long as I'm not wearing out my welcome. At some point I should check in with Chantal, but my schedule is pretty flexible. I'd love to see you after your set as well. Then I can take off, you know, whenever."

Silas grinned. "Yeah. We'll see about that. How long are you on the tour?"

"Till the end. I took a leave from my job teaching music lessons."

"Music lessons? That's rad. Where do you teach?"

Krish grinned. "School of Rock. We have a franchise in San Diego. My brother knew the owners...." Krish's face fell a little.

Silas was about to ask him more when Jessica called for them.

"Morning huddle, boys."

"I'll be back in a bit."

Silas stood from the bench and started to walk out, but he turned back and couldn't help himself. He wanted another kiss, so he leaned in and laid one on a startled Krish just as the guys emerged from the back of the bus.

"Slip him some tongue!"

"Silas and Krish, sittin' in a tree—"

"Shut the fuck up and go," added Los, shooting Silas an irritated look as he passed.

"I'll be back," Silas said absently to Krish as he turned and followed his brothers out the door. Once outside, he pushed Los hard in the chest.

"What the fuck was that all about?"

Los stumbled back, surprised, and crossed his arms over his chest. He chewed on his thumbnail as they gathered around Jessica for the day's schedule. Oh, they'd be having a conversation later.

"Set time is three thirty, so everyone needs to be ready by two. Brains, your workshop is at one, so that gives you enough time to eat after. Okay?"

"Yeah," he answered. He rubbed at his head and shifted his weight between his feet as though he had to piss or something.

"You okay?" Silas asked him quietly.

"Yeah. Just got a funny feeling about today. Remember last time we played Mountain View?"

Silas had to dig back through the last couple of years of fog to recall their last summer of Warped. Mountain View had been toward the end that year, and everyone had been on each other's nerves by then. Los and Brains had actually come to blows, and Gavin….

"Fuck. That's right. He broke up with Mel after that show."

Mel was from Australia, and he'd been working for Warped in the production office. They'd known each other for a couple of years before they finally started dating in 2014. It was the longest Gavin had ever been with one person, and he was convinced Mel was it. Then midway through summer 2016, Mel decided he'd had enough of life on the road. He told Gavin after Warped he was moving home to Sydney and he wasn't interested in continuing their relationship long distance. There was obviously more to it than that, and Gavin's emotional state was a fucking wreck. He'd been getting more and more hateful emails and social media comments the more public he was with Mel, but Gavin refused to cover it up anymore. The band all supported him, but his mood swings were off the fucking chain. Mel's news was the last straw.

The tour ended August thirteenth in Portland, Oregon, and the band returned home to Oakland the next day. Two days later, Silas showed up at Gavin's and found him.

"I don't want to jinx it or anything—"

"Guys? I'm still going over the schedule. Is there something—"

"No," they both answered at once.

Jessica continued. "And then your meet and greet will go from five to five forty-five. After that, you're done for the day. Tonight we drive back down to Ventura, play tomorrow, and then we have three days off. But we've got an appearance at a Hot Topic store in the area."

Jordan and Los started plotting what they could do to get in trouble in SoCal. They even mentioned Disney, but Silas and Brains remained silent. Neither of them was able to shake off the bad feeling that easily. When they split up, Brains put his arm around Silas.

"It'll be okay. We'll be fine. And hey," he leaned in closer. "You have fun with your guy?"

Silas beamed. "So much fun, dude. He's pretty damn incredible."

Brains patted his shoulder. "That's cool. He seems cool. Just… you know. I don't want to see you get hurt or anything."

Silas shrugged off his arm. "Why is everyone always so convinced I'm going to get hurt? I know what I'm doing."

Brains stood to his full height, which was about four inches taller than Silas, and he frowned. "You figure out whether he's the Guru yet?"

Silas shook his head and looked down at his feet. "I don't think so. But I don't know. It doesn't really matter, does it?"

Brains gave him a look to let him know that yes, it very much *did* matter.

"Fine. Fuck. I don't know. And right now, I don't care."

"Fine," Brains answered.

"Fine."

Brains stayed behind to talk about his workshop with Jessica, and Silas returned to the bus. He climbed the steps and apparently interrupted a serious conversation between Krish and Jake. They both leaned back with guilty expressions on their faces.

"Uh-oh," Silas said, trying to regain some of his good mood. "Who broke the Xbox?"

The friends broke out in nervous laughter. "It wasn't me," Jake said, pointing at Krish.

"I didn't touch it," Krish said, his hands up. Buzzing sounds came from his pocket and he pulled out his phone. "It's my mom," he said, his face going pale as he answered it. "Everything okay?"

Silas sat down next to Krish and watched as his whole body relaxed and he sighed. Silas heard a woman's voice through the phone.

"Yeah, I'm fine. What's wrong? You sure? Yeah, we're safe." Krish answered her questions and shot a quick wink at Silas.

Silas took his hand and watched the emotions play across his face. He'd gone from worried to exasperated to amused in about a minute.

"Yeah, he's right here. C'mon. Really? All right." Krish handed Silas the phone. "My mom wants to talk to you, and you will get me in big trouble if you don't—"

"Krishnan, give the boy the phone."

"Boy?" Silas took the phone from Krish and put on a serious face. "This is Silas Franklin. May I help you?"

Krish elbowed him.

"Silas, this is Krishnan's mother, Meera. Are you boys being safe on that bus?"

Silas's eyes bugged out. "Safe? Uh, yes, ma'am—"

"Your driver is getting the right amount of sleep and abstaining from alcohol and drugs? Because I know those buses can be very dangerous, and I don't want any of you to be hurt. And how old are you, Silas?"

"Uh, twenty-eight?"

"Is that an answer or a question, Silas? Don't you know how old you are? Now, I wanted to tell you that the new album is very good and I hope that you have a wonderful time on the tour this summer. My Krishnan was very excited to see you yesterday."

"Is that so?" Silas said making faces at Krish, who rolled his eyes.

"Yes. We listened to the new album together the day it came out. I've always enjoyed listening to music with my sons, and since his brother—"

Krish snatched the phone away and put it back up to his ear. "Mom, Silas has to go now." He broke into some other language with his mother that seemed to get heated before he hung up and exhaled.

Silas and Jake looked at each other wide-eyed and then back at Krish.

"I'm sorry. My mother is a little overprotective."

"Don't apologize. What language was that?"

Krish slid his phone back in his pocket. "Hindi. She made sure my brother and I both spoke it, even though we haven't been back in years."

"Were you born in India?" Silas asked, curious to know more about the guy who had captivated him.

"I was born in San Diego. My parents both moved here as little kids."

"His mom is awesome," Jake chimed in. "She's like an Indian Michelle Obama."

Silas laughed. "She sounds wonderful. That's so cool that she listens to music with you. You should bring her to a show."

Krish ran his hands through his hair. "Oh, she doesn't like to come to shows. She likes to be able to control the volume."

"Yes, and she's too busy cooking for Krish and doing his laundry."

Krish kicked Jake in the shins as he was trying to get away. "Shut up, Barrett. I cook for myself and do my own laundry."

Silas licked his lips. "I love Indian food."

Silas wasn't above a little temptation. Krish's eyes hadn't left his lips. But he was starting to have some concrete desires, like Krish cooking Indian food for him, Krish at his house, Krish in his bed. He'd love to do a lot of domestic shit with Krish. And they were still staring at each other.

Jake apparently realized Krish and Silas were having a moment. "Anyhoo. I'm going to get dressed in some of Jordan's clothes. I hope he's got something clean." Jake ducked into the back, humming loudly.

"I'm sorry if that was uncomfortable. I love my mom, but she tends to be very involved in my life."

"You should be glad. My mom couldn't give a shit about mine."

Krish frowned at him. "I'm sorry. I don't know anything about your life other than the band. You're careful not to talk about it in the press, aren't you?"

Silas shrugged and leaned back against the couch. "Nothing much to talk about, but yeah, I don't like to go there in interviews."

Krish nodded and leaned forward, his elbows on his knees. "I can understand that. You obviously don't have a lot of privacy," he said, looking around the bus. "Does that get to you?"

"Not really. I don't give a shit what people think, but I don't like when anything interferes with the band either. I want the focus to be on our music, not whatever, or whoever else we're doing at the time. But I also don't curtail my activities. So yeah, I guess I have mixed feelings about it."

Krish nodded and held his gaze. Silas thought he was even more beautiful today, and despite the weirdness of the morning, he really wanted to get back to the easy feeling he'd had with Krish an hour or so before.

"Let me get dressed, and then let's go check things out, okay? We can go see everything getting set up before the fans are let in, maybe catch a couple of sets, and then come back here before we go on."

"That sounds great. As long as I'm not—"

"If you say that again, Krishnan," he warned, emphasizing the end of his name like his mother had on the phone. He crawled onto Krish's lap, straddled him, grabbed a handful of Krish's hair, and pulled his head back. "I might have to spank you."

Krish wrapped his arms around Silas's back and gazed up at him with that sleepy grin Silas couldn't get enough of. "Promise?"

Silas tugged his hair a little more and then went in to kiss Krish thoroughly. He loved this position. It gave him access to all of Krish's mouth and allowed him to control the kiss. And when Krish grabbed his ass and squeezed, Silas couldn't remember why they weren't still in the back lounge with more of their clothes off. He was ready to make an exception to his rule for this guy, which scared him enough to pull back. He needed them to spend some time not making out. He had a feeling Krish was much more than someone he spent a night cuddling with, and he wanted that, wanted more. Besides, they had time. The tour would last two more months, and then….

"You feel so good." He dropped one more kiss onto Krish's waiting lips. "But you're testing my willpower. I need to get you off this bus."

Krish blinked as though he too was realizing how strong this chemistry was and the implications. "Yeah. Maybe you're right. I could get so lost with you, Silas. So lost. But I'd also like to get to know you better. I have so many questions."

Silas laughed. He gave one last playful grind against Krish's lap, feeling just how much they were in sync. Then he climbed off. "I'll be right out."

"Hey, Silas? I'm going to, uh, find my bus and change clothes. I can come back—"

"Hurry." Silas kissed him once more and then forced himself to walk away.

He heard the bus doors close as he locked himself into the tiny bathroom and splashed some cold water on his face.

First, he needed to slow his heart beat and calm another part of his anatomy down.

Second, he needed to clean up and look presentable. Having hardly any hair helped immensely with that. He was beginning to think he might never grow his hair again. He shaved and cleaned up his eyebrows of the stray hairs.

Third, he needed to figure out what had crawled up Los's ass, but he didn't want to waste any of his precious time away from Krish. If Los wanted to pout, let him. He'd say something when he was ready. Silas wasn't about to encourage his passive-aggressive behavior.

And last, he needed to make sure the drama stayed far away from his band today. They had history with Mountain View, and it wasn't pretty. Besides the breakup, they'd had to fire their previous tour manager after they discovered, in this very venue, that he'd been doing some shady shit, including bringing underage girls and drugs onto their bus. Gavin had flipped the fuck out and threatened to call the police. They almost got kicked off the tour. Brad agreed to leave, and they'd been able to keep it quiet, but after he reported back to their management company, he was fired and ended up going to jail for rape a year later. Fucking disaster, that guy.

Perhaps that was what had Los down. He'd been the one to find out about the shit Brad was doing, and after that he'd been leery about anyone coming around the band who hadn't been properly vetted. Los didn't like anyone poking around, especially after Gavin died. Every piece written about it had commented on how the band had gone into seclusion, that they were so broken they might never play together again. And then there were the fucking rumors about Gavin and drugs, which were total bullshit. It pissed them all off, but Los had been furious.

"They're just morbid fucking voyeurs. I don't need them seeing me in pain. I lost my best friend. I should be able to grieve for him on my own without people sticking their fucking noses where they're not wanted."

The only one who wrote about them and really seemed to get what they were going through was the Guru. He'd talked about his own loss and how sometimes he wished the world would forget about him and let him figure it out on his own.

Well-meaning amateur therapists always trying to tell you what will make you feel better become like a bad rash. No matter how much you try to ignore it, sometimes you scratch, and it makes it feel worse.

Grief requires support from loved ones, but sometimes it requires some good old-fashioned tears, a pint of ice cream, and a binge session with your favorite playlist.

Maybe part of what Silas found so attractive about Krish was that he seemed to be wise, like the Guru. Krish had an old soul for a guy younger even than Silas. He'd had the most kissable lips, and his hands…. This wasn't getting Silas through his list.

Approaching his twenty-ninth birthday, Silas knew it was time for some changes. Their profession was never a stable one, but the band's success had given him a bit of a nest egg. At some point he needed to buy a place of his own, not just crash in a flop house in Oakland with the rest of the band. He wanted their run at success to continue, but he also needed more than endless parties on the road. The guys were his best friends, and he didn't want the band to end anytime soon, but he needed to have a life outside of their world as well. He needed more than them for his support base, and since he didn't have a family to speak of anymore….

Could Krish be the kind of guy Silas could bring into his inner circle? Trust with his life and his love? He sure as hell felt like it, even after only one night. Only time would tell, and their time was ticking away as Silas had a fucking existential crisis in the tiny bus bathroom. He hurried through a quick shower and threw on some black skinny pants and a Judas Priest T-shirt he loved. He'd had it on yesterday before they took the stage, but it was his favorite and it didn't smell bad yet, so he was good. Who knew when they'd have time to get their laundry done?

Chapter Eight

KRISH WANDERED the rows of buses until he found the one with the pink dice. The doors were unlocked, and he immediately heard voices as he climbed the steps.

"There you are," Chantal said. "I'm on my way out but let me introduce you to the rest of the bus."

Two women and two men sat at the table eating and having a heated conversation.

"Guys, this is Krish. He's interning with me this summer."

Krish shook hands with them all and tried not to feel self-conscious about their probing looks.

"You're kinda young, aren't you?" Margeaux asked him. She was the eldest of the group from what he could tell, but he got more of a mom vibe from her than one of criticism.

"Yes, ma'am. I just finished my undergrad."

"You don't need to give her your résumé, kid," Casey said, rolling her eyes. "She's feeling her age around us young'uns."

"You're only two years younger than me," Margeaux shot back. She elbowed Casey and finished her coffee in a long gulp.

"And I feel great. If you'd quit smoking and go vegetarian, you'd look ten years younger."

"So now I look old?"

Tim put his arms out like a referee. "Ladies, ladies. It's too damn early for this debate. For the record, you both look lovely. Now Casey, would you mind getting me some more coffee?"

Casey raised her eyebrow. "What's wrong with your legs?"

"You're sitting on the outside. I just—"

"As you can see," Chantal interrupted and turned to grab Krish by the arms, "this group is a volatile bunch. It's better to simply smile and nod this early in the morning." She pulled him a little closer and grinned. "You have a good night?"

Krish couldn't help his stupid smile. "I did."

Chantal kissed his cheek. "Wonderful. And seriously, you do you, whatever you want. Just let me know if you're not riding with us. Will you be riding with us tonight?" She wiggled her eyebrows, and Krish burst out laughing.

"Let the poor guy be," Vinh said. "He'd probably like to change clothes, since I recall seeing him in that very shirt last night, leaving the party with Silas Franklin."

There were *ooo*s from everyone present, and Krish suddenly went from feeling giddy to a little too much under the microscope.

"I'm going to change. Nice to meet you all." He waved to them and then stepped behind the curtain that blocked off the sleeping quarters. Their bus didn't have the power doors like Hush's bus, but he had to admit he was glad it was cleaner. Although he hadn't minded the shape their bus was in last night.

He'd spent the night with Silas. Remembering how Silas's touch had felt, how his kisses had tasted, how his tongue had driven Krish crazy, Krish sucked in a breath. Something pretty magical had happened last night, at least in his mind. He had no way of knowing how Silas felt about it except to take him at his word that he wanted more. He could have just been saying that, trying to let him down easy, but then he'd asked Krish to stay with him today, to walk around....

Krish sat in his bunk for a few minutes, jotting down his thoughts from the day before so they'd be fresh when he wrote his first blog. Perhaps touring the grounds with Silas would give him the kind of perspective that he'd need to write something special.

Krish changed clothes and put his dirty ones into a separate zipper bag inside his duffel. He'd brought enough clothes for twelve days, mostly shorts and T-shirts with daily changes of socks and underwear. Chantal had told him there would be occasional opportunities to do laundry.

When he emerged from the back, only Vinh and Casey remained at the table.

"You got everything you need for your blog?" Casey asked him. "If you need any introductions or want any insider information, either of us can tell you who to talk to. I'm also happy to collaborate with you on any interviews or pictures you might need for your pieces. We've both contributed to *Alt-Scene*, so just let us know."

Krish stared at them stunned. "I… uh."

Vinh smiled at him. "We figured it out. Sorry. I swear Chantal didn't tell us. I had a hunch."

He was outed. *Fuck.* If someone other than Chantal knew he was the Guru, that meant anyone could know. Silas could find out at any time.

"It's okay," Casey said, frowning at Vinh. "We're not going to say anything. I think it's cool that you're anonymous. People will be more willing to talk to you."

"Yeah, but it's not—"

"People love your blog, Krish," Vinh said. "The artists respect you. What does it matter if they know who you are?"

"I don't know. I've always been anonymous. It feels like I can be more honest that way, you know? People don't have preconceived notions, and they don't try to influence what I have to say."

"But you plan on going to work for the magazine, right?"

His gaze shot to Casey. How the hell? That was supposed to be confidential that he'd even been talking to them.

She shrugged. "Word spreads. I heard you were in talks to go work for the magazine, and then you showed up here. It wasn't too hard to figure out."

Someone had yanked the floor out from under Krish, and he felt himself listing sideways. He reached for the counter for support. He knew he couldn't stay anonymous forever, but he never imagined it would be like this.

Vinh and Casey looked at each other as though they realized what a landmine they'd thrown him onto.

"I'm sorry, kid," Vinh said. "The only ones who know for sure that I know of are us and Chantal. And Kevin Lyman, of course. But he doesn't share that kind of shit. We won't say anything. But you might want to think about letting folks know, especially Silas. After everything they've been through, you don't want to be seen as yet another person in the media ready to fuck them over."

"I wouldn't. I swear—"

Vinh held up a hand. "We're not going to say anything. But you should think about it." He got up out of the booth and rinsed out his coffee cup. "Silas is a friend, but I understand how confidentiality works. Just think about it."

"I will," Krish said. "I have no idea what I'm doing yet. This is all super new to me."

Casey and Vinh looked at each other and smiled. "Oh, to be young and foolish once again," Casey said with a sigh.

"Speak for yourself," Vinh said. "I'm still young and foolish. Ask Margeaux. She tells me that all the time."

They laughed conspiratorially, and Krish thought they would likely both be great connections to have as he moved forward… if he could trust them. He thought it wouldn't hurt to pick their brains for a bit.

"I was wondering, do you have suggestions for can't-miss sets on the tour? I'm thinking about collecting a series of anecdotes about people's favorites."

"Underoath," Casey said without hesitation. "Their new music is fucking brilliant. I can't wait to see them. I missed their set the first two shows, but I'm seeing them today."

"Hush, of course. I'm also anxious to see The Amity Affliction," Vinh said. "I've got shoots scheduled with both bands. I'll let you know when. Maybe you can come along."

"That would be great, Vinh. Thank you. Both of you. I'll be sure to check out their sets."

Krish said his goodbyes and rushed out of the bus in search of Silas.

Silas Franklin. The guy he spent the night with. The one who wanted to spend the day with him today. Unreal.

The guy you're keeping secrets from.

Krish stopped in his tracks. He hated this feeling. If he didn't say something and he continued to spend time with Silas and the rest of the guys, it was going to eat at him.

He had to tell him. Somehow. Today. Before they got any closer.

Chapter Nine

SILAS LEFT the bus after an impromptu writing session. He couldn't resist jotting down some of his feelings about the last twenty-four hours. He took a deep breath and felt good. He'd been able to shake off some of his dread about being back in Mountain View and couldn't wait to spend more time with Krish. Vertical. And with clothes on.

He found Krish outside his bus, typing frantically on his phone. The sight brought a twinge of fear to Silas's consciousness.

Had he been stupid and impulsive to share his body with Krish? He wanted to trust his instincts that Krish was a good guy, but Los's words echoed in his head. He hated that any negativity was sneaking into his thoughts where Krish was concerned, but was that because he was desperate to find that connection? Could he trust that Krish was who he said he was? *Only one way to find out.*

"Hey, good-lookin'."

Krish's head jerked up, and he hurriedly shoved his phone into his pocket. "Hey. Mmm Priest. *Painkiller* is my favorite album, maybe of all time. That and *Point of Entry*."

Silas beamed. *I knew you were perfect.* "*Painkiller is* their best album. The fact they wrote it when they were coming back from their darkest hour really inspired me while we were writing this current album. An angry comeback."

Krish accepted Silas's extended hand and linked their fingers. "I couldn't believe what they went through with that court case. Did you ever see the documentary *Dancing with the Devil*? I can't find it anywhere anymore, but it was about several artists accused of Satanic shit back in the eighties. There was footage from their trial and everything."

An affinity for Judas Priest too? Either that was an incredible coincidence, or maybe he really was the Guru. Silas hadn't come right out and asked, but he wished he knew for sure. He didn't want to waste any more time worrying about it.

"Come on. Let's go see things come together." He shook his head and Krish chuckled. "That came out wrong. Let's go watch the festival building. We can grab a schedule and see who we should check out."

"That would be great," Krish said. "I only saw a few bands yesterday, and I got some recommendations that I'd love to see."

"Oh yeah? Who?"

Krish told him about a conversation he'd had with Casey and Vinh about their must-see bands, and that led to them discussing the other artists as two fans. Silas was in heaven. This was exactly what he'd hoped when they first sat next to each other last night... that and that they'd have chemistry. He'd solved that mystery quickly. *God, did they have chemistry.*

They walked through the back gates to check out the festival. The buses were parked on one part of the lot, and the festival took up the other half as well as the lawn areas inside and the actual amphitheater at Shoreline. Silas watched Krish as he observed all of the insanity that went into setting up a gazillion tents and seven stages for a single day before they packed it all up and moved it to set up, oftentimes the next day. They did get several days off in between some shows, but they usually played every Friday, Saturday, and Sunday, and sometimes Thursdays. By the end of the tour, everyone was cranky and emotionally and physically exhausted, but the bands played on, and the roadies worked their asses off.

While they walked and talked, Krish appeared to pay close attention to the different nonprofit groups that were setting up. "Warped is one of the only tours that invites all of these organizations along. It's going to be a shame to see the tour end. I wonder how much of an impact they make on the kids here? That would be an interesting thing to research, to figure out other ways to reach kids with this info in the flesh rather than over social media. Don't get me wrong, social media is great for outreach, but there's something about meeting people face-to-face that really makes an impact."

Silas smiled. "You're absolutely right."

They grabbed a set list and were chatting excitedly when someone crashed into Silas from behind. He spun around with a frown and then rolled his eyes when he realized who it was.

"Dude, look at your face. You want to go, Franklin?"

Silas gave Ryan Wells, the singer for Backdrop Silhouette, a playful shove in the chest, and then they bro-hugged. He noticed Krish hung back as the other guys crowded around him to chat.

"How's it going with Jordan?" Ryan asked.

"Great, actually. He's fucking astounding, and the dude can sing. Like, we were able to do some cool shit on this album that we've never tried before. It's pretty awesome."

"Yeah, man, we missed you guys last year."

Silas appreciated the sentiment. "Thanks, man. It's good to be back."

He glanced over at Krish, who'd shoved his hands into his pockets and was trying to look invisible. *Uh uh.* Silas grabbed his arm and dragged him over. "Guys, this is Krish. Krish, you know Ryan and the guys from Backdrop Silhouette."

Krish rubbed his hand on his shorts before shaking hands with the guys from the band and saying a quiet hello.

"Nice to meet you." Ryan gave Krish an appreciative once-over and then let go of his hand and turned back to Silas. "We've got the opening slot this morning on the Left Foot. I don't know how I feel about playing in all this sunshine."

It did look pretty ridiculous to be draped in black leather and chains when the sun was climbing high in the sky. That was one thing they'd all laughed about when they did their first Warped Tour. After playing clubs with their bands and then playing in the middle of the day, it took some getting used to.

"We'll come check it out," Silas said. "I'm going to show Krish around a bit. I'll see you guys later." He linked his fingers with Krish to make a point and smirked when the guys in Backdrop Silhouette all smiled in surprise. He knew them well enough to know that they would be cool. Ryan could be a prick while onstage, but he certainly understood what it was like to be criticized for life choices. Ryan had spent a year in jail after a drunk-driving incident just after the band hit it big, and they'd had to claw their way back to the top. He'd relapsed after Gavin's death, and that scared the shit out of Silas. But Ryan was very open about being sober now and had paid dearly for his sins. Silas always tried to support him and his band. He'd also been a good friend and sometime-collaborator with Gavin, which meant they had even more of a bond.

"Definitely." Ryan let his eyes roam over Krish once more.

Silas was torn between being glad his friends appreciated his new guy, but also irritated that they felt it was okay to be ogling him. Silas squeezed Krish's hand as they walked away.

"He's probably checking out your ass as we walk away," Silas said in a low voice.

Krish jerked his head around and back to Silas. "What? Why?"

Silas laughed. "Because it's impressive. But also because Ryan checks out everyone. 'For artistic purposes.' Or so he says. Did you know he draws and paints? He's hella talented too."

Krish shook his head. "I had no idea. That's awesome."

Silas gave him another squeeze. "Hey, you seem nervous." He tugged on their linked hands. "Is this not okay?"

Krish stopped walking. "I'm sorry. It's more than okay. I'm just not used to—"

"Not used to being out, or not used to being out with me?"

Krish sighed. "I don't know. Look, Silas. I live kind of a hermit life. I finished my degree, I teach at the music school, and I… I don't spend a lot of time around people. Except my family. It's been a long time. I'm a little intimidated by all this. That's all."

Silas pulled Krish behind one of the food trucks that was getting set up for the day and wrapped his arms around his waist. "Hey, I don't want you to feel intimidated. I'm sorry. I love having you with me here. This is fun. Aren't you having fun?"

Krish smiled down at him. "I'm having the best time of my life."

Silas grinned and wrapped his hand around the back of Krish's neck to pull him down for a kiss. "You're so tall," he laughed. "I like being on your lap better."

Krish laughed and bent down a little so Silas could kiss him, and immediately they were both overtaken with lust.

"OMG. Isn't that—"

And that's all it took to ruin the mood.

Chapter Ten

Krish pulled back from the kiss to see a group of kids with cell phones out watching them kiss.

"Oh, sorry. We just… could we have a picture?"

Silas smiled at his fans. "You know what? How about you guys come by the meet 'n' greet at the tent after our set? I'll make sure to take pictures with you guys then."

The girls smiled and giggled as they hurried away. Krish heard one of them squealing, "They're so cute!"

"I'm sorry," Krish said, feeling bad that Silas had been caught with him.

Silas shrugged. "It's better than in the fucking head. I've had guys ask for pictures in the bathroom, dude. That's weird."

"It doesn't bother you? Getting caught like this?"

Silas shrugged. "At least our dicks weren't out or anything. I've worked really hard to keep my junk off social media."

They both laughed, but Krish's chest was tight and sweat dripped down his back despite it not being too warm yet. Having the alone time with Silas was exceptional, and he'd seen so much of what went on behind the scenes that morning, but it was definitely strange being on display. They walked back toward the Left Foot stage.

"You were so cool about it," Krish said. "You're so good to everyone."

"Maybe. Maybe I'm trying to impress you," he said as though he were trying to brush off any seriousness in the moment.

"It's true, though. Even watching you make breakfast. You were so generous, making sure everyone else got to eat before you. You could have just fed them Pop-Tarts, but you cooked them actual food."

"They're my family. That's what we do."

"Where is your real family, Silas?"

Krish worried he'd pushed it too far, but Silas had talked to *his* mom on the phone. Asking personal questions should be part of the plan if they were to the point of walking around holding hands, right?

Yeah, but you still haven't told him.

"Um... my mom lives somewhere out near Stockton with her boyfriend, I think. We were close when I was little, but we don't talk much anymore. She's moved on with her life. My dad is in prison for armed robbery. My little sister is married and living in Texas, last I heard. Her husband is in the Army.

That's the Franklin family creed right there—scatter and survive."

Backdrop Silhouette took the stage, and Silas and Krish stopped to watch them play. Ryan was in snarky form, strutting back and forth across the stage, engaging people in the crowd as he went. He shouted for them to get the circle pit going, and they obliged him. He mocked the people along the back, encouraging them to get a little dirty as they launched into their newest hit, "Dirty Work." Then he slid off his black leather jacket and rubbed his stomach tattoo that said Alive and Kicking. He let his hand wander down to cup himself, sending the girls in the audience squealing with delight. Krish watched as Silas shook his head.

"You guys ever thought about adding a bass player? Free up your hands?"

Silas snorted. "So I can grab my dick onstage? Nah. I feel better having something to do with my hands," he said, raising an eyebrow at Krish.

"You *are* good with your hands," Krish said quietly, but Silas heard him, and they had a moment of electricity that went straight to his groin.

"Yeah, well, I think I might need to do some more practice later."

"I like being your practice."

Krish's knees went weak when Silas licked his lips. That piercing was going to be the death of him.

"You're dangerous," Silas said. "My plan to get you away from horizontal surfaces is feeling like a bad one right about now."

Krish laughed. "I know. But there's time. I'm just happy to be here with you, watching... Ryan. Is he...?"

They looked up to find Ryan with his hand in his leather pants, and they both cracked up. Ryan was a bad-boy tractor beam for temptation of the worst kind. You knew after a night with him your heart would be torn out of your chest and stomped on, and yet you would let yourself get sucked in.

"Dude is a mess," Silas said. "Hotter than hell, and he knows it." He shook his head. "He's so damned talented, though. He doesn't need the show, you know? He could stand up there in a boring suit, and his voice and lyrics would stand on their own."

"Agreed," Krish said. "Their albums keep getting better and better too. I love how much he's matured as a songwriter."

Krish took in the rest of the band and bobbed his head to the beat. Burke Dickens was fucking brilliant. Whatever happened with Jake aside, he was one of the best lead guitar players in their subgenre. Burke was a bit of a stoic dude, however. Rather than showboating, he played his guitar as though no one was watching, making love to the damn thing. He had long, straight brown hair that looked more '90s metal than the current metalcore do's, and he preferred denim to leather, unlike the rest of his band. Krish could totally see why Jake had fallen for the guy as a teen. The strong silent types definitely had appeal.

The set ended with a series of acrobatics by Ryan, including a standing back flip that made Krish suck in a breath. Ryan was built like a gymnast, ripped and stocky. He'd once joked in an interview that prison would do that to you.

"That was awesome," Krish said. "I haven't seen them live but a couple of times."

The crowd broke up a little as fans pushed closer to see the next band on the Right Foot Stage, which happened to be The Maine. Krish knew Jake wouldn't miss seeing them. He glanced around for him, but it was a lost cause.

"They always bring it live, although now that Ryan is sober, there's less potential for a trainwreck performance."

Krish and Silas walked down a row of tents, and several of the people selling merch waved to Silas. He smiled and waved even while sharing what was obviously not a comfortable subject with Krish.

"And here you are, surviving. Smiling and waving. Does it ever get too much?"

Silas's smile changed from a friendly-but-distant smile to a more private and sad one. "It does. That's when I miss Gavin the most."

Krish nodded and looked forward. Man, could he relate to that. He missed Vivaan so much it hurt. He'd been Krish's best friend, mentor, and all-around rock. Without Viv, there'd been many lonely nights.

"How do you deal?" Krish asked in a soft voice, gazing down at Silas. Silas stopped walking and sighed.

"Writing—song lyrics, poetry, whatever. Letters to Gavin. The Guru mentioned that in a blog once. He said he wrote letters to his brother who died and that helped him make it through." Silas smiled. "He's a pretty smart guy."

Krish's throat went really dry and it was like that chestburster was back. *You could tell him. You'd feel way less guilty.*

"Writing is a good outlet."

Chickenshit.

Silas stared at him for a long moment and then shook his head.

It's now or never.... Krish started to speak when Los came running up.

"Dude," Los said. "Jessica's looking for you. She needs you for an interview."

Silas looked to Krish. "You want to walk back with me? I understand if you want to stay—"

"I'm coming with you." And as soon as Silas was free, Krish was going to tell him everything.

Silas's smile touched a place that had been cold for so long, and it lit Krish up from the inside. The chestburster was still scraping at his insides, screaming *guilty, guilty, guilty*, but part of him felt warm and hopeful for the first time since Viv left him.

"Did you guys hear about Jake?"

Krish and Silas both whipped their heads in Los's direction.

"Is he okay?" Krish asked, feeling guilty he'd all but ditched his friend.

"Well, mostly. But dude, he hooked up with Burke Dickens. Like, when he was still a teenager. That's why Jordan wanted us to leave him alone. I guess it was total drama."

Silas laughed. "That explains why Burke looked so miserable last night while Jake was singing with Jordan. Did you hear what they were singing?"

Los rolled his eyes. "'Stuck In Your Head,' by I Prevail. Ohhh fuck! Now that makes perfect sense. I just thought they were being assholes."

Krish smiled to himself. Jake had told him about his fling with Burke. It had not ended well, and Jake was messed up for a long time afterward, but he said he didn't regret it. Jake thought anything you could learn from was never a mistake. It kind of brought the old saying to Krish's mind—*Tis better to have loved and lost, than never to have loved at all.* Jake felt that way. Krish had never been in love, but he hated how miserable Jake was after it happened. They were freshmen at the time, and Jake was barely eighteen. It hadn't made Krish want to put his heart out there. But here with Silas? He was ready to go all in.

"So, Krish, Jake said you teach music lessons. You any good?"

Silas snorted, and Krish could tell this was Los's way of being the protective friend. He didn't blame him one bit.

"I know enough to teach young kids the basics. It's fun."

Los made a face. "Kids?" He shuddered. "I totally don't have the patience to deal with kids."

"I love kids. I love it when they, like, get it, you know? When it all comes together."

Silas smiled at him. "That's hella cool."

Los rolled his eyes again. Krish hoped it was that he was being protective and not that he had some other reason to dislike him. *Shit. What if he knows?*

They'd made it to the back-gate area, and Krish followed Los and Silas toward the bus. Jessica came out to meet them.

"Thank goodness. I need you, Si."

Silas turned to Krish. "Would you excuse me? I'll be back as soon as I can. You can head over to the food area if you want. Or whatever. I'm sorry."

Krish tried to put on a brave smile, but he was feeling pretty awkward. "Sure. Don't worry about me. Go do whatever you need to do."

Silas pushed up on his toes, kissed Krish, and blushed as he backed away with a goofy grin on his face.

Krish could really get used to that expression.

His phone buzzed in his pocket. He pulled it out, and that chestburster broke free.

Alt-Scene was displayed on his caller ID. He glanced around to be sure no one was close enough to hear and then he answered.

"Hello?"

"Hey, Krish? This is Chaz Vella, editor in chief of *Alt-Scene* magazine. How are you?"

The EIC? *Shitting my pants.* "Good. Uh, how are you?"

"Great. Sorry to call you on a Saturday, but I spoke with Monique, and we were wondering if you could come in to our San Francisco office on Monday. I'm already a big fan of your blog, so we want to bring you in, show you around a bit, and talk some more about your plans for covering the tour... and beyond. Can you make it?"

Beyond shitting my pants to sheer panic. "Uh, sure. Monday? Where are you located?"

"We're not too far from AT&T Park. I know you are headed to Ventura next—"

"San Francisco? Yeah. I'll figure out a way to get there."

"Great. We can order you a car and put you up at a hotel if you need—"

"No, that's okay. I can manage. Can you send me the information? Like your address and a time? I don't have anything to write with at the moment."

"No problem. I have your email. It will be great meeting you in person. Monique had great things to say about you, and we think you just might be what we're looking for to head up our social justice department."

"Wow, thank you." *Holy shit.* That was way more than coming to work with the magazine. They were talking big things, and Krish hadn't even written a word for them yet. "I appreciate the opportunity to meet with you."

"Awesome. So, we'll see you Monday. Around ten sound good?"

Shit. Shit. Shit. "I'll be there."

They exchanged more thank-yous and hung up. Krish expected to look down and see his rib cage opened and his innards sprayed all over the ground. Instead he nearly dropped his phone, his hands were shaking so bad.

"You all right?"

He spun around and his phone went flying. Brains stood a couple of feet away and glared at Krish. He bent and retrieved Krish's phone and handed it to him.

"Yeah. Um… I'm fine. Great."

Brains frowned at him. "San Francisco? I thought you lived in San Diego."

Oh fuck. "Uh, yeah I do. I, um… have to meet someone in San Francisco. On Monday."

Brains cocked his head to the side. "Hey, I don't want to sound like a dick or anything, but I really hope you aren't fucking around with Silas. He's one of my best friends, and he doesn't deserve that shit. You understand what I'm saying?"

Krish backed up a step. Brains had seemed so mild-mannered at his workshop, almost like the absentminded professor. Right now, dressed all in black, staring Krish down with a cool, almost cold expression, he looked like an enforcer. His dyed-black hair was short and styled in a faux hawk that made him look dangerous. He was a little shorter than Krish, but he had broad, muscled shoulders from years of playing drums, and the look he gave Krish made his hands clammy. He swallowed hard.

"I would never—I'm not trying to hurt anybody. Silas is special."

Brains crossed his arms over his chest as Los joined them.

"What's going on?"

Brains lifted his chin in Krish's direction. "Our new friend here is going to meet someone in San Francisco on Monday."

Los mirrored his pose, and Krish seriously felt he was facing the Inquisition.

"Who's in San Francisco?" Los asked with even more attitude than Brains.

"I have a job interview," Krish said, praying they didn't ask for what.

"I thought you taught music lessons," Los said. "Were you lying about that too?"

"I wasn't lying about anything," Krish said. He really wished Silas would come back so they could all talk like rational people. "I do teach music lessons. This is for a different job."

"Oh, right." Los made a disgusted face and spit on the ground.

"Yeah, well, Silas doesn't need any more drama in his life right now," Brains said.

Krish took another step back. Were they seriously about to throw down to protect their friend?

"Hey, Krish," Jake said as he came up and put his forehead on Krish's shoulder. "It's so hot. It's already like almost eighty, and it's barely noon. How you guys can be wearing all this black shit in this heat is beyond me." He looked around with a confused look on his face. "Where's Silas?"

"He's in a meeting with our manager. He's probably going to be a while. Maybe you guys should go watch the show or something," Los said.

Jake blanched. "What crawled up your dick this morning?"

"Jake," Krish said, urging him to start walking. "Maybe we should just go."

"Go where?"

Silas came off the bus, and immediately Los and Brains lost their intimidation stance.

Krish looked between them and Silas. "I'm sorry. You're busy. I'll—"

"You'll what? What the fuck is going on?"

Brains cleared his throat. "We were just—"

"Yeah. I'll bet. Krish? Can I talk to you for a minute?"

"Sure."

Krish walked off with Silas and felt the daggers being stared into his back. Silas led him over to the motor home where their crew was staying.

"The crew is off getting lunch. I wanted to have some time alone with you before things get crazy this afternoon."

Silas ushered Krish in first and shut the door behind them.

"It's okay. I wanted to talk to you—"

Silas pushed Krish onto the couch and nailed him with a forceful kiss that knocked all thoughts out of Krish's head. Silas was much more aggressive than last night or even this morning. He slid his hands into Krish's hair and pulled his head back, just as he'd done before, but this time it felt so much more intense.

"I know it sounds insane to say this after such a short time, but I'm really into you. I feel like there's something here. Do you? I mean—"

"Silas, I feel it too. But—"

"I know. It's fucked-up. We're on the road. We're in a fucking fishbowl. I don't know what this all means, I just know *you* mean something. *This* means something. And I want to see you."

Krish smiled. "I want that too."

Silas kissed Krish again, but he was shaking. Krish pulled back, worried the kiss was about something else.

"Are you okay? Is everything—"

"Yeah, I…. God, everything's so crazy right now, and I want to get lost for a bit. You said you could get lost in me, Krish. Let's get lost."

Krish gripped Silas's arms and leaned away. "Hey, what happened?"

Silas slumped a little and exhaled. "I did an interview, and all the douche wanted to talk about was Gavin. It's like some of these fucking people only care about us because Gavin killed himself. We're a band. We make music, and we suffered a loss, but at the end of the day, we're fucking artists and our art should be what matters, right?"

"Of course it is. They're curious, though, your fans. I'm sure. They want to know you're okay. And then there are the well-meaning amateur therapists who—"

"Wait. What did you say?"

Shit. He'd just quoted himself. From the blog. Time was up.

"Silas. I need to tell you something."

Silas sat back and a veil descended over his face, cutting off the smile Krish loved. In its place was a look Krish couldn't describe as anything other than hurt. Betrayal.

"Go ahead."

This was it. He'd tell Silas, and Silas would tell him to fuck off. Whatever could have been was done, all because Krish was too much of an idiot to come clean sooner. How the hell did he expect to get close to Silas and not tell him? Maybe because he'd never dreamed any of this would happen. The dream turned nightmare.

"I… I'm sorry Silas. I didn't tell you everything. I should have told you."

Silas laughed humorlessly. "Yeah, you should have if it's this big of a deal that you can't even get it out." He got up off the couch and moved across the RV from Krish.

"I know, and I'm sorry. I never thought.... No. No excuses. I should have told you when you first asked me. I'm not a reporter, not yet. But I do write."

Silence hung in the air like a tangible threat. Silas stared at him for a moment, and crossed his arms just like Brains and Los had outside.

"The Guru."

Krish nodded and dropped his head low like the defeated loser he was. "My last name is Guruvayoor, like the temple in India. My brother always told me I was like a little old wise man and he called me the Guru. When I started the blog, it sort of stuck. I didn't say anything because I didn't.... No one knows who I am except Jake. And I guess the people on my bus. I didn't want you to think I was after a story or something, and I didn't know how you'd feel after all I've written about the band. I never dreamed you'd even read any of it. I... I didn't want to do anything to hurt you."

Silas said nothing, his face blank. It would be stupid to assume that Silas might have said, "Oh well, it's okay. I understand." But zero affect wasn't what Krish thought he'd get. He'd rather Silas threw something at him, screamed at him. Hell, they'd just been super intimate, and Krish had been keeping a huge secret. Krish felt like the lowest form of shit on the planet.

He stood up after several long minutes of Silas's muteness. Somehow that shook Silas out of his stupor.

"Well, it was great finally meeting you." Silas pushed past him and reached for the door.

"Silas," Krish said to stop his exit, but then he had no idea what to say.

Silas gave him his best fake smile. "I'll see you around."

And then he was gone.

Chapter Eleven

Silas let the RV door slam behind him and took several deep breaths. Then he plastered a smile on his face and greeted his band mates.

"So, who's coming with me to heckle Brains today? I was thinking we should make some pom pons and, like, do a cheer or something."

Los and Jordan looked at him like he'd grown a third eye.

"You all right, bruh?" Jordan asked him. "You drink enough water today? Maybe you're dehydrated."

"I'm tight." *You're a fucking liar, Silas.*

"Riiiight. So what about Krish—"

"I'm starving. There any lunch left after you guys laid waste to the catering?"

Silas strolled off in the direction of the catering tent, hoping a few minutes to himself would allow him to get his center back.

One of the things he loved most about Brains was his actual brain and the fact that he often knew what the fuck he was talking about. Back in the early days of the band, before Silas had any control over his temper, Brains used to talk him down from his desire to throat punch whoever was in the way of what he wanted at that moment. Brains taught him some meditation tricks that helped him breathe through the anger and find that place within himself that had kept him sane for all these years—the place his music came from, the place he felt the safest.

He walked and breathed, and by the time he got to the tent, he wasn't shaking anymore. He didn't feel like he might fucking cry.

"Hey," Ryan said as he joined Silas in line. "Who's your new guy?"

He should have known it wouldn't last. "You wouldn't believe me if I told you."

Ryan by himself could be pretty cool. He looked around to see if there were big ears around and then got in close. "You okay?"

Silas smiled at him and shook his head. "I'm really not, but I will be. Just had my world kind of knocked off its axis. I need a minute."

Ryan pounded on his back and nodded. "I'll run interference."

Silas laughed, and his eyes filled with tears. *Shit.* This was not getting himself centered. He needed to be alone, and that wasn't likely to happen. Ryan kept talking as they got their food and sat at a bench away from others.

"So, what'd he do? Have a boyfriend? Steal your shit? Misrepresent the facts?"

"The latter," Silas said, concentrating hard on his barbecued chicken.

"Mmm," Ryan said between bites. "Lying is the worst. It's hard to come back from that."

"He didn't exactly lie," Silas said, and then he wondered why the fuck he was defending him.

"Well, did he have a good reason?"

Silas thought about that for a minute. "I don't even know. I left before he could make any fucking excuses. Why…?"

"Hey, I'm playing devil's advocate here. Maybe he was trying to protect you or something."

Silas snorted and took a drink of his water. "That makes it worse. Why the fuck can't people quit worrying about me and just let me fucking be?"

Ryan held out a hand and finished chewing his food, which Silas appreciated. Ryan was pretty with all of his makeup on, but he was a hard motherfucker underneath. There was this edge to him, and Silas had seen very few people push him when he was on that edge.

"Because they can't, Silas. Come on. Everyone was worried you would be next after Gavin."

Silas dropped his food on his plate and wiped his hands with a napkin. It was starting to taste bitter, like this whole fucking ordeal. "Say it like it is, asshole."

"How else you expect me to say it, huh? We've lost too many talented fuckers in the past couple of years, and everyone knew how close you two were. I mean, fuck, I lost my shit too."

"Yeah, we were close, but not like suicide-pact close. Not like 'I can't live without him' close. I'm not fucking stupid, Ryan."

"Not saying you are, only saying people were worried. People close to you. You locked yourself away, and then you were partying pretty hard for a while. Word got around, you know."

He wasn't wrong. Silas had definitely cut loose for almost a year after Gavin died, but then he'd read the Guru's post about how he was tired of letting his grief stand in the way of what he loved most in his life—music. Silas had cried when he'd read those words.

My guitar has mocked me from across the room since the day my parents sat me down to tell me my brother wouldn't be coming home. I was staring at it as their words sank in, and it seemed to change in front of my eyes. The sunburst's golden waves looked like the fires of hell to me as they told me what happened to his platoon. I pictured the flames from the fires caused by the IED looking eerily like the grain on my guitar, and when my parents left the room, left me to process what they'd told me, I wanted to throw the damned thing out the window. I even stood from my chair and made like I was going to touch it, when I saw the goofy rainbow strap my brother had given me, and I fell to my knees. I couldn't destroy the instrument that embodied so many memories of him. Instead I let it destroy me.

I refused to touch it, play it, or tune it for well over a year after my brother died. I threw myself into school and added the journalism major, figuring eventually I'd finish my music degree or I'd leave it behind. I didn't really care anymore. But I stared at that guitar every night and grew more and more angry. My parents wanted me to see someone, and my friends all gave up on me, save one. He refused to let me hide and forced me to acknowledge him. In fact, it was him that I used as my escape. We drank, we caroused, we went out on the town together, and it was almost normal... save for the fact that I'd go home and cry every night, wishing I could get rid of that fucking guitar.

A week ago, I came home from the bar, walked upstairs, and started to climb in bed when I noticed the guitar was gone. I jumped up and flipped the lights on to find it on the floor. The molly bolts that supported the holder my brother had put in for me had come loose from the plastered wall, and the whole thing had fallen. I crouched beside it and touched it with one finger, as though it were a dead or dying creature. There was a nick in the bottom of the curve and one of the volume knobs was gone, but otherwise it had survived the fall. Or so I thought. I had to know. I plugged it into my amp and tried to tune it, but it was stubborn and refused to make the right notes.

I must have been at it for an hour before my mom came upstairs and asked why I was still playing "the tuning song." And I cried. And she held me. And we cradled the guitar my brother had given me as though it were him we held in our hands. I told him how sorry I was, how much I missed him, and while my words were directed at the guitar, I was finally speaking to my brother.

The next day I took it to a repair shop I've gone to for years, and the owner promised me he'd make it sound like new again. And he did. I picked it up tonight, and it sounds phenomenal. I played all of my old favorites, and you know, my heart felt a little lighter. I have to think that, instead of being the fire that mocked my grief, that sunburst is the light at the end of my grief tunnel. And by playing it, speaking the language my brother and I spoke to each other, I just might someday be okay again.

"Hey, man. I'm not trying to be a dick, here—"

"No, you're right, Ryan. It's…. He's the Guru, man."

Ryan put his fork down and stared at Silas.

"No fucking shit?"

"No fucking shit. I wish he would have told me." It would have been perfect. *The meet-cute the guys wanted me to have. The man I've been dreaming about, wondering about, turns out to be him.*

They finished eating their lunches in silence. Silas forced the food down because he knew he needed the sustenance, not because it tasted like anything other than his sorrow.

Ryan wiped his mouth and pulled out his phone to check his teeth and hair. He put it away and pulled out some lip balm. "Is this something you can't forgive? Like, you guys can't get past this?"

Silas shrugged and stood. He piled his garbage on his plate and took it over to the bins. "I don't know, man. Doesn't matter, I guess. We have Ventura tomorrow, and he's going to San Francisco."

Ryan put his arm around Silas's shoulders. "That's why God invented airplanes, my friend."

Silas barked out a laugh and fought the tears that were so close to the surface. "God didn't invent airplanes—"

"He invented the dudes who invented the planes, right? I'm right, aren't I? Damn right. Now, you get your head out of your ass. You've got a show in less than an hour."

Silas looked at his phone. "Shit. Yeah. I better go get ready."

Ryan pulled him in for a bro hug that lasted a little longer than normal. "Listen. I don't know the guy, but we've been friends for a long time, haven't we?"

Silas nodded, sucking in a shaky breath.

"And we've been friends long enough for me to tell you when you're being a dumbass, right?"

Silas pushed him away and wiped at his eyes. "Probably. You did kick my ass at *Call of Duty* last time we played. Not many dudes get away with that."

"Well, remember that. And think about it, okay? Everyone's got reasons for fucking up. Not excuses. Fuck excuses. But reasons matter."

"Yeah. I'll think about it. Later, man. Thanks."

Ryan gave him the middle-finger salute and sauntered off to a group of young women who'd somehow managed to get invites to the back area. Silas hoped they were prepared for Ryan on the prowl. He also hoped they'd met the condom guy somewhere along the way.

Silas wandered over to Brains's workshop, but he wasn't in the mood to mess with him. He stood against a tree and listened as Brains got into a serious discussion with an older guy. The dude looked military, like, he had a short haircut, and he had some sort of symbol tattooed on his impressive bicep that looked like one of the nautical tattoos Silas's grandfather'd had. He was asking Brains some pretty technical questions, and Silas chuckled as he watched the heads of the kids in the group bounce back and forth like a tennis match as this guy and Brains conversed. It wasn't exactly an argument or a pleasant exchange of ideas. For real, it was kind of like verbal foreplay. Maybe Brains would get some action this time out.

Which made it necessary for Silas to move on. He couldn't dwell on whether or not he'd ever have that kind of exchange with a certain someone who he thought was meant for more.

Chapter Twelve

Krish's iPhone battery was at 20 percent, so he went to one of the charging stations in the venue, sank to the ground, and started to clean up his mess. He searched for a hotel that wouldn't max out his meager credit card and tried to figure out the cheapest way to get to the city. He was going to have to find something to wear, as well. It would have helped if he weren't hundreds of miles from home and his stomach wasn't threatening to revolt.

Make a plan, keep moving. Forget that you just fucked up everything with the one person besides your family who'd done the most to get you through the past three years.

He wiped at his eyes and checked the email once more to get the address for the magazine office. One step in front of the other.

And then he heard the familiar chords played onstage, and his heart gave up trying to pretend it wasn't breaking.

Krish pulled himself to standing and followed the flock of screaming kids who were running for the Left Foot stage to watch Silas Franklin and Hush. Krish stayed toward the back of the crowd, as though he didn't deserve to be any closer to Silas after what he'd done.

Silas either hadn't been that affected or he was even more of an actor than Krish thought. He was in rare form, riding that edge of insanity the way Krish had always loved to see him. He'd donned tight black-and-white striped pants with suspenders hanging from the waist and no shirt. The pants barely covered his ass, and when he turned around and jumped, Krish's breath caught at seeing all of that pale flesh.

If he wasn't mistaken, the band played a little faster than usual. They all looked as though they were working hard to try and keep up with Silas's frantic pace. His bass line was tight, but rushed. Silas's manic energy was dizzying in a regular performance, but today the whole crowd seemed to be swept up. The mosh pit was larger than usual, and at any given time there were at least ten kids being tossed above the crowd from hand to hand until they ended up in the arms of security up front. And then Silas did something he never did.

While he was singing "Never Step Back," he got to the part where he recited his lyrics in a spoken-word growl, and he took off his bass and threw it to an unsuspecting guitar tech. He hovered on the edge of the stage, crouched down, his face red from exertion. His voice was lowered to a whisper as he cried out to the crowd. He gestured over to security and stepped into their waiting arms. Krish's heart dropped into his stomach. *What is he doing?*

Will you catch me if I fall?
Will you answer if I call?
Will you love me after all?
Will you catch me if I fall?

He ended on a scream, turned his back to the audience, and fell backward like a dead man. The band continued their brutal rhythm, and Los and Jordan carried the vocals as Silas lay still as a corpse being passed over thousands of fans. Not once did they let him dip down. Not once did even a foot leave a hand. And then he was back in the arms of security. They lifted him over the barrier, and he ran around to the steps to climb back onto the stage in time to sing the last chorus and end the song.

The crowd went insane. Krish was knocked around by people trying to get closer, even though he stood at the back. He didn't know how to feel in that moment. Thrilled to see Silas being loved by his fans? Angry that he'd put himself in harm's way like that? Or ashamed that he may have had something to do with Silas's erratic behavior?

"That was wild."

Jake stood next to him, looking incredibly un-Jake-like.

"What happened to you?"

Jake looked down at himself as though he hadn't noticed he was dressed like one of the guys in the band, only way fucking sexier. He wore a black New Year's Day tee, sliced and diced to show off bits of his pasty white torso. Someone had done a complete makeup job on him, enhancing his already handsome appearance. The results were striking. His hair was stylishly tousled with some sort of glitter product, and the front stood about four inches off his head. Krish was stunned silent.

"I let Roxanne and Jessica play. Jordan was all pissy about something and took off. The rest of the band was brooding, so I let the girls have fun. What do you think?"

"I think you look hot. I think your brother would flip the fuck out if he saw you."

"Let him. He's not my keeper." Jake looked him over and frowned.

"What happened this morning?"

Krish sighed. "I have an interview with *Alt-Scene* on Monday in San Francisco. And I told Silas the truth."

Jake turned to face him and rested his hands on Krish's arms. "Tell me he didn't freak."

"He didn't freak. He… left. Said 'see you around.'"

Jake frowned. "That's it?"

"That's it. Listen, I'm trying to find a way to the city and a hotel…. Can you get home okay on your own?"

Jake's eyes bugged out. "You mean you're going to *leave*? You can't leave like this. You have to say something."

"What's there to say? I fucked up. I should have told him who I was, and I didn't. I had plenty of opportunities."

"But you guys are…. You can't…. Krish, I need you to have a happy ending. One of us needs some romance."

"Well, I guess it'll have to be you." Krish smiled sadly. "You look ready for it. I'll be okay. I didn't mean to hurt him. He means so much to me."

Krish's eyes burned, and he needed to get out of there. He ran his hands through his hair. "I'm going to go back to the bus, and, I don't know. I've got to tell Chantal and figure out how to rejoin the tour after my interview. Then I'm going to head out."

Krish hugged a surprised and exasperated Jake.

"But Krish…."

"You sure you'll be okay?"

"Yeah, but—"

"Call me when you get home," Krish said as he walked away. Hush still played onstage, but he couldn't bear to watch anymore. He didn't deserve to.

He flashed his badge to security, and they let him through. He hurried over to the bus where Clarence sat jovially in the driver's seat, his silent laugh mocking Krish. He climbed on the bus and stalled out.

What the fuck was he supposed to do? He contemplated leaving a note for Silas, but that would be cheesy. Or would it? Maybe he could apologize in a forum where he was more comfortable.

His phone buzzed, and he saw it was his mother calling.

"Krishnan, darling, how are you? How is Mountain View?"

"It's okay. I'm actually getting ready to leave. The magazine called. I have an interview Monday."

"That's why I was calling. They left a message at the house as well. Oh, that is wonderful news. How will you get there and where will you stay?"

Krish sighed as he looked around once more. "I'm not sure. I think I can Uber to the hotel and then into the city on Monday. I found a place by the airport—"

"Do whatever is safest, dear. Your father and I will help you if you need anything."

"I'm fine. I can do this on my own."

"I know you can, but we want to support you. How did things go with Silas?"

And Krish's can-do attitude bled out.

"I think I really hurt him, Mom. I didn't tell him the truth about the blog, and then I did and… he left."

"That's terrible. How are you going to fix this, Krishnan? Meeting him is something you wanted to do for a very long time. You cannot walk away if something wonderful was beginning to happen. Now apologize to the boy and make things right before you go. Even if you don't have a relationship with him, you owe it to him to apologize."

Damn, his mother was smart. "Fine. I'll see what I can do."

"You'd better. He's a nice boy, and you don't want to hurt his feelings and become fodder for an angry song on his next album like Taylor Swift writes."

"You're right."

He told her he loved her, and they hung up. He knew what he needed to do.

Chapter Thirteen

ALL SILAS wanted when they got offstage was a shower. And a beer. And more beer. Their group hug was tense, and none of the guys really said much. They looked at him as though he were one scream short of a straitjacket, so he disentangled himself and took off with Jessica on his heels.

"You have something to say, or are you following me to make sure I don't pick up any more random strangers who aren't random at all?"

Jessica had to jog to keep up with him, and he didn't fucking care. He was still riled up from the performance, even though he had blown off some of the steam he'd been accumulating all day. He figured it was a perfectly healthy way of coping with huge disappointment, but everyone around him evidently thought he was losing it.

"Will you wait up one second, Silas? What is wrong with you? The other guys might be too afraid to hear your answer, but I'm not."

"What do you want to hear, that you were right? That I never should have gotten involved with someone who could hurt the band? Well, congratulations. You were right. Happy?"

Jessica put a firm hand on his shoulder and made him stop. "No, I'm not happy. Not if you aren't. What happened?"

Silas finally slowed down and allowed the feelings he'd been avoiding to catch up. They nearly knocked him on his ass.

"He's the Guru, Jess. For real."

"Holy shit."

"Yeah, but don't go telling anyone. I'm pissed he didn't tell me, but I don't want to fuck things up for him. I don't know why he didn't tell me. I gave him ample opportunities, but he didn't, not until…. Fuck. I may have just laid eyes on him for the first time, but you have no idea—"

"Yeah, I do. You've been pining for this guy for years. And you seemed happy with him. Maybe he was worried about you?"

"God, why can't everyone trust me to live my own life? I'm fully capable of making decisions and cleaning up my own messes. Just because I tend to go off the rails every once in a while, it doesn't mean I won't make it back."

"But Silas—"

"I'm not Gavin. I'm not going to bail when shit gets rough, all right? If I was going to kill myself, I would have done it when I was a teenager and had no one to give two shits about me. Gavin never had nothing. He always had people around him, and we always took care of him. He never had to deal with life. He went from his parents' place to living with me and being in the band, and I did everything for him. Mel was his first real love, and no one had ever said no to Gavin before. God. There's a million reasons he killed himself. I don't have a single reason, nor the desire. Why can't you guys believe me and stop treating me like I'm going to break?"

Jessica stood staring wide-eyed at him. They were surrounded by buses and not many people, but there were a few stragglers around shooting curious glances in their direction. Thankfully no one had cell phones out. That's all he needed. Jessica stepped closer and exhaled.

"No one thinks you're Gavin, Silas. But you also haven't let anyone in to see whether or not you're okay. You soldiered on through this whole album process, and all you'd ever say is 'I'm fine.' Your brothers, they don't expect you to be superhuman. They expect you to be Silas. They want to protect you because they love you."

"Yeah, well they can just tell me," he said, laughing a little. He wiped at his eyes and cursed when his eyeliner came off on his hands. "This shit is messy. I liked that other stuff we used to use. The Urban Decay or the NYX."

"I'll get you some more, I promise. Now, Silas. Did this guy really screw up, or do you think maybe, oh, I don't know, he was a little intimidated by all of us and was afraid to say anything?"

Silas rubbed at the fuzz on his head. "I don't know. Maybe. But why would he be intimidated by me? He could have told me."

Jessica pressed her lips together. "You're right. He could have. But he didn't. And then he did. Are you sure this isn't something you can come back from?"

Silas sighed and rested his hands on his hips. "I thought you guys were all against me seeing this guy. Why do you care?"

Jessica put her arm around him and led him to keep moving toward the bus. "Because I saw how happy you were this morning with him. And maybe I'm a sucker for a happy ending."

"I'll buy you a massage," Silas cracked, and Jessica delivered a hard elbow to his side.

"Ow. Okay, fine. But I don't even know how to reach him or anything."

"I'm sure Jake can help. Come on. Let's get you cleaned up for the meet 'n' greet. The rest of the guys will be right behind you, wanting a shower. Shall I see if I can find Krish?"

Silas sighed and shrugged. What was the right move? He'd had such a great time with him, better than he even thought he would, and before the show…. Maybe he should've heard him out. It was kind of a dick move to walk away like he had, but he hadn't wanted to explode on him either. That was his usual MO. It meant something that he hadn't.

Silas rushed his shower, and when he came out of the back room, the rest of the guys were milling about quietly.

"I'm sorry," he said to no one in particular.

"No, we're sorry," Brains said. "We were the ones who gave him shit and told him to leave."

"What do you mean?"

Brains sighed and stood up. "We overheard him on the phone saying he was meeting with someone, and to be honest, we were all worried about you. You seemed so happy, and I thought he was going to fuck you over, so we kind of strong-armed him maybe."

Unbelievable. Silas shook his head. After his talk with Jessica, he figured he should accept that his brothers in metal were trying to watch out for him and not bash them over the heads.

"I get it. Thank you for watching out for me, but I'm okay. We just, um… yeah, we had a disagreement. Sort of."

"See? I knew he was trouble," Los said.

"No, it's not like that. He's—"

"Guys! You've got like ten minutes to get to your tent for the meet 'n' greet. Hurry up in there."

They all got busy fixing themselves up and were out the door with five minutes to spare.

"I wish our day off was tomorrow," Brains said. "After that speed metal session today, I could use a break."

Silas shoved him as they were walking and knocked him into Los, who shoved him back into Silas.

"How'd it feel getting groped out there, Si?" Jordan asked. "You know, if you wanted a hand job, I'm sure we could have found someone to do it."

Silas cracked up. "Fuckers. Someone did reach down my pants, dude. I swear I got fingered, and I'm pretty sure it was a girl."

"No lube?" Jordan asked. "Damn. Well, you probably shouldn't have crowd-surfed in those pants, then. You fucking flashed me your ass every time you squatted down. I feel intimately acquainted with your crack at the moment."

Silas threw an arm around his neck and kissed his cheek. "It's a nice ass, though, isn't it? Hey, I saw your brother all dolled up. Mmmm. Maybe we should keep him." He flicked his tongue at Jordan and received a sock in the gut.

"I told you, lay off him, asshole. He might be pretty, but he's my little brother, and if you touch him, I will break you. I don't even care, dude."

"Your brother is safe from me. Don't worry." *There's only one person I want to touch right now, so where the fuck is he?*

The line at their tent stretched quite far down the aisle and around the bend. There had to be two-hundred-plus kids waiting to meet them. He'd have to be sure Jessica brought them food. He should have grabbed a protein bar before they left the bus, but he'd been preoccupied with making up with his brothers. His heart felt quite a bit lighter, and he hoped Jessica found Krish before he left the venue. If he hadn't had the meet 'n' greet, Silas would have been scouring the grounds.

Instead he sat patiently at the table in their tent and signed poster after poster, shirt after shirt, pleased to see the amount they were making off of merch and feeling sorry for their merch girl, Mischa, at the same time.

"It's so good to see you guys onstage again," a young girl was saying to him. "I'm sorry about

Gavin." She looked scared to death—as many kids did at these gigs—which was weird to Silas, but then he remembered how he'd felt meeting his idols. It was hard to accept someone saw him like that, even after all these years. He appreciated how brave she must have been.

Silas smiled at her and stood up to give her a hug over the table. *Fuck it.* It looked like it took a lot for her to say that.

"Thanks, sweetie. I appreciate it."

Her friend snapped a pic of them, and he had Jordan take a pic of them with his phone too. "I'll put this on my story later. You follow me on Snapchat?"

She blushed. "Yeah. Thank you, Silas."

"Thank you for being here."

For some reason he couldn't explain, he knew she understood how he felt.

A half hour went by and there was still no sign of Jessica or Krish. He tried hard to engage with everyone who came by. They deserved his full attention, but he was distracted. If Krish left, he was going to be devastated. He'd have to get his number from Jake, and if Jake didn't give it up, he'd beat it out of him.

"Hey, where's your boyfriend?"

Silas finished shaking hands with some young guys, and his eyes landed on two fat fucks in camo shorts who looked totally out of place in Warpedlandia.

"Excuse me?" Silas looked them over and wondered what they were talking about.

"Yeah," Fat Fuck Number Two chimed in. "We saw you guys making out earlier. Why ain't he here with you?"

They'd stood in line this whole time just to be assholes? Silas put on a nasty smile. "Why, *your* boyfriend can't keep you satisfied? I don't share. Sorry." Silas gave an exaggerated wink.

Their smug smiles slipped, and the first guy muttered "fag" under his breath as he walked away with his fat fuck friend. They were arguing about something at the side of the tent, started pushing each other, and one of them slammed into the pole.

"Watch out," Mischa yelled at them. They told her to fuck off, and they continued their argument.

"We should probably get security," Los said quietly as he continued to sign posters and T-shirts. The band was becoming overwhelmed. The line bunched up right in front of them, and there were several kids leaning over the tables.

Silas stood and looked around. "Let me grab someone."

Then he spotted Krish. He was just outside their tent typing on his phone and not paying attention. Silas shouted his name and he looked up, his dark eyes full of sadness.

And then chaos erupted.

Chapter Fourteen

"Krish!"

Krish looked up to see Silas's smiling face seconds before the tent collapsed. The pole Krish was standing near hit him in the head on the way down, leaving a stinging swipe down his scalp.

"Krish!" Silas untangled himself from the tent and ran toward him, pushing people out of the way.

The band all jumped back from the table... except Brains.

A group of kids fell onto the table, and it collapsed on top of him.

Fans scattered, and shouts filled Krish's ears as something warm ran into his eyes, clouding his vision. Someone knocked into him, and he tripped over the curb and fell onto his ass. At least two people stepped on him before he scrambled back out of the way.

"Krish. Oh my God, you're bleeding."

"Silas, I'm so sorry. I wanted to tell you—"

"Stop. Let's get you some help."

Krish sat holding his head, stunned by the amount of blood that was running down his arm and feeling a bit faint. His father was a cardiologist, but he'd never done well with the sight of blood. It was a good thing he was sitting down, because his vision was spotty all of a sudden.

"Silas. Brains is hurt bad," Jordan said as he ran toward them.

"Go to him," Krish said. "I'm okay."

Silas looked torn, and for a moment he stood and watched the chaos. He muttered, "What the fuck?" before attempting to reach Brains.

Security took several more minutes to settle things down. Krish saw several kids with scraped up legs who'd fallen in the ruckus. Medical personnel rushed to the tent, which several men were now trying to clear.

Krish's blood turned cold when he heard Brains scream.

When the tent was finally pulled away, the scene was horrifying. Brains's legs were under a now-flattened table. Mischa was on the ground as well. The first to get to Brains was an older man in plain clothes who said he was a medic. Brains grabbed for his hand and spoke to him as the medical staff worked on him. They moved the table away, fitted a neck brace on him, carefully loaded him onto a backboard, and then did the same with Mischa.

"He's going to be okay," the medic said to Los, who had tears running down his face.

Brains said something to the man, and he nodded and continued to hold his hand as they put the backboard on a stretcher and carried him to a waiting ambulance.

"Krish!"

Krish turned his head to find Jake running toward him. He was at his side in an instant with a woman on the medical staff, and she began looking at his head. Krish saw Silas run to Jessica. The two of them had a frantic conversation, and then they returned to Krish and Jake.

"God, Krish, what happened to you?"

"The tent came down and caught me on the side of the head. There must have been something metal sticking out. I'm okay, though."

"Actually, this is going to require sutures, or staples maybe," the medical staff said. "Is there someone who can take you to the hospital?"

"We will," Silas said. "Brains and Mischa are going by ambulance. We're going to follow in the bus. Can you stand?"

Krish tried to nod, but his head went fuzzy again. Silas took his hand and slowly pulled him up. He stumbled a little, and Silas steadied him.

"I got you," Silas said softly. "I got you."

Krish felt those three words were a little like "I forgive you," but he didn't want to get his hopes up. Silas kept a steadying arm around Krish's back, and he was grateful.

"I'm coming with," Jake said.

Jordan wandered over and leaned on Jake. He looked as dazed as Krish felt.

"What happened to you?" Silas asked, concern evident in his expression.

"I fell down. Hard. On my ass. The tent collapsed and fell over, and I kinda tripped over my own big-ass feet. I'm okay, just sore."

"Anyone seen Los?" Jessica said, searching around frantically as they began to move in a group toward the bus. She called out his name, and he whistled from by the ambulance where they were loading Brains.

"I'm going to go grab him. You guys get to the bus and stay put. This place is a fucking disaster right now."

"If you need to go with her, I'll be okay," Krish said. "You should go check on Brains."

Silas once again seemed conflicted. He walked Krish over to Jake's other side. "I really want to see him before they leave. Jake, don't let him fall."

"I won't. I might trip him, but—"

"Not fucking funny," Silas said. He gave Krish an exasperated look and squeezed his arm. Then he ran after Jessica.

They jogged together to the ambulance, and Krish saw him hug Los for a long time. He poked his head in the ambulance door and reached up to touch Brains's foot, but had to step back as the paramedics closed the doors. Then he walked to the other ambulance and checked on Mischa. Theo was with her, holding her hand for support. When they lifted her inside, Krish saw Theo climb into the ambulance with her.

"Come on," Jake said, moving their trio forward. "Let's get you both on the bus. Krish, you're bleeding through that bandage. We better get you to the hospital quick."

"I need an ice pack," Jordan moaned. "Damn, that hurt. I think I landed on something. My ass hurts like fuck."

A couple of minutes after Jake got Krish and Jordan settled on the bus, Jessica and Silas made it in with Los, who thankfully was uninjured. The driver had to maneuver a bit to get them out of the line of buses, but they were soon on their way. Jessica sat up front with the driver to give him instructions. Jordan took a bunk with some ice from their freezer in a bag and moaned for a while until he got comfortable. Jake stood by him, a frown marring his face.

Silas sat next to Krish without speaking, but the rapid rate his leg was bouncing let Krish know how stressed he was.

"Who's the guy with Brains in the ambulance?" Jessica asked as she joined them in the back.

Los shrugged. "I don't know. He was at his workshop earlier."

"You mean the guy he was having the crazy debate with?" Silas said, laughing. "I wondered if he knew him or something."

"Who knows? When the paramedics started working on him, he grabbed the guy's hand and was, like, not letting go." Los crossed his arms over his chest and frowned.

"They think his leg might be broken," Jessica added. They all exchanged worried glances at that news. "What even happened? I was just coming back from trying to find Krish when everything went to hell."

"All I know is some drunk assholes were causing issues at the front of the line, so I told them to fuck off, basically. They were arguing when they moved to the side, but I don't know what happened. I saw Krish, called to him, and was headed his way when the fucking tent got knocked to the side and fell over. I ducked out and found Krish bleeding, but there were people everywhere. How'd you get out?"

"I was headed to get security on those two bastards," Los said. "I stepped out the back to wave someone down, and everything went crazy. They started beating the shit out of each other, and they knocked into a couple of kids… like, fell on them. One of the kids was with the guy that went with Brains. Like, maybe his kid or something."

"Shit," Silas said quietly.

"Silas?" Krish asked. "Can you help me—"

He held out his bloody hands, and Silas jumped up. "Let's get you over to the sink."

Krish stood while Silas scrubbed the blood off of his hands and arms. He was careful and gentle, and he muttered under his breath a few times, but Krish couldn't tell if he was frustrated with the whole mess or something in particular.

"I'd get you a shirt, but you're probably not done bleeding yet," he said with a humorless laugh.

"Silas, I'm so—"

"Don't fucking worry about that right now. Okay? All I care about is getting you to the hospital and stitched up, checking on my merch girl, and making sure my best friend is okay."

"What about my ass?" Jordan whined from his bunk.

"Your ass comes fourth."

There were a few snickers, but everyone was in shock and too out of it to joke around.

The bus was quiet the rest of the way to the hospital. The driver pulled up as close to the entrance as he could and still be able to get out. He told Jessica he'd be parked and ready for whatever. One by one they left the bus and Jessica counted heads.

"All right. How many of you need medical attention?"

"Jordan and Krish, I think, is it," Silas said. "Jake?"

"I was with Jessica, watching all of the chaos unfurl."

"Great," Jessica said. "Let's get everyone inside and see if they'll tell me anything about Brains. Silas? They're going to ask about next of kin. Do we know?"

Silas shook his head. "He won't want them contacted. Guess you're his sister or something."

"I'm so glad you didn't say his mom or I would have socked you, so help me God. Okay, Jake? You'll get Jordan signed in?"

"Ain't the first time and won't be the last," Jake said, rolling his eyes. "Krish, you need me to call your parents?"

"Not yet. I don't want them to worry. I'll call when we actually know something."

"I can call for you," Silas said. "I promised your mom I'd keep you safe, and I fucked up. Better if I tell her."

"Silas—"

"Besides, you'll just bleed all over your phone." He offered a half smile.

Krish thanked him and went to sit with the others. His head still felt fuzzy, and he felt gross. A shower would have been heavenly.

What a mess. And poor Brains. A broken leg would be devastating to the band, sure, but he could have been killed. All because two drunk guys decided to get into a stupid brawl next to their tent. That type of stuff never happened at shows Krish had been to. He'd seen a couple of tussles, but this was like a mob scene. He hoped and prayed that none of the kids in line got hurt. He knew the band would feel awful if they had. Krish planned to write a blog post about what happened when his brain stopped spinning, so he could reassure folks that concerts are safe, relatively, and that anytime there was a large gathering of people, something like that could happen. It had nothing to do with the band or even the show. But that wouldn't make the band feel any better if someone other than them got hurt.

"Okay, Mr. Guruvayoor, let's take you back."

Krish stood up shakily, and Silas walked with him, a hand supporting his lower back. His presence reassured Krish that all hope was not lost, but things were still incredibly awkward between them.

"Right in here," the male nurse said as he guided Krish to sit down in a chair. "Okay. What happened?"

"A pole fell on me. I fell. I got stepped on. I don't really know what else."

The nurse chuckled and removed the bandage. "How long ago?"

Silas pulled out his phone. "Shit. Maybe an hour ago? I don't know. It all happened so fast."

The nurse kept sneaking looks at Silas as though he maybe recognized him or at least knew he was an important person.

The bandage came off, and Krish winced as Silas sucked in a breath.

"Holy fuck, Krish. That's big."

The nurse laughed a little louder this time. "I'll say."

"I'm serious, babe. That's huge."

"Stop," Krish said, laughing a little bit too. He couldn't look up at Silas as he was being worked on, and that was probably a good thing.

"I haven't seen one this big for a while. Yeah, the doc is going to have to staple this."

Krish looked at the guy's badge. Garrett Chu. Garrett was a bit of a flirt, which normally wouldn't bother Krish, but if he started flirting with Silas, he was going to tell him where he could stick his staples.

"And I have worse news. I'm going to have to shave around the wound."

"Awesome," Krish said, his head starting to pound. "Didn't realize I'd be getting a makeover."

Silas reached over and squeezed his shoulder, and the gesture made Krish breathe a little easier. As long as things were salvageable with Silas, he could handle this, even if it meant a new haircut.

Krish zoned out while the nurse got to work, first cutting his long curly locks and then shaving around the wound. They must have given him some numbing stuff, because once it came time for the doctor to staple him together, he just felt tugging on his skin and heard the clicking sounds. It was surreal.

When they finished, Krish looked up at Silas. He had his arms crossed over his chest and was chewing on a nail. He made eye contact and smiled a little at Krish.

"Okay, let's finish cleaning this up, put some goo on it, and you're good to go. Do you have someone to watch you—"

"Yeah. He does."

The boldness in Silas's tone made Krish's wishful heart thud, but he didn't want to read too much into it. For all he knew, Silas was doing what he did best, being good to others. If only they could get a moment alone to talk, but it was selfish of him to even think that while the band's future was threatened by Brains's injury.

Once Krish was fixed up, he excused himself to go to the restroom, and Silas said he was going to check on Brains. Their parting was awkward. Krish wondered if they would ever be able to have that easy way between them again.

He used the bathroom, and while washing his hands in the sink, he cringed over his appearance. He wasn't a vain guy at all, didn't really care much for his appearance, but having a big chunk of his hair gone on the side of his head was ridiculous. The staples, all twenty of them, were severe. His scalp was somewhat lighter than his face. Wow. Not attractive. And what if he had a huge scar? And what if his hair didn't grow back right?

Yeah, and Brains might have a broken leg, and God only knew what had happened to Mischa, so get over yourself.

That thought sobered him enough to end his pity party and send him back to the waiting room.

No one familiar was around, so he took a seat in the corner by the door and rested his head against the wall with his eyes closed. He listened to the sounds of children fussing and adults scolding them, of sick people moaning softly, coughing, or even crying in one case.

It was the first time Krish had been on his own during a crisis, and he hadn't fallen apart. His head hurt and he was going to look funny for a while, but he'd survived. He was making adult decisions and taking steps toward a self-sufficient life with his interview Monday—

The interview.

How the hell was he supposed to show up with his head stapled together? How could he leave Silas and the band in this state? And would Silas even want him to be there for him? So many questions with no answers, so he just sat there, trying his best to block out the noise and concentrate on what he *did* have control over.

"Hey, you're not supposed to be asleep, are you?"

Jake nudged Krish's foot, which had fallen asleep. Krish opened his eyes and tried to shake out his foot.

"I can sleep. I just have to be woken up. But honestly, I don't think I have a concussion or anything."

Jake laughed. "Well, you're awake now. You look fantastic," he said, brushing some of Krish's hair to the side. "Like Indian Frankenstein."

"Shut up. How's your brother?"

"Bruised but fine. Mischa broke her wrist, they think. Waiting on X-rays. Brains is bad, though. He fractured his femur. They don't think they need to do surgery, but they need to do more X-rays once the swelling goes down and see if there's anything else going on."

"That's awful," Krish said, any humor between them totally evaporated. "They just started the tour."

"Yeah. The guy with Brains, his name is Paul, he said he's taking Brains back to his house from here. I think we're going to follow in the bus."

Krish frowned. "Okay. Yeah. You're going to stick around?"

Jake nodded. "Jordan was pretty stressed about everything. I'll stay long enough to make sure he's hanging in there, and then I'll go home. How about you?"

Krish shrugged. "I'm supposed to go to the interview Monday in San Francisco."

Jake beamed. "I'm excited for you. That's exactly what you were hoping for. I want everything to work out," he said, looking around. "Especially with Silas."

Krish smiled. "Thanks." He wanted to be excited about the job, but he wanted to know where he stood with Silas even more. Maybe he had his priorities mixed up, but that's how he felt.

Krish's phone buzzed. Chantal. He was doing a terrible job so far on his internship.

I heard about what happened, and I heard you went to the hospital with Hush. Are you okay?

Krish sighed. How was he supposed to answer that?

Mostly. Staples in my head. Being watched for concussion, but I don't think I got hit that hard. I'll be okay. I'm sorry.

Her answer came back shortly.

Don't be sorry! I'm glad you're okay. Kevin said to please pass along his well wishes to the band and for them to keep us posted. Do you have any updates?

Krish was faced for the first time with a conflict of interest involving his relationship status with Silas. People would expect him to give details on the band, and he was absolutely not going to do that. He would never be like one of the assholes who did them wrong in the media. This was one of his worst fears moving into journalism from what he'd been doing. He'd never wanted to put the story before humanity. Humanity *was* the story for him, and he wanted to do everything in his power to help people, not hurt them. It was one of the tenets he'd been taught to live his life by. Do no harm.

Chantal wanted an answer.

It would be best to ask Jessica. I don't have any updates on the band. Thank you for checking on me, and again, I'm sorry I'm falling down on my intern duties.

Shit. San Francisco. Speaking of duties. He needed to let her know.

I have been asked to come to San Francisco to the Alt-Scene *offices on Monday morning. I'm going to get myself there, and then I'll let you know when I will be rejoining the tour. I'm sorry if this causes any problems. I feel like I haven't really earned my intern badge.*

He hoped he wasn't blowing his opportunity, but he had no control over any of it. He was an unpaid intern only because the tour and magazine had to do something to get him there. He couldn't worry about it right then. His head was pounding.

OMG Krish your poor head! Don't worry about us. Just take care of yourself. The 'intern' duties are all taken care of. Are you sure you don't need anything? I can come to you if you need. I'm responsible for you.

They'd barely had any time together, but she'd been so nice to him.

I'll be okay, but thank you. I can't tell you how much I appreciate all you've done. I'll see you soon. I'll keep you posted.

She texted a final goodbye, and Krish's phone gave up the ghost. He hadn't even told his parents anything yet. He was just so tired....

Chapter Fifteen

"So how long are we talking, doc?"

Silas saw the tension around Brains's eyes as he asked the question that not only affected his life, but their band's future. Jordan, Los, Jessica, and this stranger, Chief Petty Officer Paul McNally, stood by as the doctor went over Brains's prognosis.

Silas wanted to rage against the injustice. They'd only just gotten their fresh start. If they pulled out of Warped Tour, there went their comeback. Not to mention the money lost, the fans disappointed, their crew out of work….

"You're very lucky it appears to be a hairline fracture. I think we're looking at three to four weeks in the brace with physical therapy, and he should be able to start resuming normal activity. Slowly. He's going to be in pain."

Assorted groans and curse words escaped, none of which were going to make Brains feel better.

"Hey, guys. Brains is the priority here," Silas scolded. "We'll figure everything else out. Don't fucking lose it now."

The assembled group was adequately admonished, and the doctor continued.

"We'll get you fitted for a brace, and you'll need some crutches. We can recommend a medical supply place nearby where you can pick some up. Don't worry, son. You'll be back out on the road in no time."

Yeah, but by the time he's well enough to play, Warped will be over.

"I'm sorry, Silas," Brains said, tears in his eyes as he reached for his best friend. Silas bent over the bed and held him as he cried.

"I'll go talk to the admissions folks about billing and everything," Jessica said, excusing herself. Silas heard the curtain swish as she left. Los and Jordan followed her, mumbling as they walked.

"I'll leave you two," Paul said, making to leave.

"Please? Paul? Will you stay?"

Silas looked up questioningly at Paul. He appeared to be similarly confused.

"What's going on?" Silas asked.

Brains looked down at his hands and picked at his nails. "I just want him to stay."

"Brains?" Silas had known Brains for close to twelve years, and he knew the dude was often way up in his head. Sometimes his actions didn't exactly make the most sense, but this time….

"Do you two know each other?" Silas asked, cutting through the bullshit.

Brains looked up at Paul, and for a moment, Silas saw some unspoken connection pass between them. Paul gave Brains a reassuring look.

"He found me first. And he knew what I needed."

Silas knew more about Brains than anyone in their close-knit group, but he didn't know his whole story. What he did know was that Brains's coming out had been the nail in the coffin for his toxic relationship with his parents. He left home at sixteen and never looked back. He'd told Silas he spent days in the library and nights on the street learning everything he could to survive. He joined Sullen when he was only seventeen. They had a few hits before falling apart, which left Brains on his own again. Forming Hush was his way of making a new family, and he'd seemed satisfied with his circumstances. Silas didn't have a relationship with his family either, save the occasional phone calls on birthdays and holidays, so the two of them had spent nearly all of the past twelve years together. Which was why Silas was so confused by his behavior.

Jessica came back in with a nurse to go over instructions, and Paul stepped forward and put his hand on Brains's arm.

"I'm going to step out for a moment with Silas. I'm not going anywhere."

Brains nodded, but his eyes filled with tears again.

"We'll be here," Silas said, his heart breaking at the look on Brains's face. "I'm not leaving you."

Brains's bottom lip quivered as he turned his attention to what the nurse was telling him.

Out in the hallway, Paul turned to face Silas, and Silas sucked in a breath, somewhat intimidated by the older man.

"I don't want to be a dick here, Mr.—"

"Paul. And it's fine."

"Paul. Okay. Do you have any idea why my best friend is hanging on to you like a security blanket?"

Paul crossed his arms over his muscular chest. "I have an idea, but I don't know for sure, no."

"Then give me your idea," Silas said. He attempted to keep the agitation out of his voice. "Because we're in a pretty fucked-up situation right now, and I need all the information I can get."

"When I found him, he was under the table still, and the pain hadn't hit him yet. I was afraid of the worst. He's really lucky. He asked me to keep talking to him, said he was scared, and he needed me to keep talking. So I did. I told him I'm a Navy Corpsman—"

"Is that like a medic?" Silas hated to interrupt, but this whole situation was insane.

"Something like that. I take care of injuries for a living, oftentimes in hairy situations. We'd had quite an exchange earlier in the day when my son and I were at his workshop and then, I don't know. Sometimes an injured person just needs someone to focus on. When I told him about my job, that seemed to calm him down. Then when the paramedics arrived, he panicked and started to fight them." Paul rubbed at the back of his neck. "They told him they'd have to sedate him if he didn't stop. I held his hands, and he settled down."

"Are you serious?" Silas leaned back against the wall as though Paul's words had punched him in the gut.

"Yeah. He ever have any episodes like that with you?"

Silas shook his head. "Not at all. I know he had a really fucked-up childhood, but I don't know the whole story, but he's never lost it like that. He has no contact with his family, refuses any calls from anyone about them. He hasn't even been sick since I've known him, which has been over twelve years, so there was no reason for paramedics or doctors or anything. Jesus. You think you know a guy."

Silas was beside himself. He wanted to be there for his best friend, but he hadn't been the first one to him. Some stranger had to see him through this traumatic experience. After all Brains had done for him when he found Gavin, and he couldn't even return the favor?

"My son, Bowie, he has anxiety, so I kinda knew how to talk Billy down, but I'm not sure what else I can do. I offered him our place so he could be comfortable. I can't imagine the bus being fun on crutches, or sleeping in a bunk, for that matter. I've done my time on bunks, so I get it. You all are welcome to crash at our house. I've got three bedrooms and a pullout couch. And my sister lives next door and has an extra room, so if you guys want a place to kind of regroup or whatever, you're welcome."

Silas thought about his offer. The guy was a stranger, but for whatever reason, Brains trusted him.

"Yeah, we've got some big decisions to make. If he's laid up for three to four weeks, that's almost the whole Warped Tour for us. We're probably going to have to pull out."

Paul nodded and kicked his heel against the toe of his other shoe. "That's gotta be awful for you guys after everything you've been through," he said quietly. "Look, come back to my place, you guys can rest and make a plan tomorrow or something once the adrenaline wears off."

Brains would be incredibly uncomfortable on the bus, and with all the jostling around, he'd be in pain. Silas didn't want to put his best friend through that, but their place in Oakland, while not too far away, required climbing a flight of stairs and the bedrooms were up another flight. They could get hotel rooms, but they needed to be together to figure this out. They were well and truly fucked.

"Paul, we're really in a jam here, but this is crazy. I can't just send my best friend home with some dude who looks great in a muscle shirt."

Paul coughed and his cheeks turned a shade of rosy pink that wasn't from the sun.

"Look, I know you have no reason to trust me, but I'm a twenty-four-year Navy Corpsman. I take care of people for a living. I have a twenty-one-year-old son who's crazy about your music. And my sister and her twins, one of whom is on the spectrum, live in a duplex with me. I'm bringing you to my sanctuary too, right? I'm trusting that you guys won't bring drugs or violence into my house, and you have to trust that I'll take care of your friend the best I can."

Paul held out a hand, and Silas accepted his handshake.

"All right. I guess we're going to your place. You'll ride on the bus with us?"

Paul nodded. "And I've got crutches back at my place. I had ACL surgery a couple years ago. I think they're still in the garage."

"Thanks," Silas said. One less thing for them to worry about. "At least this happened in the Bay Area, not some back-asswater place where he wouldn't have gotten good medical treatment."

Paul laughed. "Try Afghanistan."

"No shit," Silas said, figuring the guy had probably seen a lot. He felt a little safer about taking his whole horde to the guy's house now—the horde he needed to take charge of. Jessica was good, but he needed to step up.

He also needed to talk to Krish. There was a lot left unsettled between them, but just knowing he was near gave Silas a little boost of confidence that they would get through this clusterfuck. Somehow. He had to have faith.

Silas made his way to Mischa's room next. Theo was holding her hand, and they had their foreheads pressed together.

"Hey, sweetie," he said. "What happened?"

She sniffled a little and smiled. "Those assholes. When they started fighting, they hit the pole, and the whole tent shifted. I went over to tell them to knock it off, and one of them shoved the other one into me. I fell backward and caught myself. My wrist is broken, and the doctor said I'm going to have to have surgery."

Silas's heart sank. Poor thing. She was a college student, and Silas knew this summer gig was helping to pay for her tuition.

"Don't worry, I swear. We'll take care of you. You got that? I don't want you to worry."

She nodded. "Thank you, Silas. I gotta go home, though. I'm going to have to leave the tour. I'm sorry."

Theo sat back and sighed. "I want to stay with her through the surgery."

Silas knew they were close, figured maybe they were even involved, but they'd both been professional about it, so he didn't care. It wasn't like they needed Theo if the band wasn't playing, so he nodded at him. "Of course."

Silas kissed Mischa's forehead. "Don't worry about us. I mean, worry, because no one else is going to keep our merch organized and be as good a salesperson."

She went to punch him, but then winced when she moved her injured arm.

"I promise you can beat me when you feel better. I'll even hold still."

"Thanks, Silas."

"You need a ride home?"

She shook her head. "My sister is coming to get me. I have to go see an orthopedic doctor tomorrow, and then they'll decide on surgery."

She was in for a long recovery. Silas remembered when Gavin broke his hand during a fight. He'd been devastated, thinking his guitar playing days were over. Luckily it healed right, and with physical therapy, he was good as new.

"Keep us posted. Jessica will make sure everything is taken care of. Just take care of you, okay?"

She smiled and thanked him again.

Silas shook hands with Theo and headed back to the waiting room, hoping to find Krish… and an answer to his new dilemma of what the fuck they were going to do.

AN HOUR and a half later, they had Brains loaded carefully on the bus with his leg up on the couch. Every bump in the road, every time they stopped and started, his face would screw up in pain. Paul sat across from him, watching him carefully, at the ready to spring into action if needed.

Los, Jordan, and Jake all sat at the booth and moped. Jordan, it turned out, had a really bruised asscheek and would be fine, just in a lot of pain. Jessica sat up front with the driver, speaking in a low voice that Silas couldn't quite make out. She was probably telling the Warped folks that Hush was royally screwed. Everyone was exhausted, and with the near future uncertain, the tension in the bus was incredibly thick.

Silas sat beside Krish, who had his head in his hands. The poor guy had a big hunk of hair missing, and the staples looked hella harsh.

"You know," he said, trying to add some humor to their dire straits, "you could start a whole new hair trend like this. Chris Motionless had his head shaved with metal studs in his scalp, but I'm really thinking this look could work for you."

Krish rubbed at his eyes and sat up with a grin. "I don't think I could come close to Chris's level of cool, but the staples do look intense."

Silas nudged his knee with his fist. "I've got clippers. I can take care of you when we get to Paul's."

"Yeah, outside, though," Paul cut in. "My son got the bright idea to shave his head in the bathroom once, and I was picking hairs out of the rug and finding them in the cabinets for months afterward."

They all chuckled, and the tension seemed to bleed out a little. Jessica came back and stood holding on to the counter for a few breaths before she spoke.

"I told the production office we're out tomorrow. We're in Phoenix on Thursday. I told them we'd be in touch tomorrow after you all had some time to regroup."

"Thanks, Jess," Silas said, and they all murmured their thanks.

"I don't know about you guys," Los said, "but I could really use a beer."

The group burst into laughter and took a collective deep breath for the first time. Even Brains smiled a little.

Jessica handed water to Krish, beers to the three at the table, and then to Paul and Silas. Brains waved his away, asking for food and water instead, so he could take more pain medicine. Paul grabbed him some pillows and tried to make him more comfortable. He was so tall he couldn't exactly stretch out. Silas grew more grateful by the minute that they were going to be at a real house in real beds that night.

It took them about an hour and change to pull off the freeway in San Ramon, an affluent community on the other side of the hill from Oakland. The two cities were worlds apart in culture, architecture, and atmosphere. Paul gave the driver his address, and within minutes they were parked outside of a quaint duplex at the base of the foothills. It was close to midnight by that time, and the only activity in the neighborhood was an occasional car and a herd of deer happily munching on grass across the street.

"Hard to believe we're still in the Bay Area," Los said as he stepped down from the bus and joined Krish and Silas on the sidewalk. Paul carefully supported Brains to the top of the steps, and Los and Silas held on to his arms as Paul helped him down the steps. Once they reached the street, Paul swept Brains up into his arms and carried him like a fairy princess up to the front door.

"Is that guy fucking Captain America or something?" Los asked as they all gaped.

Paul wasn't huge, but he didn't even strain under Brains's weight, which was probably around a hundred and eighty pounds. He got to the porch, and the door opened from the inside.

"Come on in, guys," Paul called over his shoulder as he gently maneuvered Brains through the door without bumping his bad leg. Silas grabbed Brains's bag with his toiletries and some clothes and brought it in. He placed it on the floor next to the couch where Paul carefully set Brains down.

"I'll get you some water, okay?"

Brains nodded to Paul and watched him closely as he walked away. Silas and Krish sat on the couch across from him. Jake asked Paul where the restroom was and where he could stash a now very sleepy Jordan.

"You two can take my spare room, if you want. Two of you can have my son's room, and we can pull out this couch. I'll put Billy in my room. My son and I will go next door so you can have some space."

Brains blinked, and Silas could swear he was about to cry again. He watched Paul move around the house getting things set up for guests. He looked like a lost puppy.

"Brains?" Silas knelt down on the floor next to the couch. "Babe. What's going on? We got you. It's okay. Everything is going to be okay."

Brains looked at him, and Silas teared up seeing the pain in his eyes.

"I'm sorry, Silas. You guys gotta find someone to replace me, okay? You have to stay on the tour."

Silas shook his head. "No decisions are getting made tonight. Let's all get some sleep and see where we are in the morning. Sound good?"

Brains sniffled and nodded, looking down at his hands in his lap. "If only we didn't have all those kick-drum parts, huh? Stupid double bass. Too bad we don't have like conga drums or something."

Silas was relieved that Brains could joke about their situation. "We could try that on our next album maybe." He reached for Brains's hand and squeezed it. "Hey. When Paul gets back with those crutches, let's get you to bed. We'll all be able to function better with some rest."

Brains squeezed back.

"We're about the same height, so you can try these tomorrow," Paul said as he brought in the crutches. "I can adjust them if they're too tall."

"Thank you," Brains said quietly, his big blue eyes still on the verge of leaking. "I'd like to go to bed, if that's okay."

Paul smiled at him. "Yeah. Sounds good. Let's get you set up."

He bent again and picked Brains up from the couch. Brains whispered something, and they both chuckled softly to each other. Silas watched in awe as Brains wrapped his arms around Paul's neck, and Paul carried him down a hallway toward the back of the house.

"Uh, good night?" Silas called out, exasperated.

Once they were out of sight, Brains called back, "Good night."

That left Silas and Krish alone. Krish had his left arm on the arm of the couch and his head rested on it with his eyes closed.

"Let me get you to bed," Silas said.

Krish stood up and listed to the right. Silas guided him down the hallway and into a large bedroom with a huge drum set in one corner and a queen-size bed on the other wall. He pushed Krish down gently onto the bed, removed his shoes and his clothes down to his underwear, and started to urge him to lie down when his deep brown eyes opened.

"Silas." He tried to speak, but Silas shushed him with a finger to his lips.

"I'm going to check on Brains, but I'll be back. You go to sleep. I'll have to wake you up every couple hours, okay?"

Krish nodded. "I'm sorry," he said once. Then he turned over and faced the wall.

Silas smiled down at him and gazed longingly at his back. He wished for nothing more than to curl up naked against it, but they had work to do before they could go there. He pulled the covers up over Krish's bare shoulder and turned to leave.

Then he heard voices from the end of the hall.

"I'll be down the hall. I'll hear you if you—"

"Please, Paul. I'm sorry. I wish I could explain it, but I just need you to stay."

"Okay, but I'm taking the floor."

"But it's your bed—"

"Billy, I don't want to hurt you. I'm liable to bump you in the night."

"Paul?"

Silas turned the corner to find Paul with his hands on his hips and Brains sitting up in bed.

"Can I come in?"

"Yeah," Paul said. "I'll be right back. I'm going to check on Bowie."

He left the room with a frown on his face, and Silas moved to Brains's side of the bed.

"Hey, man," he said, smoothing Brains's hair back. "You want me to stay with you?"

Brains sighed. "I promise I'm not losing my shit here, Si. There's a reason for all of this. I just can't talk about it."

Silas nodded. "It's okay, my brother. We have time. You'll tell me when you're ready. We've been through it, you and me. I'm not going anywhere."

Brains smirked. "Except you need to go to your guy."

Silas threw his shoulders back. "You're my priority, Brains."

"I know that. But he needs you. You need him. You and I will always be brothers, but you need love."

Silas smiled. "I need *loooove*," he crooned, quoting the old LL Cool J song. Pretty soon they were both rapping along to it and laughing. When Paul returned, Silas was doing his best impression of the sexy rapper while Brains laughed so hard he made no noise, just had tears streaming down his face.

"You're killing me, dude," Brains finally squeaked out and grabbed gratefully for the water Paul had brought him.

"Yeah, I know. I don't quite have his abs." Silas lifted up his shirt and tried to flex. Some tiny abs popped up and some mini triceps, but nothing compared to LL Cool J.

"Look! There's one," Brains said, holding his stomach. Then the hiccups started.

"Well, that's my cue," Silas said. "Thanks again, Paul, for letting us stay here. I promise we won't trash the place."

Paul waved at him and grabbed some extra blankets out of the closet. "I'm not worried. I still don't think a bunch of musicians can do as much damage as sailors on leave." He turned his back to lay out a bed on the floor.

Silas and Brains wiggled their eyebrows at each other, and Silas mouthed, "sailors." Paul turned back around and caught them looking guilty.

"Right. Well. Brains? You sure?"

Brains smiled at him, and the frightened, teary look was gone. In its place was an appreciative gaze toward Paul and a reassuring one toward Silas. They'd deal with the rest in the morning.

They all said good night, and Silas went back to the living room to find Jessica making the bed on the pullout couch.

"Hey," she said. "Lester is going to go to a hotel and park the bus there. Logan followed him in the RV. Theo went home with Mischa and her family. This is a safe enough area. I think the stuff will be okay."

Silas waved at her. "I'm not worried about it. The gear made it into the trailer fine with Logan in charge, right?"

"I already talked to him. Everything is taken care of."

Silas went to her for a hug, and she collapsed against him.

"I'm so exhausted I can't even think straight."

"Then don't think," he said, chuckling. "Sleep. We'll figure this shit out tomorrow. Brains is adamant we stay on the tour."

She stood back to look him in the eye. "You sure?"

Silas nodded. "We'll have to find someone. I'm already thinking."

She sighed. "All right. Get some sleep. It's you and me, kid."

"Hey, what about me?" Los called out as he exited the bathroom. "I have ideas too, you know."

They both laughed. "Right. We'll let you sit at the grown-ups' table tomorrow." Silas ducked a punch from him, and then they hugged.

"You sure you're good on the couch?" he asked.

"Yeah. I ain't bunking with the brothers, and I don't think you'll let me snuggle with you and your guy, so it's the couch for me."

"Los, I said you could have the pullout."

Both men turned to Jessica. "No."

"Absolutely not," Silas added.

He said his good-nights and had nothing else to do but return to watch Krish sleep.

Chapter Sixteen

Krish woke up as gray light filtered into the unfamiliar bedroom. His head hurt, more from the staples than from getting hit, but that didn't bother him as much as seeing Silas curled up in an easy chair in the corner. He looked awfully uncomfortable. Krish stood from the bed and approached him to shake his shoulder.

"Hmmm."

"Silas. Take the bed. Come on."

"No, I'm fine. Go back to sleep."

Krish stood up and cursed. He used the adjoining bathroom and returned to Silas's chair.

"I'm not going back to sleep unless you get in that bed."

Silas grumbled and stood up, keeping the blanket wrapped around his shoulders, and flopped facedown on the bed. "Get in here," he said.

"Silas."

"Krish, I'm too fucking tired to argue with you. Just get in the bed, dammit."

"Fine, dammit."

Silas chuckled and rolled over toward the wall. Krish took a chance and ran his hands up Silas's back, hoping to work the kinks out with his thumbs along Silas's spine.

"Fuuuuuck, that feels good."

Krish smiled to himself and continued working on Silas's knotted shoulders. He'd taken some classes with his mother when she decided to go back to work as a massage therapist, and he really enjoyed the peace he could provide others with his hands. He wanted to do that with his writing as well.

He massaged Silas's back, neck, and shoulders until he couldn't keep his eyes open anymore and drifted off. When he woke next, Silas was lying on his back with his hand resting on his chest. He was staring up at the ceiling, his brow creased in concentration, tapping his thumb along to some rhythm only he could hear. The motion made his bracelets jingle enough to have awakened Krish.

"Good morning? Or is it afternoon?" Krish asked.

Silas turned his head and smiled. "It's around nine, I think. I don't hear much movement out there, though." He turned on his side. "You get any sleep?"

Krish yawned, covering his mouth. "Yeah. Some. Until I'd roll over and bump my staples. I usually sleep on that side, so it's going to take getting used to."

Silas winced. "Yeah, it looks kind of angry." He moved some of Krish's hair away from the wound and shook his head. "Damn."

"It's not going to be fun, but I'll live. How's Brains?"

Silas sighed. "He was better before bed last night, but I don't know. He doesn't do well when all he can do is sit. He's a health freak—he exercises every day, meditates and shit. Guess he'll do a whole lot of meditating now."

"I'm so sorry, Silas. For everything."

"I know." Silas smiled, brushing more hair out of Krish's face. "I'm sorry too. I could have handled it better."

"No, I should have told you. It was stupid. If I were you, I'd never speak to me again. But for selfish reasons, I can't help but hope you can forgive me, even if I don't deserve it."

Silas was quiet for several beats, long enough to make Krish squirm.

"I forgave you yesterday, after I left. I talked to a friend, and he reminded me that people have reasons why they fuck up. Not excuses. I don't hear you making excuses, but I'd like to know your reasons, for real. The shit I make up in my head about it is probably worse than your reasons."

"Totally fair. My reasons are simple. I don't tell anyone. Jake knows because we were roommates for a while. And my parents know. And my brother knew. That's it."

"But Krish, your writing is so important. It's bigger than you. You've touched so many people. Don't you know that?" Silas leaned forward and kissed Krish on the forehead. "You touched me with your words before *you* ever touched me."

Krish didn't know how to respond, so he tried to focus on breathing and waited for Silas to continue.

"Were you afraid I'd influence your writing? Or have something to say about it?"

"Maybe. I worried you'd be angry over things I've written."

"How could I be? You've written such beautiful reviews of our albums and shows."

Krish smiled, and his cheeks warmed from the praise. "I've always been able to keep my feelings about the person separate from the music… except with you. I can't do that with you. I've wanted to know you for so long, but it was never going to happen, which is why I let myself write the things I did, hoping somehow you'd read them and know how much you meant to me. As more than a musician. As a man."

"Krish—"

"But I also didn't want to seem creepy. I swear I wasn't stalking you or anything."

"I almost wish you would have been. Then maybe we would have met sooner. I certainly tried to find you."

Krish balked in surprise. "You tried to find me?"

Silas rolled his eyes. "I did. It's kind of embarrassing."

"What do you mean, embarrassing? What did you do?"

Silas pressed his lips together and blushed. "I figured out early on that you didn't answer emails. Then I tried to make a fake email account so you wouldn't know it was me, but that didn't work either. I searched all the socials, DM'd you on Twitter. Nothing. At one point, I was so desperate to find you, I almost hired a private investigator. Then I met a guy who claimed to be a hacker, and he said he could find you. But that would have involved some illegal shit, and I had to draw the line there. So I don't want to hear you were worried about creepy, because I went all kinds of creepy trying to find you."

Krish burst out laughing and rolled over to bury his face in Silas's shoulder. "You couldn't have DM'd me on Twitter. I have them turned off."

"Shit. Then who was I messaging?"

"Beats the hell out of me," Krish said. Then he paused. "Wait. Did you send dick pics?"

Silas pushed him away playfully. "No. God, I'm not that desperate."

Krish sighed dramatically. "It's too bad. I might have answered if you had, especially now that I've seen it."

That led to play fighting, which led to Krish's head getting bumped and both of them wincing in pain. "Oh, shit. I'm sorry, babe."

"It's okay," Krish said, taking advantage of their closeness to press a gentle kiss to Silas's lips, to see if he'd respond.

Silas immediately melted against him and stuck his tongue in Krish's mouth, once again refusing to be thwarted by morning breath. They embraced and rolled each other over, taking turns being on top, kissing like they hadn't kissed in millennia.

"I'm really sorry, Silas. Can we try this again? Can we start over?"

Silas shook his head, brushing his nose against Krish's. "No way. I don't want to start over. I want to pick up where we left off. If we weren't in some stranger's bed, I'd fuck you right now," Silas growled against Krish's neck. "We've got to find a hotel soon. I need to—"

"Wait, Silas. I'm supposed to go to San Francisco. I—"

"What do you mean? Are you leaving?"

"I don't know. I don't want to. But yesterday I got a call from *Alt-Scene* magazine. They want to meet with me."

Silas sat up. "You're going to work for a magazine? Why? The blog is fantastic."

Krish sat up to face him. "I double majored in music and journalism. I want to be a music journalist. I want to write about things that matter, and *Alt-Scene* is growing their social justice section. I want to be a part of it."

Silas frowned. "That sounds… but a reporter? I don't know, man. I think your blog is awesome. I'd hate to see you change because you're a member of the press, you know? Is this what you want?"

"It is. I think. I want the experience of writing for a magazine—in my style, in my voice. I've been holding out hope, waiting to see if they would offer me a permanent position and not only guest posts on their blog. I have to meet with the managing editor to work out the details."

Silas's expression was hard to read. "When is your meeting?"

"Tomorrow at ten. But I can call them. I don't want to leave you with everything up in the air."

Silas rubbed at his head, sat back, and rested his forearms on his knees. "Yeah. Things are definitely in flux. Brains wants us to find someone to replace him, not pull off the tour. It makes the most sense businesswise, but it feels weird."

Krish took his hand and squeezed. "That's got to be a lot. So many changes. You just got Jordan."

Silas perked up. "See? You get me, Krish. You're absolutely right. We were just getting into the groove with Jordan, and now someone else? At least the sets are shorter, though, so it would be fewer songs for someone new to get good with. God, I can't even believe I'm talking about this. It feels like a betrayal."

"I can understand that, but at the same time, there's a lot more at stake if you *don't* continue with the tour, right?"

Silas nodded and put his head down on his arms. "Yeah. A lot of people will be impacted." Then he lifted his head, and that wary expression was back.

"Does this mean I have to start watching what I say around you? And the band—"

"No, Silas. I won't do that. I'd already decided I won't write about the band anymore. It's not right. You can trust me. I know that's kind of presumptuous on my part after what happened, but it's true."

The door burst open, and they both turned their heads.

"Oh. Shit. You're… um…. Hey, are you busy?"

Okay? Los really was awkward. Either that or he was simply used to them all being out in the open.

"What's up?" Silas said, patting the bed next to him.

Krish pulled his legs in and scooted back to the wall to make room for Los, who sprawled on the bed between them.

"Nothing. I heard talking in here. Jessica's on the phone. Paul left to go get food, and I was all by myself."

Silas petted Los's long, dyed-black hair, and Los put his head down on the pillows and closed his eyes.

"Did you sleep?" Silas asked him.

"Sort of. The couch was okay, but you know I can't sleep well at other people's houses."

"True." Silas kept stroking Los's hair, and Los sighed happily, burrowing his head into the pillows. Within seconds he was snoring.

Krish laughed softly. "Does he always crash this fast?"

Silas leaned down and kissed Los's forehead. "Yeah, if he's tired. He probably lay there all night last night staring at the ceiling. When we moved into our flophouse in Oakland, he slept with me for the first couple of months because he was freaked out."

"Something scare him when he was a kid?"

Silas sighed and nodded. "Yeah. Lots of things. He actually really likes it when we're on tour and he can sleep in his bunk with all of us together. He'd be happiest if we had a room-sized bed and all slept together. But yeah, puts a cramp in the sex life."

"He's straight, yeah?"

"Totally. But I fuck with him all the time, and he takes it well."

"Yeah, like when you kiss him onstage."

Silas nodded and then looked down at Los and flicked his tongue at him. Krish snorted, and Los stirred.

Silas held a finger up to his lips and shushed Krish. Then he gestured for him to move forward so he could kiss him as they leaned over Los's body.

"You're crazy," Krish whispered as he kissed Silas long and deep. He wished they were alone, but he also thought it was damn cute that Los was curled up with them.

Silas pulled back and sighed. "Hey. Let me figure out what's what, and then maybe I can come with you to San Francisco, if Brains is settled. Jessica will be here, and his security blanket." Silas rolled his eyes.

"His what? What do you mean?"

"Paul. He has, like, fixated on him or something. I can't explain it, but Paul doesn't seem to mind at all. I think it's cute. I'm not sure of Paul's status, though, and I don't want to see Brains disappointed."

"Right. Well, it worked out great that they met, though. Seemed like it was kind of meant to happen, huh?"

Silas grinned. "Yeah. There's a lot of that going on."

Los mumbled something about them doing something quieter with their mouths so he could sleep, and they took that as their cue to exit.

"Let me see if Paul's got some clothes for you. With yours left behind, we're gonna need to go shopping," Silas said as he walked Krish into the bathroom. "And I'll get my clippers out of—shit. They're on the bus. Let me see if Paul's got some, and we can cut your hair and then get you showered. You trust me to give you a new do?"

Krish laughed. "I don't really have a choice, do I? It looks pretty ridiculous. I guess I could wear a hat to my interview?"

Silas turned him to face the mirror and stood behind him. "That could be hot. But we could also give you a rad-ass-motherfucking mohawk. What do you think?"

Krish couldn't help but laugh at Silas's enthusiasm and feel grateful they were "picking up where they left off," as Silas called it. Yeah. It felt right. They'd fallen into something really comfortable that Krish could let himself ease into. If only they didn't have a time limit or lingering issues of trust. God, why did this have to happen now? If he'd met Silas earlier, before he finished school and decided on this track? Krish had never foreseen his passion for music and writing would intersect with his personal life like this. Everyone has a fantasy of meeting their celebrity crushes, but no one prepares for the possibility of a reality with them. And that's what Silas was talking about—a reality where they were together.

They'd known each other less than forty-eight hours, but in that time, they'd certainly checked off many of the items on the compatibility list. The one that remained unchecked was that Krish was on a career trajectory that could interfere with Silas's, and Krish remained unsettled about that fact. He *wanted* Silas. And he *wanted* his words to reach those who needed to hear them. How could he do both and not hurt Silas or Hush?

They went to check on Brains and found him sitting in the kitchen at the table with his leg carefully propped up on pillows watching Paul cook breakfast. Well, he was watching Paul, period. Paul wore low-slung sweats and a tight tank top that revealed a whole lot of muscle and some very cool nautical tattoos.

A younger guy, who Krish assumed was his son, Bowie, sat at the table quietly drinking a cup of coffee, looking wide-eyed between the two. Paul introduced them all, and they shook hands.

Silas draped his arms around Brains's neck from behind and hugged him. "How you feelin'?"

Brains shrugged. "Hurts, but I'll survive." He looked at Krish and winced. "What the hell happened to you, dude?"

"The tent pole caught me in the head on the way down. Someone must have fallen on it, though, for it to have cut this deep." Krish and Silas took seats kitty-corner from each other, with Silas closest to Brains.

"Yeah, the scalp is pretty easy to slice through," Paul said, flipping bacon in the pan. It smelled so good, Krish's stomach growled. How long had it been since they'd actually eaten anything?

"Remember when you got cut on top of your head, Bowie? Your aunt bought you guys that stupid trampoline, and you caught the corner of one of the springs pretty serious."

Bowie blushed and rubbed absently at the top of his head. "Yeah, but it was fun."

They all laughed, even Brains, who drank from some sort of smoothie that looked and smelled nasty but was probably healthy.

Jessica walked in and sat down at the last empty chair. "The Warped people want to know what's happening. They've given me today."

Brains cleared his throat. "You're going to tell them you guys will be in Phoenix by Wednesday night. That's what you're going to do."

"Brains," Silas said, but Brains held up a hand.

"We've come too far to fuck this up right now. We can't afford to back out."

Krish knew Brains was right, but Brains's hands shook as he took another drink of his smoothie.

"Who are we going to get?" Silas asked, taking a plate from Paul and thanking him. Paul handed one to Krish, and he wanted to worship at the man's feet. Scrambled eggs, bacon, pancakes. Perfect.

Jessica sighed. "I've already called everyone I know. How about someone already on tour? Someone could do double duty, couldn't they?"

Brains snorted. "No one I'd want touching my fucking drums. Besides, who's going to learn all the songs in a couple of days? No, we need someone closer. What about Theo?"

"Drum-tech Theo? We could ask, but I don't know. He's not fast enough," Silas grumbled.

"No one's fast enough for your speed metal version of the set," Los said, joining them by sitting on Jessica's lap. "You gonna pull that shit again?"

"Really?" She shook her head. He leaned down and kissed her hair and they both graciously accepted plates from Paul.

"Yeah, sorry about that," Silas said, ducking his head to eat some scrambled eggs. He winked at Krish, and they all started laughing.

"I guess let's get him over here so we can try him out. Anyone else we can get? Paul? Is there room, like, in your garage or something, for us to set up Brains's kit?" Los asked.

"How about the kit in his room?" Silas said, pointing his thumb at Bowie, who was sitting on a bar stool at the counter. "How long you been playing?"

Bowie's eyes went wide, and he kind of looked around like maybe Silas was talking to someone else. "Um, a while."

"About ten years," Paul said. "Give or take. He started guitar first, but he picked up drums soon after."

Brains looked him over, and Bowie immediately got very interested in his food. He ate a couple more bites, and then carried his plate to the sink. He whispered something to his dad, who patted him on the back of the neck. Bowie gave them a small smile and hurried out of the kitchen.

"Paul?" Brains asked as soon as Bowie was out of earshot. "Can he play?"

Paul leaned his hips against the counter and crossed his arms over his chest. "Yeah, but that's not the issue."

Krish and Silas watched as Brains and Paul seemed to have a silent conversation that ended in Paul politely excusing himself from the kitchen, but obviously disturbed by something.

"You sure you guys just met yesterday?" Silas asked Brains.

Brains continued to stare in the direction of where Paul had stood moments before.

"I can't explain it," he said in a soft voice. "You'd make fun of me if I tried."

Silas gave Krish a look that he felt all the way through his chest to his heart. It took his breath away.

"Like you've found someone who gets you?" Silas asked. "Who understands your fears and needs and isn't deterred when you freak out? Yeah. I kinda understand." Silas reached over and took Krish's hand on top of the table.

Krish's face hurt from smiling so much.

Brains looked between them and shook his head. "Anyway, it's all crazy right now, but I'm not anxious or worried, really. Not like I should be. I feel like everything's going to be all right."

"I think you're right," Silas answered.

PAUL HAD clothes that were a little big but the right height. He also had a nice set of clippers, so an hour later, Krish found himself on Paul's back patio with a towel around his shoulders, completely at Silas's mercy.

"So, are we going with the rad-ass-motherfucking-mohawk? Or the full buzz?"

Krish sighed. "Shit. My mom's going to flip out. She hates it when I cut my hair too short. I think sometimes I'm the daughter she never had. She let it grow so long when I was a kid. It was always a mess."

"Well, why don't you let the master work, and we'll see what you like."

Silas flicked on the clippers, and Krish shivered when Silas touched his bare shoulder under the towel.

"A shower is going to feel so good when you're done."

"I bet. You ready? 'Cause here we go." Silas started singing under his breath, some unrecognizable tune. Krish closed his eyes as Silas made the first pass with the clippers, the buzzing against his skin only mildly uncomfortable.

"It is kind of a shame. Your hair is so gorgeous. But you'll love being shaved. It's very freeing."

Krish laughed. "We'll see. My brother thought so."

Shit. He hadn't meant to bring up Vivaan. He'd been gone for three years, and Krish still missed him every day, but it didn't hurt as bad to talk about him. It wasn't like he talked with anyone other than his mother or Jake on a regular basis about anything of consequence, but for some reason he'd brought it up. That must mean something about Silas.

"Your brother who passed away?" Silas asked gently.

"Yeah. Vivaan. He was a Marine. His unit was hit by an IED in Afghanistan." His breath came out in a rush, as though getting past those memories had actually required physical exertion. The words continued to come out, and Silas proved to be a good listener.

"He was eight years older than me. He didn't make it home. Our parents had been so proud of their American soldier son, and the Marines had been happy to have a soldier who spoke Hindi and some Urdu, since he spent summers in Northern India with my mother before I was born. He also picked up some Pashto in Afghanistan. Vivaan was a whiz with languages. Unfortunately, that didn't save his life. I'm still bitter about his sacrifice."

"Wow. I'm so sorry," Silas said quietly as he placed his hand gently on the top of Krish's head, pushed it forward, and brought the clippers to the back of his neck. He'd told Krish he'd use the #3 first and they'd see how it looked before they went shorter.

Krish watched his hair fall around him, and it mirrored his feelings. Some of the weight he'd been carrying fell along with it.

"He was the one who introduced me to music at a very early age. He knew a lot of musicians, hung out with them when he was in high school and college. He enlisted as an officer."

"That's huge," Silas said. "He took you to shows?"

"Yeah. And I would write in my journal about them afterward. Vivaan asked if he could read what I'd written and I showed him. He told me I needed to keep writing, that I had a gift."

"He was right. I kept a copy of your post about your guitar for a long time in my wallet. I'd take it out and read it whenever I felt like I couldn't deal with Gavin's death. You have no idea how much it meant to me."

Silas squeezed Krish's shoulder, and Krish reached up to take his hand. A sob wracked Krish's body, and he couldn't speak for a moment. Silas stopped shaving and held his hand.

"I'm glad we were there for each other," he finally said.

"How do you mean?" Silas asked, stepping around to look at him.

"Your music got me through so many nights. I killed two iPods in that first year with how much I listened to music. Then Gavin died, and I hurt so much for you."

Silas went back to work on Krish's head. "It was awful, for sure, but thankfully Los, Brains, and I had each other. I still had my brothers. I'm sorry you were alone dealing with it."

Krish shrugged and wiped at his eyes. "My mom was great. My dad spent a lot of time at work. It was really hard for him. They struggled as a couple, and I feared their marriage might not make it, but when I started to get myself together, she finally started to grieve, and the two of them went to counseling together. They're happier now, I think. He'll retire in a few years, and they're already making plans to travel. He wants to go run with the bulls in Pamplona or something crazy like that."

Silas barked out a laugh. "That *is* crazy, dude."

"I know. My mom will put her foot down, I'm sure, and he'll go along with her because that's what we do."

Silas finished his first run and brushed hair away from Krish's face. "She sounds awesome. I'd love to meet her."

Krish was quiet. Meeting the parents. Krish had only brought one boyfriend home. His father hadn't accepted his coming out at first. It wasn't until he lost his eldest son and realized what was really important in life that their relationship improved. His mom had been his biggest supporter, but she was protective, and she found his boyfriend lacking. Jonathan was premed and was quite vocal about his opinions, which were super conservative, and Krish's mother had a lot to say about it.

Jonathan broke up with him shortly after Vivaan died. He said school was too intense for him to be with anyone, but Krish knew better. Jonathan couldn't handle helping others grieve, which didn't bode well for him as a doctor. It was just as well. Krish wasn't in any position to be in a relationship at that point. But now? With Silas? He was different. Was this where they talked about what happened when real life started back up again?

"Here," Silas said when Krish didn't answer. "Take a look and see what you think." Silas stood in front of him and held up a mirror. Krish's eyes nearly popped out.

"Oh lord, it looks ridiculous. Doesn't it?"

Silas chewed on his lip. "No matter what, the staples are going to be there. Your hair will fill in… eventually."

Krish kicked at Silas's foot, and he laughed. "What? I think you're hot however your hair looks. Although with it gone, your features are so…. Damn. You are so gorgeous."

Krish shook his head. "You sure *you* didn't hit your head?"

Silas smacked his shoulder. "Shut up. So what are we doing? You want another opinion?"

"Take it all off. Why not? I'll get to see what it's like when I'm an old man."

Silas snorted. "All righty. The full buzz, coming up."

Silas started up the clippers, and Krish worked up the nerve to address the elephant in the room. "Hey Silas?"

"Yeah, babe?"

I love hearing that. "Um, so you guys will be going to Phoenix, then."

"Uh-huh. Somehow. Even if I have to play bass and drums at the same time, apparently."

Krish chuckled and then chickened out. He'd wanted to ask what would happen when he got back to the tour, but what was the use? Silas would probably reassure him, but starting a relationship while on tour would be tricky and would probably remind him that being with Krish was a complication he didn't need in his life. Besides, the others still didn't know his big little secret.

"Whoa. You look hella different, Krish."

Jordan and Jake had finally awakened and now stood in the doorway staring at him.

"Yeah, well, the uneven thing wasn't really working for me," Krish said, wishing they'd quit staring. It was going to be weird enough as it was. He was going to be in the spotlight… with a shaved head and staples. *Yay.*

"Hey, Silas? We know anything yet?"

"Only that we're trying to find someone to fill in until Brains can join us. He doesn't want us to leave the tour. And then there's the fact we lost our merch girl." Silas switched off the clippers and brushed more hair away. "Okay, you're done. How about we get you in the shower? You can't get your staples wet, but I think I can at least get your head clean. Here, let me look."

Krish stood up and shook the hair off. He turned to face Silas, expecting the worst and hoping for the best.

Silas beamed at him. "Even more gorgeous. Damn. Uh, we'll be back."

Jordan and Jake laughed. "Hey, Krish?" Jake looked uneasy. "I'm taking off this afternoon. Paul said I can take the rapid transit thingie to the airport. I booked a flight out at six."

Krish's heart felt heavy. Soon he'd have to say goodbye and leave for San Francisco. He didn't know if leaving would end things, end the magic. He didn't want his time with Silas to be over, but truthfully, what were they going to do? They were just getting started, and now that his identity was out of the closet, a whole new set of issues would arise.

"Okay. I'll give you a hug when I'm not covered in hair."

He forced a laugh, but his insides were in turmoil. What the hell was supposed to happen next?

Chapter Seventeen

SILAS HELPED Krish clean off the top of his head with a wet rag and then left him to take a shower alone when it seemed he wasn't totally comfortable with Silas being there for the whole show. *Pity.* But they had time. Silas had all kinds of plans where Krish was concerned.

He found Brains, Paul, Bowie, Los, Jordan, Jake, and Jessica in the living room in what looked like a serious conversation.

"Paul, he can play the songs. Like, well. Like, better than me. He's super clean."

"Billy, that's not the issue, I told you."

"Dad, I'll be okay."

Silas plopped down next to Jessica, who looked about as comfortable as someone sitting in on a lover's dispute between a couple they'd just met.

Because whatever this weirdness was between Brains and Paul, it was starting to feel a little like that.

"What's going on?"

Brains turned his upper body toward him, wincing a little. "The kid is phenomenal. He's taught himself all of our songs—"

"But he's never played in front of anyone except for school—"

"But, Dad—"

"Whoa. Okay, hold on. Bowie? You can play our songs?"

"Yeah," he said, ducking his head and looking up at his dad from under long lashes. "But I don't know how I'll do in a crowd." He swallowed hard and looked at Silas for the first time in the eye. "I have anxiety. Sometimes I can't function."

Silas sat back and slung his arm around the back of the couch behind Jessica. "That makes you no different than anyone in this band, frankly. I've got anger management issues, Los can't sleep by himself, Brains has OCD…. Jordan? Other than being a sloppy drunk and a pain in the ass to your brother, you're probably the most normal of us, but I haven't known you as long as these guys."

"I wet the bed."

All eyes shot toward Jordan, including his brother.

"What? I'm trying to fit in. Geez."

Nervous laughter broke out, and it seemed to ease the tension a bit.

"Bowie, this means being on a bus for nearly two months. And what about your job? And classes?" Paul seemed more concerned about Bowie's anxiety than the other issues. Perhaps it was a bigger deal than they thought?

"I'll call my supervisor today and see if they can give me leave. I haven't missed a day in two years. My boss is cool. If not, I can find something else when I get back. And class is over. I don't start back until September."

"And the tour will be over by then," Brains said. "And as soon as I'm better, I'll join up with them and watch out for him. Until then, Mom will watch out for him—"

"I swear to God, Brains. I don't care if you're broken, if you call me Mom one more time—"

"We'll all be there for him," Silas said. "But maybe we should play together first? See if he feels comfortable?"

And that's how they all ended up squeezed in Bowie's room when Krish came out of the bathroom. His eyes went wide and he quickly moved out of the way as Jordan, Silas, Los, and Bowie took orders from Brains, who sat in the easy chair in the corner with his leg resting on a chair from the kitchen.

Bowie had two guitars, a Gibson Les Paul and an old Ibanez. Paul reluctantly brought an Epiphone bass from his room. Seems like this family really bonded over music, but Paul didn't seem very comfortable with the scenario.

"I'm sorry, I only have the two amps," Bowie said, his cheeks mottled red.

"It's okay," Silas said. "One of those guys can plug in, and I can use the other one. Let's run through the set list. Bowie, if at any time, you have a question, stop us. And don't worry if it's rough. We've got, um, a day or two to get organized, right? No problem."

They all grumbled anxiously, and Bowie took his seat behind the drums as the guys tuned their instruments. Paul stood next to Jessica in the doorway with his arms crossed over his chest. Jake and Krish sat on the bed and whispered to each other.

"You ready?" Silas asked Bowie gently. The kid nodded and got his sticks comfortable in his grip.

"For 'Faceless,' you're going to start us off. You ready? Just the kick drum. One… two… three… four—"

Bowie laid down a flawless rhythm, Jordan came in with his note, Silas started the bass line, and Los kicked in with the opening riff. And it fucking came together.

One by one they ran through the songs in the set, with the exception of the two new tunes. Bowie had to ask questions of Brains a few times as he'd only recently started to learn them. The kid was basically fucking solid. When they finished, they all grinned nervously at each other. Except Paul. He left the room. Brains's gaze followed him out the door.

"Krish? Can you hand me those crutches?"

Krish jumped up to help him get situated, and Brains followed Paul, his movements slow and stiff as though he were in more pain than he let on. Silas watched Brains as they started up one of the new songs. They needed a break, for real, and this kid might be what they needed.

Bowie concentrated so hard, Silas was worried he might burst a blood vessel, but he barely broke a sweat. He was in good shape. He wasn't much older than Silas and Los when they joined up with Brains and started this crazy ride. It was fun watching his enthusiasm. Silas was really impressed with how much the kid had taught himself. He was a natural. He didn't play with as much force as Brains, and perhaps he was a little bit more tentative, but that would go away after some rehearsals.

They finished a couple more songs and decided an hour of playing in the tiny bedroom was enough. It was time for a break. Bowie stood from the drum set and flexed his hands.

"How you feeling?" Silas asked him.

Bowie smiled shyly. "Great. It's definitely different than playing in the jazz band."

The guys all laughed.

"You never jammed with anyone before?"

Bowie shook his head. "I mean, not anyone outside of school, and there we play what we're told and how we're told most of the time, unless we're working on improvisation. I'm in the music program at the community college here, and I play with the jazz band. This is different."

"Absolutely. Hail to the band geeks," Jordan said and high-fived Bowie. "I was in band in school myself."

"You sound fucking great, kid," Los said, fist-bumping him.

"Thanks," Bowie said. "Brains is like my biggest influence. I'm so sorry he's hurt, man."

"Yeah," Silas said. "Us too. But shit happens. We once had to postpone a series of dates because someone who shall remain nameless broke his finger being pushed into the bushes in a shopping cart *Jackass*-style."

Los coughed into his hand. "It's warm in here. Anyone else need some fresh air? Dude, you rock. Let's take a break, shall we?"

Bowie's eyes bugged out, and he pressed his lips together to keep from laughing. But Jordan didn't hold back his laugh.

"And I thought you broke it because an amp fell over while you were practicing. Wasn't that what you told me?" Jordan asked, giving Los a shove out the door.

"I *did* break my finger when an amp fell, fucker. Nearly broke my whole hand."

"Yeah, but we didn't have to miss shows for that one," Silas called to their retreating backs.

"Well, I'm going to say goodbye," Jake said. He hugged Krish and rubbed his head carefully to avoid hitting his staples. "Your mom is going to freak. You know that."

"Yeah, I know. Wish me luck."

"Luck. And kick ass tomorrow."

Jake hugged Silas and Bowie, who was hesitant, but there was no avoiding a Jake hug. He gave a shy smile, and then he left the room to follow the other guys.

"Thanks for letting me come along for the ride," Jake said. "It's been quite an experience."

"Thank you for bringing me Krish," Silas said with a wink.

Jake's eyebrows rose nearly into his hairline. "I mean, I brought him. Didn't know I was necessarily bringing him for *you*, Mr. Lead Singer of

My Brother's Band That I Have to Be Nice to or I'd Say—"

"Yes, thank you, Jake," Krish interjected. "I'll call you tomorrow after the interview."

Jake waved at Krish and then did the whole fingers pointing to his eyes and then to Silas thing that made Silas crack up. *Yeah, go ahead and watch me. Krish is mine, Jake Barrett.*

And then they were alone again. But Krish's smile looked forced.

"Looks like you guys have a plan, then. I should probably go. I need to get to a mall and buy something to wear tomorrow." Then his determination seemed to peter out, and he slumped against the wall.

Oh, this would not do. Silas couldn't have him leaving there sad. He could tell Krish was having a tough time about something. He hadn't missed his comments earlier when Silas was clipping his hair. He'd have to show Krish that they could make it work. It could happen. He'd loved him from afar before....

Well, shit. That's exactly what was happening here. Silas *could* eat his cake and have it too. The Guru came to him, just as he'd hoped, covered in the beautiful frosting that was Krish, and Silas wanted it all—the man and the dessert. Okay, that sounded wrong, but in Silas's mind, Krish was everything sweet and wonderful he'd hoped for over the years when he dreamed about meeting the Guru. The fact that they had such great chemistry, and that Krish was as incredible in person as he was in his words, confirmed for Silas that they were meant to find each other.

Yeah, now he believed in that destiny and fate shit. They'd both paid him a visit, and he intended to make it clear to Krish that this *was* happening. This, whatever they were doing, was real and was going to continue despite the shitstorm that was going to erupt when his brothers found out about Krish. Because Silas wasn't going to give him up. Period.

But he's joining the Dark Side.

The magazine gig. Silas had to admit that could be a problem. The guys in the band were going to flip out. Brains might understand. He was the mature one, but Los? After all the sordid shit that had been printed?

At least *Alt-Scene* had been good to them. Their coverage of Gavin's death was as close to factual as they were going to get with no comment from the band. The magazine loved Silas, he'd been on the cover a bunch, and at one point, he'd even had a guest column for a couple of years… until that Warped Tour. Could he trust that this could work? For now, he would, because he'd be kidding himself if he thought he could walk away.

"I could use some new clothes. And some new makeup. I told Jessica which kind I like, but I guess they were out of it at Sephora before we left. Guess I need to come with you to the mall."

Krish blinked. "Silas. What are you—"

"Yeah, and I haven't been to San Francisco in a long time. I'm due for a new photo shoot with *Alt-Scene*. Maybe Jessica can set that up while I'm there. With you. For your interview."

More blinking. "Silas?"

Silas rolled his eyes and crawled onto the bed. "Babe. This is me inviting myself to go with you to San Francisco. I want to take you shopping and hold your hand while you freak out about your interview." He reached up and cupped Krish's jaw. "I want to spend the night with you," he whispered as he leaned in for a tender kiss. Then he pulled back a smidge. "Unless I'm overstepping my bounds." He darted his tongue out and licked, making sure to connect his piercing with Krish's lips. He wasn't above manipulation, and he knew how much his piercings got Krish's engine revving. "What do you say?"

Krish sighed. "Thank you."

Silas leaned back, beaming. "Then it's settled. Let's see if Paul can get us—"

"Wait, Silas. Are you sure you can really go? What about the band?"

He sat back on his heels. "I know. If I didn't think Brains was in the best hands, I wouldn't dream of leaving. But honestly, I've been watching those two. If I told him I was staying behind while you left, he'd tell me to get the fuck out. He knows how important you are to me. They all do."

Krish frowned. "Silas, are we postponing the inevitable? What are they going to say when they find out about me?" He looked down at the bed and sighed.

"We'll deal with it. Why? What are you saying?"

Krish pulled his knees up and wrapped his arms around them, still not looking at Silas. "The guys aren't going to be so supportive when they find out who I am, what I'm planning to do. What are you going to say to them?"

"We'll tell them together. You've already told me you won't write about the band. We'll tell them, and they'll have to deal with it. Besides, are you willing to give this up, this whatever it is between us? Come on, Krish. You know it doesn't have to be like that. You know you want to see this through, just like I do. People aren't given a chance like this very often. Don't make me get all cheesy and shit here."

Krish laughed. "Sometimes cheesy is okay." A small grin from Krish was all it took for Silas to know that he was winning the argument, their first since picking up where they left off.

"Cheese belongs on pizza, in Mexican food, and in a sandwich. It does not belong in this bed, Krishnan Guru—how do you say the rest?"

"Guruvayoor. And I'm sorry, Silas. I'm not trying to be all dramatic or anything. I feel like we're only just getting to know each other, and there's so much going on. I don't want to cause problems—"

"I know. I know. We'll tell the guys. It might suck… a lot. But you're important to me, and I want you in my life."

"But what about after Warped? I know a lot can happen between now and then, but are you really going to want—"

Silas held up a hand. He'd already anticipated that argument. "Look, I can't change this about me. I tour. We have to tour, but it's not forever. In fact we have a very small window of opportunity to make it and we're taking advantage of the favorable winds. Knowing you're on the other side of the journey makes it all the better." He leaned forward and pressed their foreheads together. "Please give us a chance," Silas whispered. "I promise. If I haven't convinced you after a night in San Francisco—"

"You've convinced me, Silas. I want this too. But I'm unsure. My whole life was thrown into chaos the minute I left my house... when was it? I don't even remember. Friday. In two days, I met the guy I've been dreaming of for years, I was offered a potential job with my dream magazine, and I'm kind of freaking out, to be honest. It's a lot to take at once. But I don't want you to think for a second that being with you, making a go of this, isn't at the top of my priority list."

That was all the encouragement Silas needed. "Great. Then let's start living the dream."

Chapter Eighteen

KRISH FELT like he might vomit the second he spoke. Silas seemed so confident that everything was going to be okay, but Krish remembered being cornered by Los and Brains and how angry they were when they spoke to him.

"I really hope you aren't fucking around with Silas. He's one of my best friends, and he doesn't deserve that shit. You understand what I'm saying?"

How were they going to handle this?

Brains was reclining on the couch with his leg elevated on pillows. Paul sat on the floor next to the couch. He had an iPad in his hands, and whatever he was looking at had him frowning severely. Brains was leaning over his shoulder, pointing something out to him. Bowie sat in an armchair watching them with an identical frown to his dad's. Jessica sat by Brains's feet, looking like she needed a week's sleep.

And Los was slumped on the love seat next to Jordan, who watched the goings-on around him with interest. All of them looked up when Krish and Silas came down the stairs together.

"Oh good. You're all here. Krish and I have something to talk to you about."

Los raised an eyebrow. "You're pregnant. When's the baby due?"

"Right," Silas said, rolling his eyes.

"Silas is going to join the circus?" Los asked.

"Uh, you guys are running off to elope?" Jordan asked.

Krish barked out a laugh, and Silas turned to look at him. "Not a bad idea," he whispered.

Krish pushed him away and then rubbed his hands on his borrowed sweats.

"This isn't a guessing game, but—"

"Krish is the Guru," Brains called out.

After the chuckles of disbelief, the room fell silent.

All eyes fell on Krish, and he had the strongest urge to flee… until Silas took his hand and squeezed. Silas would take the majority of shit for this, so Krish could be brave enough to tell them.

"It's true. I'm, um… him."

The silence persisted for a few short beats, and then the room erupted.

"I can't believe my fucking brother didn't tell me after all this time."

"I fucking *knew* it." Brains slapped his good leg and laughed out loud. "I knew you guys were going to meet. I fucking told you, Silas." He gestured from the couch for Silas to come give him a hug.

"Yeah, and you were right about that fate shit." Silas squeezed him tightly, and Krish was incrementally relieved. But Los hadn't said anything.

He just stared. And then he got up and left the room.

"Shit." They all watched Los walk out the back door and onto the patio. Silas turned to Krish with a conflicted expression.

"Go." Krish knew the guilt would eat at Silas if he didn't clear things up with his friend. He knew because the guilt had already eaten through *his* insides. This was all his fault, every bit of it. If only he'd told Silas from the beginning, been honest with them…. As the rest of the group sat staring at him, he hoped he had a good enough explanation. If that even existed.

All eyes turned on him expectantly. Brains narrowed his eyes and crossed his arms over his chest.

"I never meant for this to happen." Krish's chin quivered as he spoke. "I'm so sorry. Please know, from the moment it became clear to me that Silas and I—"

His gaze settled on Brains, who was shaking his head, his anger seeming to fade. "It doesn't matter, Krish. Silas is into you, always has been. When you two met, it wouldn't have mattered. You were going to end up together, so why didn't you tell him? It's not like you could keep that secret forever."

"I know. I never thought…. This is not an excuse, I know, but I literally finished college two days before I came on the road. I got the offer to come on tour two days before that. I skipped my graduation to come here. I had been in contact with *Alt-Scene* and—"

"Hold up." Brains narrowed his eyes at Krish once more. "You're here with the magazine? Were you after a story or what? That's hella fucked-up. You knew—"

"That's right. I do know what you guys have been through, and I would never, *ever* write about anything to hurt you. In fact, the minute he—well, you know—the minute we—"

"He stuck his tongue in your mouth, okay, I get it. What?"

"Brains." Jessica put a hand on his arm and shook her head. "Don't."

"I'm fine," he said. "I just want to know what the hell—"

"I'm not writing about Hush anymore. Period. It's a conflict of interest. I hadn't anticipated this kind of a situation, you know? I planned on touring with the show this summer, writing my blog posts, and then writing about my experience for the magazine at the end. *Alt-Scene* set it up with the understanding that if they liked what I wrote about the tour, they'd offer me a full-time position with them. I thought that was what I wanted. It's what I've been working for."

"And then you fell for Silas," Jordan said. "I get it. No, Brains—"

Brains started to get up but Jordan, who had moved behind the couch where Brains was sitting, put his hands on his shoulders. Brains crossed his arms over his chest, and his frown lines deepened.

"Just listen," Jordan said. "I showed up to an audition a year ago, not having any clue who it was for, and when I saw you guys, I almost walked out. I didn't think I could handle Gavin's shadow and the weight of grief you guys were all carrying around, but then Silas took me aside and told me…. He said he thought Gavin had sent me to you."

There were a few audible gasps. Jessica teared up. Brains's nostrils flared, and his chin quivered. Paul, who was sitting on the floor next to Brains, turned and squeezed his forearm for support. Brains took his hand and wiped at his eyes with his other one.

"Yeah, that's what I thought. He never told any of you. He had this whole idea that Gavin was looking out for us, and he got that idea after reading a blog post by the Guru. He had the fucking thing folded up in his wallet. Did you know that?"

All eyes in the room shot to Krish, and he actually stumbled back a step as though an actual force had hit him. Silas had told him about keeping it, but it hadn't hit Krish how much his words had affected the man he'd admired from afar and was now falling for up close.

"If Silas thought so much of him all this time, if he trusts him and can get past it, I think we should too. Besides, my brother wouldn't be best friends with some evil fuck who was out to ruin the band. The fact that he and Jake have been friends for years gives me faith in him. I trust him." Jordan looked around, and his cheeks reddened a bit. "Not like I get a vote or anything. I just, I get it. You all had me sign that letter saying I wouldn't tell anyone I was with the band until the album was finished—"

"Yeah, in case you sucked," Los said as he and Silas wandered back in. Silas walked straight into the kitchen instead of joining them in the living room, and Krish's concern grew. Los was rubbing his knuckles. Had they gone out there—

"Thanks a lot, asshole. No, but I worried about what the hell would happen when everyone would find out. My whole life was going to change, and I didn't know how to handle that. I never said anything, but I almost backed out, right before we finished recording on that last day. Remember? I was late, and you gave me shit about partying too hard the night before?"

"I remember that," Brains said. "You were going to leave?"

"Thought about it. It was a fuck-ton of pressure, dude. Hell yeah, I almost left. But then I remembered that, duh, this is what I wanted my whole life—to join a fucking awesome band and conquer the world." Jordan gestured with both hands. "Imagine what this guy is going to deal with when everyone finds out. How long have you been writing your blog, Krish?"

"Almost six years," he said in a low voice. He appreciated Jordan standing up for him, but at this point he was so raw, he wished he could disappear.

"Six fucking years this guy has been writing about music, and he's got, like, millions of followers. How do you think that's going to go over? Not to mention the fact that some people may not be too happy with him after some of his reviews. No offense," he said, turning to Krish again. "Just... give him a fucking break. Like you did with me. Don't assume he's out to fucking hurt the band, or Silas, for that matter. You know what happens when you assume things."

Brains snorted, and his lips curled up in a reluctant smile. "You're an ass."

Jordan had gotten pretty worked up by this point, but now he unleashed that Barrett smile at full wattage. "*You're* an ass, Brains. So what do you fucking say?"

Brains looked over to Los, who was leaning against the wall, looking at the ground. "I say I'll trust him until he gives me reason *not* to trust him. What about you, Los? Can you live with this?"

Los shrugged and kept rubbing at his hand, but he didn't speak.

Krish's resolve was at its last few bars of health. He didn't think he could take much more drama. And then Silas came in with a bag of ice on his face.

"What the fuck, Silas?" Jessica shot up off the couch and ran over to him.

"I'm fine," he said, but from the redness in the one eye he could see, Krish could tell he'd been crying.

"Los? What did you do?"

Los glanced up at Silas and then looked down. "I'm sorry," he muttered. His hair hung over his face, hiding his expression.

"Let me see—holy shit! Los!" Jessica turned on him in disbelief. "*You hit him?*"

Jordan and Paul stood up to investigate. Paul's movement knocked Brains's crutches over, and he scrambled for them but Bowie, who had been silent the whole time, picked them up and held them in one hand while he helped Brains up with his other.

Krish tried to get to Silas, but Bowie and Brains blocked him on one side of the couch, and Los stood on the other looking like a lost puppy. Los turned toward the stairs, but Krish stepped in front of him.

"Los, I'm sorry, but if you're going to hit someone, you should hit me. I'm the one who caused this mess."

"No," Silas said, fighting to get away from everyone. "You didn't cause anything that wasn't going to resurface at some point anyway."

"My God, Silas, your eye!"

Silas had pulled the bag of ice away from his face to expose an awful-looking shiner. His upper cheek area below his eye had a nasty cut, and the area was angry, raised, and purple.

"Silas, let me get a butterfly on that or you're going to end up needing stitches," Paul said.

Then Krish noticed the blood all over Silas's black T-shirt and his arm. His stomach lurched and he had to look away and cover his mouth. He was so angry, he wanted to punch Los, and he'd never hit anyone in his life other than Viv when they were fucking around. That thought made him sick all over again.

"I'm sorry, Si. I didn't mean it." Los's voice cracked, and he refused to make eye contact. There was so much pain in his tone and posture that Krish couldn't help but feel sorry for him. He was obviously hurting and had done something really stupid to a person he cared deeply for. Krish could relate.

"I'm not saying I deserved it for this, but at some point, I probably had it coming. It's cool, Los. But are *we* cool?" Silas sounded as tired as Krish felt.

They'd all been through so much in the past couple of days. It was a miracle any of them could string more than three words together.

Los pushed away from the wall and approached Silas with his head hung. Silas pulled him in for a hug and held him for a long time until Los raised his arms to reciprocate. The relief in the room was tangible until Jessica stormed up to them.

"Silas, let Paul fix you up. And goddammit, Los, I should beat you with a wooden spoon right now. What the hell were you thinking?"

He shied away from her as though she really were wielding a weapon, but Los's spunk returned. "Obviously I wasn't thinking—Mom—or I wouldn't have done that." His mischievous smile was the last straw for Jessica.

"That's it. I told you not to call me Mom. You're on restriction, Carlos Jiménez Morales! I can't believe you."

Los threw up his hands and backed away from her, laughing hysterically. Krish thought for a minute she was actually going to smack him, but instead she growled.

"When Lester brings the bus over tomorrow, your ass is cleaning it *and* doing everyone's laundry."

Los stopped laughing and his mouth dropped open. "Are you fucking serious?"

Jessica tried not to laugh. "Absolutely. You called me mom. You must need a mom to get your ass in line, so I'm going to treat you like the manchild you are!"

They stared at each other for a long moment until she couldn't keep the laughter at bay any longer.

"*Man*child." Jordan had fallen on the couch and was holding his stomach from laughing so hard. "You should see your face."

Los blinked. "I'm actually turned on right now."

The room was filled with howls of laughter, including Jessica's. "You have problems," she said, her cheeks red.

"I'm serious. That was hot, Jessica."

She rolled her eyes as Los approached her warily. As he started to hug her, she laughed again and let him embrace her.

"You should be hugging Silas right now," she said, but she buried her face in his neck. It was obvious they'd all reached their breaking point, and thank God it had ended in laughter and not tears or worse. Well, there was Silas's black eye to worry about.

Krish went into the kitchen, where Paul was working on Silas. Silas reached a hand out to him, and he approached, his stomach clenching once more.

"Are you okay?"

Silas laughed and then sucked in a breath as Paul pinched the skin closed and applied butterfly strips to hold it together. Silas squeezed his hand hard, and Krish's heart went out to him. He wondered how much of his pain was from the cut and how much was because his best friend had hurt him out of anger. Krish knew some guys were used to fighting to solve problems, but that hadn't really been part of his life. He and Vivaan had screwed around, but they'd never done it out of anger.

"There. Jesus. That must have been quite a punch."

Silas shrugged. "Yeah, he hits pretty hard when he's pissed."

Paul frowned. "Silas, I don't know how I feel about all of this. Bowie's just…."

"I'm sorry you had to see this, and I swear we're not always this emotionally immature. Usually we can talk through our issues like real grown-ups, but I think Los had reached his limit, especially as tired as he is. He didn't sleep last night."

Paul stepped back with his hands on his hips, worrying at his bottom lip with his teeth. "Bowie and I are going to have to talk about this some more. I'm going to take him over to my sister's for a while and let you guys, I don't know, *adult*."

Silas laughed and shook hands with Paul. "Thanks. I'll take care of Brains while you're gone," he said with a smirk.

The tips of Paul's ears got really red and he full-on blushed. *Hmmm.*

"Yeah, okay. Let me tell him I'll be right back." The stupid grin on his face resembled the one Krish had been sporting for the past couple of days, and Silas seemed to recognize it as well.

"Uh-huh. You do that."

Paul muttered something under his breath as he walked out of the room, leaving Silas and Krish alone.

Krish gently cupped Silas's wounded cheek and winced. "Are you okay? I'm so sorry, Silas."

Silas took Krish's hand and kissed the palm. "I'm okay, I guess. That, uh, could have gone better."

Krish gave a weak smile. "Yeah, for you and me both, although Jordan saved the day."

Silas wrapped his arms around Krish's waist. "Really? Did he drop some bomb that was even more salacious than you being the Guru?"

"He told them about you pulling him aside and showing him the blog post in your wallet."

Silas sighed and rested his uninjured cheek on Krish's chest. "Yeah, my Spidey-sense said he was gonna bolt, and I couldn't have that. I had to hang on to him or else Hush would have fucking died its final death, dude. No respawning from that point. Game over."

Krish brushed his lips over Silas's head. How scary, to have put themselves out there with a new guitarist and then for Silas to see it all slipping through his fingers.

"Are you and Los okay?"

Silas chuckled. "Yeah. We were hugging it out when I started bleeding all over the damn place. His abandonment issues, man. It's, like, he trusts me as much as he can possibly trust anyone, but this was asking too much, apparently. I'm going to get him back, though, I put him on notice."

"I'm sorry to have brought all of this into your family, Silas. I'm not sure you shouldn't have just told me to fuck off."

Silas shook his head and looked up at Krish. "No way that was going to happen. I'm not letting you go." He pushed up on his toes and tentatively brushed his lips across Krish's. It was enough to unleash the emotions Krish had been holding back. He pulled Silas in closer and deepened the kiss, bending at the knees to get on Silas's level.

"*Fuck*," Silas moaned. He grabbed Krish's head, and his hand grazed Krish's staples just as Krish reached up to cup his face and pressed on his cheekbone.

"Ow." They pulled back laughing.

"We make quite a pair." Krish straightened Silas's shirt where he'd yanked the collar askance.

"We make a *great* pair," Silas said. "Hey. I still want to go with you. Let's go back in there and start the peace talks."

Krish wasn't sure it was a good idea, but he was coming to recognize that determined set to Silas's jaw. Krish didn't see the wisdom in fighting, especially when it was exactly what *he* wanted.

As they reentered the living room hand-in-hand, Krish knew that Silas came with the rest of the band, and while they'd survived this battle, he could only hope and pray they'd manage to survive those to come, that he'd have the courage to keep fighting.

Chapter Nineteen

AFTER ONE of the most drama-filled days of his entire life, Silas was ready for some peace, but first he had to run his plans by the guys and Jessica. Thankfully they all seemed to realize a little space would do them all a world of good. Brains told him to get the fuck out, as Silas had assumed he would, and Los and Jordan were already making plans to go blow off some steam at some trampoline park nearby. Jessica was all too happy to call *Alt-Scene* and get him an appointment for a photo shoot with the magazine.

"After this fiasco, it would be nice to have something positive about the band in print. Although with your shiner, I don't know if you make the best ambassador."

Brains had additional reasons to want Silas out of his hair for the next twenty-four hours. "It'll give me time to coach Bowie and to reassure Paul that sending his only begotten son off with a bunch of heathens is actually a great idea. With you here, you're bound to screw it up, especially the way you're eye-fucking your boyfriend."

"Wouldn't you?" he asked. *Boyfriend.* Silas liked the sound of that.

Brains shook his head. "Yeah. Probably."

Silas wondered if he might return tomorrow to find Brains doing a little eye-fucking of his own with a certain sailor.

"Hey, what are we going to do without Mischa?" Los asked.

"Fuck," Silas said. "I'd almost forgotten we were out our merch girl."

They all sat quietly for a few minutes until Brains once more lived up to his nickname.

"What about your brother, Jordan? Wasn't he talking about sales plans and marketing and shit when we were on the bus?"

Jordan looked baffled. "Yeah, he was. I don't know. Krish? Did he have something lined up for this summer?"

Krish shook his head. "No, not that I know of."

Brains snapped his fingers and clapped his hands together. "Then Barrett, my friend, I think you have a call to make."

Jordan pushed his hair out of his eyes and laughed. "He's not even home yet. So what, like, have him meet us in Phoenix?"

"Get on it. Get Barrett Junior to come be our merch girl."

Jordan stood and saluted. "I'm on it. Hey, does that mean I get to call him Merch Girl all summer? It's a step up from My Bitch, which he's always hated."

They all laughed, and Jordan left the room to call their parents.

Jordan and Los agreed to help Brains on his mission to convince Paul to let Bowie come with them for his indoctrination into heathenhood. Then they would head out to find some trouble. Jessica promised she would supervise when Silas started to protest.

"It's fine," she said. "We're in fucking San Ramon. How much trouble can they possibly get into?"

Bowie and Paul returned a short time later, and they both appeared as worn out as the band. Bowie dropped Silas and Krish off at Stoneridge Mall in Pleasanton and gave them instructions on how they could catch the Bay Area Rapid Transit, or BART, to the city and showed them which stop to exit the train. Krish and Silas found the address of the magazine office and the nearest hotel and made a reservation. Bowie loaned them both beanies—Krish so he wouldn't look like Frankenstein's monster and Silas so he'd be less likely to be recognized. Krish nixed Silas's plan to wear sunglasses, since all he had were aviators and that made him look even more like a rock star, and he suggested Silas leave the makeup off as well, especially with his still-angry shiner. Silas reluctantly agreed and even wore a long-sleeved shirt to cover his tattoos.

The mall trip proved to be a success. Silas took Krish into Nordstrom and they both walked out with new suits and shoes as well as some new casual clothes, only getting a few wary looks from employees. At one point a security guy started shadowing them, which pissed Silas off. Krish had to hold him back from making a scene. Instead, they were followed to the cashier, where Silas made a big production of pulling out his Black Amex card. The customer service women fell all over themselves asking if they wanted their purchases gift wrapped, did they want any other accessories, and would they like some personal assistance. Krish bit his lip as Silas slid his hand around to Krish's ass and let it stay there as he continued to flirt with them.

"You're too much," Krish said as they walked out.

"What? That?" Silas's innocent act was so full of shit, and Krish told him as much.

"I can't help fucking with people," Silas admitted. And Krish was so fucking gorgeous, Silas couldn't help how much he enjoyed watching other people gawk at him, knowing he'd finally be alone with his boyfriend that night.

Boyfriend. Sounded so good to Silas.

A stop by Sephora scored Silas the makeup he wanted and almost got them discovered when the guy working the Urban Decay aisle seemed to have recognized him but chose to stay quiet.

Silas behaved when they were in the dressing rooms, but he was anxious to get Krish out of the mall, into the city, into a hotel room, out of his clothes, and….

"You all right? Your leg hasn't stopped bouncing since we got on the train."

Krish placed his hand on Silas's knee and applied pressure enough to make Silas realize he was that keyed up.

"Sorry. I'm just anxious to get you alone." He linked his fingers with Krish's and sighed. "And maybe I'm a little anxious, period."

Krish squeezed his hand. "You have every reason to be anxious. Tomorrow is going to happen regardless of what we do. And the next day and the next. I'm anxious too, but having you beside me helps keep me in the moment."

Silas felt some of the tension bleed out of his body. "You really are a smart little old man in there, aren't you?"

They both laughed, and Silas leaned a little more into Krish's side. The train sped under the bay, it grew too loud to hear each other talk, and then they were in the city. They took the Montgomery Street exit and used Krish's phone to guide them on the four-block walk to the Omni hotel. Krish had bickered with Silas over paying for the hotel, but Silas won when he said it was a business expense and he'd write it off. Krish seemed to take several calming breaths, but he allowed Silas to win. They were probably the first of many Silas would see him take.

The walk from the front desk, past the ornate staircase, to the elevators that would take them up to the third-from-the-top floor was painfully long. By the time they made it to their Signature room, both Krish and Silas were tired, but the thrill running between them was a live wire with nothing to ground it. Silas couldn't keep his hands to himself. Even if it was simply a touch to Krish's arm or a squeeze of their hands, he had to be in contact with Krish. But he had to put down his shopping bags to unlock the door, and he gestured for Krish to step inside first.

"Wow," Krish said, looking around with wide eyes. "This is incredible." He walked to the window, looked out over the bright lights of San Francisco, and took a deep breath. "It's so beautiful," he said.

Silas closed the door and flipped the lock. In the faint light from the desk lamp and the city skyline, Krish's features were illuminated in a manner that made him look even more alluring. His long, thin nose, his thick lashes above high cheek bones, and the silhouette of his lips all made Silas desperate to touch him.

"Did you want to order room service? Or shower or anything? Did you need to sleep?" He hoped the answers to all of those questions would be no, but a shower might be fun.

Krish turned to face him with a lust-filled gaze. "Does this count as not being on tour?"

Silas approached him slowly, removing the long-sleeved shirt and beanie in one tug over his head. "That rule doesn't matter anymore. Not with you. This isn't just some tour fling. This means way more to me."

Krish smiled shyly and slid his own beanie off. "And you're sure you want to make it with the monster?" He touched the bandage they'd carefully put over his staples and then dropped his arms at his side.

"I want us to fuck, Krish. I want us to be as close as we possibly can. I need that. I need you."

Silas placed his hand on Krish's cheek and caressed his lip. Krish turned his face to kiss his thumb.

He closed his eyes and took the thumb into his mouth and sucked. Silas's eyes rolled back in his head.

"I want you to fuck me," Silas whispered.

Krish opened his eyes with a questioning gaze. "Are you sure?"

Silas nodded. "Yeah. And I want to fuck you. I want it all with you."

Krish smiled. "Oh. I assumed—"

"Yeah, I know I can be bossy, but you also know I like to be held. I need that closeness, Krish. Does that make sense? If I'm going to be intimate with someone, be in a relationship with someone, I'm all in when it comes to sex. I trust you with my body and my heart, Krish. Otherwise we wouldn't be here."

Krish pulled Silas in for an embrace and sighed. "I trust you too, and I love that you're so affectionate. I'll give you whatever you want," he said with a smile.

"Yeah, you will," Silas said, kissing his neck. "But first, let's get horizontal. You're too fucking tall."

Krish laughed. "And let's shower. I really want to shave or you'll be covered in beard rash tomorrow for your photo shoot."

"That's what makeup is for, but yeah. A shower sounds great."

The bathroom wasn't as huge as Silas would have liked, but it would do. They undressed completely in front of each other and Silas couldn't get over how gorgeous Krish was, nor how self-conscious he was. His skin was so beautiful. Without his hair to hide behind, his big brown eyes seemed to glow with the warmth of his personality, and he smiled so brightly. Silas was determined to keep him smiling. They stared at each other for a long time, giggling nervously but not touching.

"I can't believe we're here and alone," Krish said.

"I know, right? Bus living leaves something to be desired when you're getting to know someone."

Krish ducked his eyes away and looked at himself in the mirror. "Geez, I need to shave. Mind if I shave first?"

Silas shook his head. He laid a towel out on the counter and hopped up to sit next to the sink. "Nope. As long as I get to watch you."

"You're going to give me a complex," Krish said as he took the few toiletry items they bought out of the bags—small can of shave cream, disposable razors, lotion, lube, condoms. Silas had a Pavlovian response to seeing the lube and condoms. He couldn't wait to use them.

Krish ran the water in the sink until it was warm and then lathered his face up with cream. The only razors they could find were kind of shitty ones, but Krish had said he'd make do.

"You'll have to let me do that for you sometime," Silas said.

"Yeah? You did a good job on my head, so maybe I will. Sorry, I have to shave every day unless I want to grow this thing out."

"I think it looks sexy as fuck. Either way, you're gorgeous. But I like having easy access to your lips and your neck."

Krish looked down at his semierect self and back to Silas. "You're making it very difficult to concentrate."

"Sorry," Silas chuckled. "But damn, I can't wait."

Krish seemed to pick up the pace with his shaving. He peered down at Silas, who was fully ready to get things moving, and he smiled. "I could shave you. You ever have someone shave you?"

Silas's eyes flared. "Ooo that's hot. And no, I've never let anyone near my balls with a razor, but I might change my stance on that for you."

Krish laughed and made one last pass with his razor. "That will have to do." He rinsed his face with water, and before Silas knew what he was doing, Krish bent over and rubbed his face on Silas's cock. "How's that? Smooth enough?"

Silas leaned back to give him more access. "Mmmm, I'm not sure. Maybe you better—ah!"

Krish swallowed him down until Silas couldn't breathe. God, this man was so good with his tongue. He reached for Krish's head but paused when he remembered Krish's injury. He was surprised he could remember anything as Krish's mouth did such astounding things that Silas couldn't concentrate on anything except the feel of Krish against him, around him, over him. He loved all of the sensations. Krish kissed his way up Silas's torso, spending several long moments worshipping his nipples and tugging on the piercings. Silas never wanted it to stop, never wanted Krish to let him go.

Krish stopped long enough to lead them into the shower, and once in there, he cleaned Silas lovingly and then turned Silas to face the wall. He stroked Silas's cock gently while eagerly attending to his hole with his tongue. Silas's legs shook so badly he could barely hold himself up. When he started to collapse, Krish's strong hands held his hips in place.

"God, Krish, I need—"

"I need you," Krish said, slowly and gently pressing a finger inside Silas when all Silas wanted was to feel Krish's length inside him.

"Now. I need you to fuck me."

Krish pulled away only long enough to turn off the water and grab towels for them. Once he wrapped Silas in one and helped him step from the tub, Krish pushed him up against the wall and kissed him deeply.

"How do you want me?" Krish asked. He caressed Silas's face while brushing their arousals together. "Tell me how you want me."

"Bed," Silas answered, breathless. "I want to be on a real bed with you where we can be as loud as we want without having to worry about who's outside the door."

Krish chuckled. "Bed sounds good, but I'm game for anything. I want to be inside you."

They made it clumsily to the bed, and Silas pushed Krish down onto his back.

"Shit. I didn't dry off," Krish laughed.

"It's okay. I plan to mess up this bed good with you tonight."

"Let's get started, then. Where's—"

"On it." Silas dashed back into the bathroom, slipping on a towel on the floor and nearly crashing into the counter.

"Be careful in there," Krish called out. "We don't need any more injuries."

Silas trotted back to the bed laughing, dropped the lube and condoms on the bed, and then straddled Krish's hips. He leaned down to suck Krish's bottom lip into his mouth. "God, you taste good. I want to taste all of you, but right now I need you in me."

Silas was so ready to go. He crawled off Krish long enough to roll a condom onto Krish's dick, and then he was right back on top of him, loving the feel of taking all of Krish, slowly and steadily.

Krish grabbed on to Silas's thighs and sucked in a long breath, his body straining underneath Silas.

"God, that feels divine," Silas said as he was fully seated.

"I can't breathe," Krish said. "So intense."

"Yeah," Silas said as he began to move. Krish let him set the pace, and soon he was rocking back against Krish and moaning.

"It's too much. I can't… I'm going to—"

He came in a rush, covering Krish's chest with his load. Krish's answering smile kept him moving until Krish took over. He gripped Silas's hips and pulled him down hard until Krish came just as strong, his back lifting off the bed with the force. Silas couldn't even hold himself up. He collapsed onto the bed next to Krish and threw an arm and leg over him.

Chapter Twenty

"I can't move," Silas moaned.

"Good," Krish said, kissing his forehead. "Means I did something right."

Silas barked out a laugh. "That was a whole lot of right. You turned me inside out." He ran a finger through the mess he'd made on Krish's chest and sighed. "I love seeing you like this."

I love you. It would be so easy for Krish to say it, just put it out there, but he still worried Silas would think him clingy or too invested in what they had. Silas could say all he wanted that they were going to make a go of it, but Krish was still nervous.

Silas's steady breathing beside him let Krish know that his lover was done for at least a while. Krish extricated himself from the bed and cleaned up in the bathroom. When he was done, he wandered out to the sitting area of the suite. He was drawn to the windows, nearly floor to ceiling in height, and he stared out into the night sky.

So many thoughts jumbled in his mind, he thought he should get some of them out before trying to go to sleep. He picked up his phone, saw he had two missed texts from his mother, and shook his head.

In San Francisco with Silas. Don't worry, I got a suit to wear. I'll send you pictures tomorrow.

He hit Send and then realized that, *shit*, he still hadn't told his mom about the injury. She was going to flip out. Maybe he'd wait until after the interview, when he'd hopefully have good news for her as well.

Silas had talked him into getting a fedora to wear to the interview, and he had to admit it looked rather dashing paired with the black pin-striped suit Silas had picked out for him. He'd fit right in with the hipsters in San Francisco, and no one would question his stapled head.

Luckily the suit and the shirt he bought were on sale. The shoes were ridiculously expensive, but he didn't have anything nice at home and he'd probably keep them forever. The last time he'd had to dress up was at Vivaan's memorial service, and he'd worn an old suit of their father's. Buying his own suit for his first major interview with a magazine felt like he was finally growing up. He'd allowed Silas to buy him a bloodred tie he insisted looked stunning against Krish's skin. They'd had so much fun shopping together that Krish found himself longing for more adventures like that. Silas had talked about how cool it would be on tour when Silas had a couple of days off, how much fun it would be to explore new places together, and Krish wanted all of those things.

Krish began dictating into his phone his thoughts about Warped Tour and the new changes in his life. He wasn't sure if he would publish it or not, especially the part about Silas. He would never put Silas's personal life out on display like that, but it was hard to completely keep him out of it. His entire Warped experience so far was wrapped up in Silas, and his feelings for Silas would forever be tied up in the memories they'd made, both good and bad.

He stood in front of the window, baring his thoughts and feelings into a document that he'd then go back and polish. It seemed appropriate that he was naked, and totally outrageous that he was in a suite in one of San Francisco's swankiest hotels while preparing his blog post. Despite the seriousness of what he was sharing, he felt a little giddy.

"Who are you talking to?"

Krish turned to see Silas sprawled naked on their bed. He could stare at that picture for hours. He almost wished he could snap a picture so he'd have it forever.

"Sorry if I woke you. I'm dictating for my blog post."

Silas crawled across the bed toward him and joined him at the window.

"That's cool. You can, like, write on the go that way, huh?"

"Yeah. I do a lot of blogging from my phone."

Silas pretended to peek over his shoulder. "Can I see it, or is that taboo?"

Krish laughed. "It's not taboo. It's rough like this, though. I go back and clean it up before I post. I'm not sure I'm going to post this one, though."

"Why not?" Silas leaned against the window frame, facing him.

Krish shrugged. "I guess this one got really personal, and I would never publish anything about you, about us like this."

Silas's eyes bugged out. "You wrote about me? About us?"

Krish waited for him to get pissed, but he laughed.

"Read it to me," he said.

Krish sighed. "I don't know. It's kind of embarrassing—"

"Oh, come on. I've read every one of your blog posts since I found you three years ago. I love your voice."

"Fine," Krish said. He cleared his throat. "Warped Tour has always been an escape for me. A day of fun in the sun and time to commune with the music I love. But Warped Tour 2018, this last hurrah for the franchise, wasn't an escape for me. It was a 'come to whatever deity you believe in' moment. Instead of letting myself go, I let someone else in. Instead of being an outsider, enjoying the music, the music brought me inside. I laughed, bled, and loved with the people I've written about for years, and this surreal experience has changed me forever. Not only do I have a totally different view of what goes on behind the scenes, I have new friends, a prospective new career, and someone special who wants to share his life with me." He turned off his phone and set it down on an end table. "That's all I have so far."

Silas stared at him for a long moment and then stepped forward and brought Krish's head down for a kiss. Slow, sweet brushes of Silas's tongue made Krish's knees go weak. The feel of Silas's hands working their way down his back to his ass nearly knocked him off his feet.

"Silas," he whispered against his lips.

"Please tell me you meant all of that and that you'll publish it?"

Krish pulled back. "I wasn't going to use your name, or any identifying information about the band."

"I trust you, Krish."

Krish grabbed his arms and pulled him back from the kiss. "I would never invade your privacy like that."

"I won't keep you hidden, though. I want everyone to know you're mine. Guru or not."

"Silas, come on. You don't need any more drama in your life right now. Just give it some time. I'm sure there are already going to be pictures of us on the internet after getting caught making out."

Silas's blank look had Krish nervous. Had he royally screwed up again?

"I appreciate that you don't want to cause problems for me, but I honestly don't care about any of that. All I care about is you."

He was so sincere. Krish's heart melted a little bit more at Silas's words.

He cares about me.
And I believe him.

Krish kissed him and pulled him closer—so close their bodies were flush together. "I want you, Silas. I want you."

Silas growled and kissed him harder. Krish's lips tingled from the pressure. Silas pulled away and told him to stay put. He walked back to the bed, grabbed their supplies, and returned to the window. He turned Krish around to face the wall and pressed kisses and licks along his spine, spending extra time on the globes of his ass.

"I can't stand up, Silas."

Silas stood and pressed against Krish's back. "I love it that you're taller than me, but *damn* you're tall. Here," he said, grabbing the ottoman for the wingback chair. "Kneel on this. You can hold on to the chair for support."

Once he had Krish in position, he ran his fingernails down Krish's back, causing him to suck in a breath. He was so turned on. Every single nerve ending was screaming for Silas's touch.

Silas spent an achingly long time playing with Krish, using one hand to prepare him for Silas's entry and the other hand to stroke his balls and his cock until Krish wanted to sob from the pleasure. Silas's hands left Krish's body for the millisecond it took him to roll on the condom, and then he was back, leaning over Krish's back as he pressed against Krish's tight muscle, begging for entrance.

"You're mine, Krish, and I don't care who knows it." He pushed in and Krish shouted. It was so much. Silas was so much. Silas held him, giving him time to get adjusted before he began that slow rocking that had driven him crazy before when he was inside of Silas.

Silas kept whispering in Krish's ear the whole time, telling him how tight he was, how good he felt, how much Silas wanted to be in him until neither of them could walk. How much he loved him....

Love. He actually said he loved Krish, and Krish was too far gone to know whether he meant it or not. But damn, he did love Silas, and in that moment, with their bodies as close as they could possibly be, he wanted to believe Silas felt the same.

"God, babe. I'm so close... it's so good...." Silas pulled out, and Krish heard the snap as he pulled the condom off. Krish turned and looked over his shoulder to watch as Silas stroked himself only two or three times before he came all over Krish's back.

"Don't you come yet," Silas moaned. He turned Krish around to sit on the ottoman and dropped to his knees. Silas went down on him, flicking that damn ball in his tongue against Krish's cock until Krish felt his orgasm come screaming out of his body and into Silas's gorgeous mouth. He'd never experienced so much pleasure in his entire life. Silas was everywhere, was everything.

The wicked smile on Silas's face as he licked his lips made Krish bark out a laugh.

"You're crazy," he said, panting. "That was crazy."

"Crazy good. I loved that." He stood up and pulled Krish to his feet. "Let's clean up, and then I'm cuddling the shit out of you."

Krish leaned on him for support. "That sounds like heaven." He kissed the top of Silas's head, and

Silas gave him a squeeze. They cleaned up quickly in the bathroom and then sprawled together on the bed, foregoing the blankets until their overheated skin cooled down.

"Yeah, we can work around our height difference," Silas continued. "I've got this great chair in my room back home, and I'm going to love taking you like this again, coming all over your back. Fucking hell, Krish. You've completely ruined me. This is all I'm going to be thinking of until we get to do this again."

Krish's chestburster woke back up. "Good. I want you to be thinking of next time."

Silas turned to face him. "All the next times. Krish, I mean it. I want you. I want this."

"Me too. I want this with you." And yet he fell asleep worrying about those next times.

SILAS HAD thought ahead to order room service, so when the knock on the door woke Krish at 7:30 a.m., Silas was already dressed in one of the robes from the bathroom and at the door before Krish could pull the covers over him. Silas signed the bill and took care of getting the food set up on the coffee table in front of the couch in the main area of the suite.

"Babe, come get some of this. Man, I love room service. Not having to cook breakfast for all the hooligans on the bus is heaven."

Krish dug around in his new-clothes bag and put on a pair of silk boxers Silas had insisted he get to wear under his suit. For confidence. *Right.*

"I hope you like waffles. We have a shitty waffle iron on the bus, so I love to get big flaky waffles when I go out to eat."

"Yeah, waffles are great." He sat down next to Silas and kissed him on the cheek. "Thank you for, well, not just last night—"

"But particularly last night. You're welcome," Silas said, kissing him back. "It was epic. Man, I wish we had more time. I woke up thinking I'd really like a repeat."

Krish fell back against the couch and smiled lazily. "That sounds fantastic. I could use a couple more hours of sleep too."

"Nonsense. You need to get ready for your big interview. You sure I can't put on some eyeliner, make you look a little more mysterious?"

Krish's smile fell a little. "No, thank you. I think makeup is your thing."

Silas frowned at him. "What's wrong?"

Krish sighed. "I don't know. How weird is it going to be, me walking in with Silas Franklin, into the office of the biggest alternative and rock magazine on the West Coast? I'm worried how that's going to look."

Silas sat back, one leg tucked underneath him. "Let me get this straight. You're embarrassed—"

"No. No no no, that's not at *all* what I meant. I don't want it to seem like I'm trying to ride your coattails into a job."

Silas rolled his eyes and scooted over to sit on Krish's lap. "Babe. Your writing got you this interview, remember? What did they say to you on the phone?"

Krish looked down at his lap. "That they liked my voice."

"Exactly. Now, did they know we were seeing each other?"

"No," Krish said. "Of course not."

"Exactly. You getting this interview had nothing to do with me. Besides, it's not like I have any pull with them."

"Oh, come on. You're one of their favorite artists to put on the cover. How many times have you been on the cover of *Alt-Scene*?"

Silas shrugged. "I don't know. A few?"

"Try seventeen times in the past ten years. I counted. I probably have all of them in my room."

Silas's eyes bugged out. "Do you ever take them out and, you know—"

"Silas! I'm serious."

Silas leaned over to kiss Krish and licked at a spot of syrup he had on his lip. "Babe, none of that matters to me. And I'm sure it will have no bearing on whether you get the job or not. Which you will. Because you're incredible. You have no clue how much your blog means to people, do you? I've had people mention the Guru's posts to me on tour. Our label A&R guys follow you, especially your reviews of up-and-coming bands. Your reviews are often the clincher in bands getting signed. I bet you didn't know that. You're so respected in the industry. I wish you could see that. You and me? Us being together? Yeah, some people are going to talk, but let them. I don't care, Krish. I only care about you."

Krish's heart couldn't take much more. He wanted to tell Silas how he felt—not in the middle of sex, but in a moment like this, right here, right now. Unfortunately, he was much better writing it down than actually saying it.

"So what do we tell them when we show up together? Don't you think they're going to ask questions?"

Silas took a bite of bacon and raised an eyebrow. "You can tell them whatever you want." His wicked smile had Krish remembering what he'd looked like early that morning, and that had him tenting his boxers, and—

"Pity we don't have time for that," Silas said with a wink.

They finished their breakfast, fed each other bits of eggs and waffles until they were both stuffed, and then they dressed. Silas tied Krish's tie for him, and Krish blushed when Silas mentioned what he'd like to do with it later.

They checked out of the hotel and left their bags at the desk so they wouldn't look like total tools walking down the street. It only took them about thirty minutes to find the magazine office, which was in a new development down by the AT&T ballpark. Krish and Silas clashed over baseball teams—their first major disagreement, according to Silas. Krish loved the Padres and Silas was an A's fan first, and then a Giants fan if they weren't playing the A's. They talked about the possibility of catching a game together at some point. There were so many things Krish wanted to do with Silas, so much fun they could have together, if only he could quit worrying about it.

The receptionist greeted Krish with a smile and greeted Silas by name.

"Mr. Franklin. Josanne will be here shortly for the photo shoot. Can I get you some coffee?"

"No, thank you. I'm fine. We had breakfast already." He winked at Krish. The guy was too much.

"Mr. Guruvy—"

"Guruvayoor. I'm here to see Chaz Vella?"

"Yes, of course. He'll be right with you. May I get you some coffee?"

"No, thank you."

She showed them to a waiting room that had an entire wall of covers from the magazine going back several years. Krish said thank you as he sat down next to Silas with space between them.

"One… two… three…. They have at least eight covers of you hanging in here," Krish said.

Silas rolled his eyes. "Whatever. I'm sure these pics won't end up on the cover. I think this is the first time I've worn a suit, though."

"Yeah, I think I like the shirtless ones the best," Krish said.

"I bet you do. You can get me shirtless when we're done here. Pantsless too. I don't need to be back to San Ramon until tomorrow, actually—"

"But I have to get to Phoenix. I need to get some work done."

Silas's excitement vanished. "That's right. Damn. I forgot. I'm going to miss you. I know it's only a couple of days, but—"

"Me too."

"Mr. Guruvayoor. Silas. What a nice surprise to see you here."

Chaz offered his hand to Krish, who shook it vigorously, and then he hugged Silas.

"I figured since we had a little unplanned hiatus, I'd make it over for that photoshoot you guys were asking for."

"Excellent. Josanne just walked in. She'll take care of you. It would be nice to get a statement about that fiasco on Saturday. I'm so sorry about Brains. He doing okay?"

"Yeah, he'll be fine, but he's out for a few weeks. We've got a replacement already lined up. We're rejoining the tour Thursday in Phoenix."

Chaz's eyes widened. "There's a story there for sure. And how do you two—"

"Krish and I met over the weekend."

Silas's smile was infectious. That smile was everything. It said I love you, I'm here for you, and I'm never letting you go, all at once.

"Yeah. We, uh, just met." Krish's voice cracked a little, but he shared in that stupid smile with Silas and didn't care much that he sounded like an idiot. His potential new boss looked back and forth between them with a curious expression.

"Great. I'm glad you both could come," Chaz said. "Well, Mr. Guruvayoor, wait, can I call you Krish?"

"Absolutely. I know my last name is a bit of a mouthful."

Silas snorted. Krish felt his cheeks getting hotter by the moment.

"Great. Uh, shall we? I've invited Monique to sit in with us. Frankly, I couldn't keep her out. She wanted to meet you in person, and since she'd be your direct supervisor, I thought it was a good idea."

"Sure, I'm happy to meet her. She had a lot of great things to say about working here when we spoke on the phone."

"She better," Chaz said. Then he burst out laughing. Krish laughed too, but his was out of nervousness. As Chaz led Krish away from Silas, Krish looked back once more.

Silas winked and blew him a kiss, and Krish stumbled over his new shoes and nearly fell.

Once inside the conference room, he was introduced to Monique, who he'd talked to on the phone already.

"So, Krish. Wow. You're the Guru. How does it feel to be out?"

Krish laughed at Monique's question, rubbing his hands on his pants as he sat down. He hadn't sweated this much in a long time.

"Quite strange. Friday morning I woke up anonymous, and here I am, three days later, about to tell people that yes, I'm that guy that's been writing about your music for the past several years."

Monique and Chaz looked at each other knowingly.

"And you met Silas," Chaz said. His tone sounded ominously like he was about to start digging for information.

"Yeah, um, my best friend Jake is Jordan Barrett's brother. That's how we met." He figured they could probably see right through him, but for whatever reason, he didn't feel comfortable telling these people about his personal life. It shouldn't matter, right?

Monique smiled conspiratorially and leaned forward. "I have to say you two looked adorable sitting out there. Did he know who you were?"

Krish shook his head, feeling even more unsettled. "No, no one knew but Jake. And Kevin and Chantal because of the internship. Thank you for setting that up, by the way."

Chaz and Monique looked to each other and then back at Krish and leaned forward. "Followers of your blog would be titillated to hear about your time with the band," Chaz said.

Krish cleared his throat. "I won't be writing about Hush anymore. Not reviews of their albums or shows, nor anything personal."

"I can imagine that to be a difficult decision for you," Chaz said. "But just because you, ah, just met them, doesn't *have* to mean you can't write about the band. In fact, I had an idea."

KRISH WALKED out of the office in a daze. They'd offered him a sweet deal, basically everything he'd hoped for, but he didn't feel comfortable at all with what they were asking him to do. He told them he'd have to think about it, and they seemed surprised.

Silas was nowhere to be seen when he came out, so he asked the receptionist.

"Oh, he and Josanne took a walk to find some spots outside. They should be back soon."

Krish turned away from the receptionist, his stomach churning. He couldn't take it anymore. The chestburster was coming out for real this time. He pulled out his phone to text Silas.

And realized they'd never exchanged numbers.

Fuck.

He approached the receptionist once more.

"I'm sorry to bother you, but can I leave a message for Silas with you?"

She looked at him in disbelief. "You don't have his phone number?"

Krish felt his cheeks flush, and he thought he might cry if he spoke anymore.

"Can you please tell him I went back to the hotel?"

"Sure. No problem."

"Thank you," Krish said, and then he stormed out of the office, trying to keep his feet from running down the hall.

Silas would be pissed that he left, but what else was he supposed to do? He couldn't sit in that office one more minute without losing his mind. He needed some time to think.

Once he got outside, he couldn't hold back the tears. His heart was about to break. He couldn't do what they wanted. It would be going against everything he'd stood for when he decided to reveal himself as the Guru and start writing for a major magazine. And if he did do what they wanted, he wouldn't be being true to the man he loved or the guys in the band who Krish hoped would come to accept him. Krish had no choice but to say no and start over again.

Back at the Omni, Krish called his mother and told her everything. She listened quietly, only slipping into Hindi when he told her about his injury. He assured her he was fine, but that he was too shook up to make his travel arrangements home.

"Can you please help me?"

"Krishnan, darling, are you sure you want to leave like this?"

"No. But I can't do this. I won't do this to Silas."

She agreed to book him a flight and text him the information. He would ask the hotel if they had a shuttle to the airport, and if not, he would take the BART train as he'd noticed the day before that it went that far. Her text came fifteen minutes later. He had an hour and a half to make his flight.

"That's the only flight I can get for you today. The rest were sold out."

He couldn't wait for Silas to get back. He'd have to leave without saying goodbye.

Krish went to the desk and asked for his bag. The valet brought both of their bags, and Krish wrote a note on hotel stationary and slipped it into Silas's bag.

The valet flagged a cab for him, which dropped him at the BART station, and he followed the signs to the train that would take him to the airport.

He needed to go home and regroup. Then he could make a new plan. He decided he needed to talk to Chantal, so he texted her.

Hey, I think I'm going to be gone for a couple more days. I just

How the hell did he describe what had happened? He'd walked into that interview with the naïve expectation that he was going to be able to set his own limits. Obviously he wasn't going to be able to operate like he had on the blog. He knew that. Editors had requirements, and there were journalistic rules he needed to follow. He never thought....

need to get home. Something has come up. I'll be in touch.

He hit Send, and a few moments later, his phone rang.

"Krish! What's going on? Are you okay?"

He exhaled and went to rub at his hair, which he'd forgotten was gone, and he hit his staples.

"Not really."

Could he trust Chantal? He needed to talk to someone, and if he called Jake, he wasn't going to get an objective perspective.

"Krish? Are you there? Honey, if you need to talk...."

"If your boss asked you to do something that went against everything you believed in... and basically threatened you...."

"Krish, what the hell happened? What are you talking about?"

So he unloaded the entire tale on her during the BART ride to the airport and during his wait in the security line. When he finally stopped, she was cursing out loud.

"You listen to me. You have a job with Warped Tour regardless. I'll make sure of that. If you need a couple of days to cool down, I get it. Let me talk to Kevin and tell him what's happened. Call me tomorrow, and we'll talk about when you'll meet back up with us." She chuckled. "I'll make sure no one on the bus says anything. Casey and Vinh told me about your conversation, and I could have knocked their heads together. We told you you'd be anonymous. They will not be telling anyone."

"Thank you," he said. "I need time to think. I don't know what I'm going to do. I don't think I can work with *Alt-Scene* after what happened."

She cursed under her breath. "I wouldn't. I can't believe…. Look. You get home. Rest. Call me tomorrow. Everything is going to be okay."

He thanked her once more as he hurried through security. He dashed to his gate with only minutes to spare, and he was fine until he got to his seat. Then his chest, his heart, broke open. He pulled out his phone, ignored the texts from his mother and Jake, and started pouring out his feelings onto a doc that eventually he'd edit to become his blog.

Chapter Twenty-One

Silas returned to the magazine to find Krish had left without him. He jogged back to the hotel at a quick pace. No Krish. Just a note in his bag.

The only flight I could get home means leaving without saying goodbye. I'm sorry. I hope your photo shoot went well. I'll look forward to seeing the pictures in the next issue. I don't know when I'll see you again, but I want you to know that this weekend meant the world to me. I love you. Krish

Stunned, Silas gathered his belongings and sat staring at the note. He was so raw. He'd thought for sure his time in San Francisco with Krish would have cemented their relationship, that they would have left together, and that they'd somehow be all right.

He said he loved me. What the hell could have happened? Everything was great until—

Silas marched right back to the magazine and insisted on seeing Chaz.

"Silas! What can I do for you?"

"I want to know why my boyfriend left here so upset."

Chaz sat down slowly behind his desk. "He's your *boyfriend*?"

"Yeah. My boyfriend. What happened?" Silas remained standing with his arms crossed over his chest.

"Well, we knew you'd met and that he'd spent time with the band, but I had no idea you two—"

"It was a recent development." Silas was vibrating with anger. He knew in his heart something had to have happened for Krish to leave like that. He couldn't accept that he left without saying goodbye for no reason.

Chaz sighed and folded his hands on his desk. "We thought if anyone could get the story behind Gavin's suicide and how the band was dealing with it, it would be the Guru." Silas started to speak, but Chaz held up his hands in surrender. "We were hoping to have it kick off our social justice feature. When I saw you guys come in together, I thought—"

It all made sense now. Krish had been adamant that he wouldn't write about Hush any longer, and Chaz tried to pull this shady shit.

"Listen, Chaz, I've always had respect for this magazine, but lately you've been coming dangerously close to crossing a few lines. I was willing to let it go when you published that piece on Ryan's prison term, which had some factual errors in it, and your treatment of Roxanne for her choice to come forward with a #metoo article. Your reporter basically tried to discredit her instead of supporting her like you should have after all she's done for your magazine. Your staff could use some sensitivity training. It's one thing to cover these issues from a standpoint of wanting to be a part of the solution, but when you do it just to sell copies, that's wrong. And I know for a fact that Krish would never do anything he didn't feel was part of the solution."

Chaz swallowed hard. "I'm sorry you feel that way, Silas. But Krish seemed to think he would be able to stay anonymous, and I told him that after this tour, there was no way people *wouldn't* know who he is. Now that he's with you, he'll for sure have no privacy."

Silas frowned. "Are you threatening to out him?"

Chaz shrugged. "Not intentionally, but there are people who know he was working with us. Word's bound to get out now. Look, if he wants a career in journalism, he's going to need that name and his reputation."

"That is his decision. Not yours. And let me tell you what else…."

Chaz was much more understanding after Silas left. It might have had something to do with the fact that Silas threatened to sue, that he threatened to go public with the fact that Chaz tried to use his boyfriend to get an exclusive insider story on the grieving process of one of *Alt-Scene*'s darlings, a band that had made so much money for the magazine it was pathetic. Chaz saw the error of his ways and agreed to rescind that part of the job offer he'd made Krish.

At least that might fix Krish's employment situation.

But Silas wasn't sure if their relationship was salvageable at that point. Krish walked away from him. That's not how this shit worked. At least that's what he very drunkenly tried to explain to his brothers back at Paul's house, drinking Paul's whiskey.

"He leaves me, writes in a note that he loves me, and then gets on a motherfucking plane. That ain't the way love goes. That's not what Janet sang about. Miss Jackson if you're nasty."

"I think he's had enough," Jessica said, trying to take the bottle from Silas as he hugged it to his chest.

"No. I need to cuddle it."

"You can cuddle with me, all right? Geez." Los took the bottle from Silas and carried him upstairs to Bowie's room, where he spent the night listening to Silas's drunken ramblings and helping him to and from the toilet where he puked most of the night.

"I'm sorry, Los," he said when he'd finally purged his body of the last bit of alcohol.

"Don't apologize to me," Los said. "I hate that you're hurting."

"Thank you. I'll be okay. It just sucks, man. We were supposed to have our comeback, bruh. We were supposed to have a great summer, and it's kind of off to a rocky start if you hadn't noticed." He brushed his teeth and then followed Los back to Bowie's bed.

"I really thought Krish and I—" He wanted to cry, but he was so exhausted it came out as a long exhale.

"I'm sorry Brains and I gave him such a hard time. I like you two together. I thought he'd stick around."

"It's okay. You guys were looking out for me."

Los didn't answer. Silas looked up at him. "I promise, Los. I'm going to be okay. I got my heart hurt. Please don't worry about me."

Los took in a shaky breath. "I do, though. I can't lose you too."

Silas wrapped his arms around Los and kissed his head. "You're not losing me."

"I mean, I know that, but I get scared."

Silas knew it took a lot for Los to tell him that. Los didn't do the whole sharing-feelings bit, but Silas knew how hard he'd taken the loss of Gavin.

"What can I do to make you feel better, my brother?"

Los grimaced. "Quit breathing your puke breath in my face."

Silas snorted. "I'm sorry. It's pretty bad, huh?"

"Yeah, you smell like minty-fresh death. Just… I don't know. I want you to be happy, Si. I don't like seeing you get hurt."

"I know. And I don't want to worry you either. This would be so much easier if we agreed to be life partners. We'd make each other happy, wouldn't we?"

Los sighed. "We've been over this. I don't want your dick, Silas."

"But it's so—"

"Dude."

"Bruh."

"Go to sleep. We'll figure it out in the morning."

"I love you, Carlos Bro-rales."

"I love you too, Silas Bro-dumbass."

SILAS WOKE up Tuesday morning with a headache but a clear conscience. He wanted to text Krish, but he realized, in all the time they spent together, they hadn't exchanged numbers, and Krish hadn't left his number in the note. That seemed to indicate he wasn't meant to contact him yet. He and the guys practiced for hours, had a long discussion with Bowie and Paul about compensation, etc., with contracts that Jessica had drawn up, and prepared to leave Wednesday morning to ride the bus to Phoenix. When they arrived, he was disappointed to find out that no, Krish hadn't returned to the tour. *Where the fuck had he gone?*

Thursday's show there went off with only a couple of miniscule hitches. Bowie made a couple of mistakes, but the audience was so insane no one seemed to care. They were so fucking excited to see Hush after everything that happened. Bowie apologized profusely and promised it wouldn't happen again.

"Dude," Los said, slinging his arm around Bowie. "It's totally fine. You know how bad Jordan screwed up when we played—"

"Shut up, dick. I didn't fuck up that bad."

Bowie would soon learn that the guys busted each other's balls on the regular and he'd be expected to do the same.

Silas wished Krish was there to share.... Fuck. All day he'd wanted to turn to Krish for a smile, a kiss, a laugh. He'd stepped up and been there for his brothers without Brains to keep them in line, but could he really pull this off? With Krish by his side he could. Well, if Krish wasn't coming back, he was going to have to do it without Krish, now, wasn't he?

SILAS WOKE Jordan up Friday before daylight to find out when Jake was coming.

"Tonight. Fuck, Silas. It's five in the morning."

Silas couldn't stand it anymore.

"I have to talk to Krish. Call Jake and get his number. Please, Jordan."

They'd driven all night to Las Vegas and would be playing early in the day. If he could make the stars align for him, he'd grab a plane to San Diego after the show and get his man.

But Jake wouldn't give up the digits unless he talked to Krish first, and he couldn't get hold of him. Friggin' honorable good friend.

Silas did his best at their performance and prayed it didn't suck, but he was having a difficult time getting to his center. He'd even called Brains before the show and asked him to talk him down. Brains sounded happier than a dude with a broken leg should sound.

After their set Silas went back to the bus to see if he could make flight arrangements that would get him either back tonight or to Salt Lake City by show time tomorrow. Jessica did her best, but there was no way they could make it work.

"I'm sorry, Silas, but maybe you can go Sunday night. We have Monday off. You can meet us in St. Louis on Wednesday."

Silas sighed. She was right. He didn't need to take the chance of missing a show. They were on thin ice with the Warped management as it was.

"Thanks for your help, Jessica." He gave her a hug and went to the back of the bus—not to drink, not to cry, but to think. Come up with a plan. Some way to make Krish see—

"Hey, Si?" Jessica called. Silas turned to see her looking down at her phone. "Theo needs you. He's over in the RV."

Silas frowned. "What is it?"

Jessica exhaled. "I don't know. He needs you! I'm guessing it's something in your purview, something above my pay grade."

Silas barked out a laugh. "There's nothing in my purview that's above your pay grade, Jessica."

"Whatever. Just get over there."

"*Fiiine.*" He tried to shake off his melancholy and put on a professional face. He'd done his best to hide it, but the longer he was away from Krish, and the more he ran through everything in his head, the more he began to doubt. Was he wrong? Had Krish not felt the same?

He climbed the steps of the RV and knocked before opening, because you never knew. No one answered, so he opened the door a crack. "Hello?"

Krish stood in the kitchenette, his hands shoved in his pockets. "Hi."

Silas approached him slowly. "It's you."

"I was hoping we could talk."

Silas wanted to hug him, but he didn't know what Krish came to say, so he figured he better wait until he spoke. And then the aroma hit him.

"You... you cooked?"

Somehow Krish had managed to whip up several delicious-looking Indian foods and had them in serving dishes on the small counter.

"I did. I wanted to cook for you. I'm sorry I left the way I did. I should have explained... I should have—"

"You cooked for me."

Krish laughed, but he wouldn't look Silas in the eye. "Yeah. It's apology food. I'm sorry—"

"I know what happened."

Krish's eyes went wide. "You do? How—"

"After you left, I went to see Chaz. He told me what they asked you to do."

Krish stood a little taller. "Then you know why I couldn't take the job."

Silas crossed his arms over his chest. "I know you refused to write an article on us."

"That's right."

"But Krish—"

"Silas, I'm not going to be close to you and write about how you're handling Gavin's death or about Brains's accident. I told you, I won't write about Hush anymore if we're going to be together."

"I understand, Krish. I... missed you."

Krish looked down at his feet and took a deep breath. "I missed you too. I'm sorry."

"Krish, I know I'm a cocky bastard and I can be an asshole, but I can't handle it if you walk away like that again." Silas wanted to give the guy a break, but he was still tender. He couldn't move forward unless they cleared up this issue.

"I won't—"

"I mean, I understand why you left but—"

"I'm staying—"

"But you can't leave a note, even if it says 'I love you,' and walk out the door. I can't.... Did you say you're staying?"

Krish grinned. "I'm staying."

Silas moved closer to him. "What do you mean, staying?" His heart skipped around in his chest like some bad jazz composition.

"I'm going to keep traveling with Warped, but I've broken off ties with *Alt-Scene*. I asked Chantal to set up a meeting with Kevin Lyman, and he asked me to write a full history of Warped Tour. He's going to do a series of interviews with me and give me complete access to his staff and everyone on tour. I'll get the archives as well. I just wanted to tell you, you know, that I'm going to be around. I'm staying on the tour."

Silas blinked.

Krish cleared his throat and shifted his weight. "I thought maybe we could, you know—"

"If you say 'start over again,' I'm going to kick your ass. Come here."

Krish and Silas embraced, and Silas held on for the longest, loving the feel of Krish back in his arms. Even though it had been less than a week, his heart had hurt from the loss.

"I won't be in your way. Chantal said I could stay on their bus still—"

"You're staying with me, and don't you even argue with me about it."

Krish chuckled and leaned back, his hands on Silas's face. "I didn't want to presume."

"Well presume, dammit. I love you, Krish. You didn't even let me tell you in San Francisco. I'm so sorry for what happened."

"I love you too. And thank you. I was really disappointed, but I decided that if they were going to ask me to do something that made me feel compromised, then it wasn't the right job for me. I plan to write this book, sell it, and freelance, or maybe find another magazine to work with. Or hell, if I can make this book work, maybe I'll write another one."

"You can do whatever you want. You're brilliant."

Silas pulled Krish down for a kiss, but he pulled back after a quick touch of their lips.

"You cooked for me."

Krish laughed. "I did. My mom sent me with the ingredients…. It was a little tricky packing this stuff, but I didn't know if I'd be able to get to a store or anything, and I wanted it to be perfect."

Silas stared at the food and shook his head. "This is perfect." He turned back to face Krish. "I can't believe you're here."

Krish barked out a laugh and sat on the couch. "I can't believe it either. My mom didn't really want me to be gone, especially after she saw my head, but then she said I had to come. I promised her I would bring you home to meet her and my father once the tour was over."

"Done," Silas said, moving toward the couch. He stopped before Krish and paused, his heart confused. He wanted to believe this was really happening, that he was going to have it all—the man and the dessert.

Krish reached for his hand and took it gently in his. "I understand if you need time. I'm so sorry I left, Silas. I promise I won't do that again."

Silas squeezed his fingers. It would be so easy to straddle Krish's lap and pull his head back for a delicious kiss, but if they were going to do this right, they needed to talk. He'd known they needed to learn more about each other after their first cuddle session together. If they had, perhaps a lot of the heartache that ensued could have been avoided. If he'd known how much Krish was dealing with, if he hadn't pushed so hard....

Silas brushed his thumb across Krish's lips. "I only need the time it takes to pick up where we left off."

Krish smiled and tugged on his hand.

"I'd like that."

Silas stepped back, dropped Krish's hand, and sat down at the table. "I believe you were about to serve me dinner?"

Krish laughed and stood. "You're right. I do need to feed you." He turned and went back to stir the skillet. "And now I can feed you every night."

Silas coughed. "Wow, and here I was trying to be all appropriate and shit, and you have to go being sexy as fuck."

"Hey, I'm trying to make sure you're well fed." Krish licked his fingers at one point, driving Silas mad with thoughts of Krish's talented tongue. He was so turned on watching Krish cook, he could barely string two words together, but he figured he should try.

"What are you feeding me?"

Krish smiled and continued testing the dishes. "I didn't know what you liked. This is biryani and paneer. I brought some naan too. It's store-bought. Sorry."

"I've never had a guy cook for me before. Just the band, and there are times when I'm truly only eating out of the necessity for food, because, for real, they can ruin anything, and one can only perform after food poisoning so many times before.... And I'm rambling."

Krish served the food onto a plate for Silas and they sat at the table.

"Aren't you going to eat?" Silas asked.

"I'm okay. I want to know if you like it."

"I'll love whatever you made, Krish. I'm.... Damn, I'm so glad you're here. Come here."

Silas leaned across the table and kissed Krish, and though he never wanted to stop, he didn't want his meal getting cold. He sat back down with a smile and dug in.

"Oh my God," he said fanning his mouth. "There's so much going on. I fucking love this. Like, I'm totally overwhelmed with awesome in my mouth."

"I know the feeling," Krish said, and Silas nearly choked on his food.

"You're extraordinary, you know that?"

Krish grinned and rested his chin on his fists. Silas normally would have been a little creeped out having someone watch him eat, but this was more like exploring a piece of art for the first time, and he couldn't fault Krish for wanting to experience it with him.

Someone pounded on the door, and Silas sat back. "Yeah, come in."

"Oh, thank God," Jessica said with a sigh of relief. "I was hoping I wouldn't... never mind. Silas, I'm sorry to tear you away, but Ryan really needs you."

He exchanged surprised looks with Krish.

"It's okay," Krish said. "I'll keep this warm for you."

Silas stood from the table and held out his hand. "Come with me."

"You sure?"

Silas squeezed his hand. "Absolutely. Don't be surprised if we're joined at the hip for at least a few days. I don't want you out of my sight. I'm still afraid this is a dream and you're not really here."

Krish shook his head. "Let me cover this up. Jessica? Did you want some? I made enough for everyone."

She smiled and asked, "Do I have to share?"

"Nah," Silas said. "Eat what you want first. Then maybe you can let the stray dogs in."

She hugged both of them and took a moment to whisper in Krish's ear before she let him go. He smiled down at her and followed Silas out of the RV.

"What did she say?" Silas asked as they jogged toward Ryan's bus.

"She thanked me for coming back. I was grateful Chantal put me in touch with her. I couldn't figure out how I was going to get back to you."

"Yeah. I'm still pissed you didn't even leave your number. We have a lot to discuss," Silas scolded but then winked at him.

"I'll take whatever punishment you deem necessary," Krish said as they approached the bus.

Silas brought him in for a quick kiss and then pressed their foreheads together. "You keep talking like that, you're really going to be in trouble."

"Bring it."

Silas leaned back and shook his head. He opened the bus door and called out, "This better be good, Ryan."

Ryan sat alone at the table on his bus. He didn't look up as Silas and Krish approached.

"What's up, man?" Silas asked. "You okay?"

Ryan took a swig from a bottle of water. He nodded to Krish and then stared at Silas.

"I had an idea, and I need you for it."

Ryan gestured for them to take a seat across the table from him.

"What's going on?"

Ryan blew out a breath and pressed the heels of his palms against his eyes as though he were in pain. "I've been having a rough couple of days. I found some old pictures." He pulled out two wrinkled photos from an old leather-bound journal and slid them across to Silas. One was of Ryan with Chester Bennington. The other was Ryan with Silas and Gavin. Silas took in a deep breath.

"I remember this one." He showed them to Krish and then placed them on the table.

"Yeah. This was before I went to jail. Gavin and I had been writing together, remember that?"

"Hell yeah, I remember that. I still wish that album would have been finished. You guys were making something great."

Ryan took another drink. "I miss him."

Silas felt that familiar ache in his chest. Krish reached over and squeezed his leg, which gave him the strength he needed.

"I miss him too."

Ryan nodded and put the pictures back in a leather journal that looked well-loved. "I talked to the guys…. Would you sing with me tonight? To close out the show? We're the last to go on. I was thinking we could do a song for them."

Silas patted his hand. "That sounds like a great idea. What do you have in mind?"

Chapter Twenty-Two

KRISH SAT in the corner of the booth as Silas and Ryan ran through a couple of songs and finally decided on "Angel's Son" from Sevendust. Ryan played an acoustic and sang lead with Silas adding harmony, and then they switched. Krish had never been so close to music being crafted like these two were doing. He was a big fan of Backdrop Silhouette and always thought Ryan was more of a genius than he was given credit for. Watching these two prepare really brought that to light. He wanted to write about it, and he would…. He needed to figure out how to write about his thoughts and feelings around Silas while maintaining some sort of integrity.

Backdrop Silhouette put on a scorching set, one of the best performances Krish had ever seen from the band. Ryan called Silas to come onstage to sing their tribute to Chris Cornell, Chester Bennington, and Gavin, and the crowd went absolutely fucking mental. It was one of the largest ones the festival had seen to date.

Before running onstage, Silas asked Krish to call and FaceTime Brains so he could hear the tribute. Krish took the opportunity to program his number into Silas's phone so at least that could never be an obstacle again. He found Brains's contact and hit the FaceTime button.

"Silas, what the—oh. Hi, Krish."

"Wow, um hey. Nice makeup. How are you feeling?"

Brains was made up like one of the members of KISS. He looked off-camera and got a silly grin on his face. "I'm in pain, but I'm pretty fucking awesome right now."

Krish laughed. "That's great, man."

"Thanks. Hey, Jessica told me what you did. Right on, man. I'm glad you're back."

Krish smiled at Brains's change in attitude. "Thank you. I'm glad too. Hey, Silas asked me to call you because he wanted you to see this."

Krish stood sidestage with an excellent view as Ryan pulled up a stool and hushed the audience.

"We're grateful to have our brothers, Hush, back on tour this year, but as we all know, there's a part of our hearts missing. It's also been a year since we lost Chris and Chester, and to be honest with you all, I'm struggling."

The crowd went silent, and Ryan took a minute to calm himself. Silas put his arm around him and said something quietly in his ear. Krish checked on Brains, and he was teared up on the screen.

"You okay?" Krish asked him.

Brains nodded and took a tissue from someone offscreen. Krish didn't want to make him uncomfortable, so he turned the phone back toward the stage. Ryan played the beginning of the song and sang the first verse. The crowd all held up lighters or phones and swayed along with the music.

Krish's eyes welled as Silas stepped forward and sang the lyrics in a heartfelt voice. It was emotional, passionate. He poured himself into the song, and the crowd screamed for him. He and Ryan harmonized so well together, Krish thought perhaps the two of them should pick up where Ryan and Gavin left off. Perhaps they could put out their own tribute, sort of like Temple of the Dog did all those years ago.

When the song was over, the crowd cheered for what felt like ages. Krish turned the phone back around and found Brains in the arms of Paul—who was also wearing KISS makeup—and he was crying.

"You okay?" Krish asked, having to shout into the phone to be heard over the crowd.

Brains wiped at his face, smearing his makeup, and Paul sat back offscreen.

"Thank you, Krish. That meant the world to me. Please tell Silas I love him and to call me tomorrow."

"I will. Take care of you."

Brains held up his hand in the devil horns and disconnected.

Krish laughed and stepped back to let the band offstage. Silas crashed into him and hugged him tight.

"You sounded like an angel," Krish said into his ear.

Silas pulled back and smiled, holding his fist to his heart. And then he was literally swept away.

Krish laughed as one of the guys from Backdrop Silhouette picked Silas up and carried him down the stairs behind the stage, where he was engulfed with hugs and high fives from members of all of the big bands at the festival. He was loved. Ryan got his hugs too, but it was obvious his demeanor was a bit intimidating to some.

So this is going to be my life. Watching Silas soar from the sidelines was definitely a gig he could get used to. Though they'd gotten off to a rocky start, he felt much more confident after Silas's words when he returned—*I only need the time it takes to pick up where we left off.*

Krish was ready to do just that.

"Krish!"

Krish turned around to find Jake running toward him, dressed in what appeared to be more of Jordan's clothes. Or perhaps the makeover stuck? He looked stunning.

"What—"

Jake hugged him tight and then stepped back. "Didn't you hear? I'm Hush's new merchandise associate. They called and asked me to come, but I had a meeting with my advisor to discuss my summer seminar project. I got permission to work remotely, so I'll be here."

They hugged again and talked excitedly about how wild the whole situation was. Krish thought it was a good opportunity for Jake. He'd always been so sheltered... with the exception of the limited amount of corruption Krish had bestowed upon him.

And it could be a great business opportunity for Jake, as well as solving a dilemma for the band.

"I'm so glad you're here."

Jake made eye contact with Burke Dickens as he walked by, and Jake looked away first.

"It's going to be one helluva summer." Jake rolled his eyes.

EVENTUALLY SILAS made his way back to him, and they shared a brief kiss.

"A bunch of folks want to get together tonight. You mind? I know we didn't have much time, but—"

"Not at all."

Silas smiled.

They joined the rest of Hush and the other bands and crew members backstage to share thoughts and memories about those no longer with them. More songs were dedicated to the fallen heroes. Drinks were passed around along with hugs. Someone lit a fire in a garbage can and busted out marshmallows and sticks. Some guys were even toasting hotdogs and other assorted sausages. Eventually it turned into insanity with partial nudity. Some of the crew put the fire out before the carousers started throwing flammable things into it.

Silas gathered up his band and took Krish by the hand to lead them back to the bus. He'd told Krish they all needed to have a meeting about Krish's joining the family, and Krish had been worried about crashing the party. But as soon as Silas told them he was writing the book and would be traveling with them, the guys gave their resounding stamp of approval.

"You guys take the back."

"I'll move my shit. You can have the extra bunk."

"Can he cook?"

The last was from Los, who, despite their near-cuddling session, was still obviously concerned about Silas's involvement with Krish. That concern was quickly put to rest.

"Dude. The skills this guy has…. He made me Indian food."

Los's eyes grew wide, and he put an arm around Krish. "I'm sold. When do you move in?"

It turned out it didn't take a music major or a genius like Brains to figure out the back-lounge bed situation. Jessica took one look at them and shook her head. She marched to the back of the bus and when she came out she was still shaking her head. "Sometimes I wonder how you guys ever got along without me."

Silas and Krish rushed back there, and somehow, Jessica had managed to turn part of the couches into a bed. It still wasn't huge, but it was better than before. Los pushed past them and flopped down on it.

"Awesome. There's room for all three of us."

Silas threw a pillow at Los, and he threw it back. That started a full-blown pillow fight. When Jordan pushed past him with a bag and an evil laugh, Krish ducked out before he got hit. He moved his duffel bag along to the bunk below Brains's, well, now Bowie's. Brains wouldn't be back for at least a couple more weeks. Krish hoped he was hanging in there. At least he had Paul. And his makeup, apparently. And when he returned, Bowie could move to Silas's bunk. Room for everyone.

"All right, all right. God, I can't take any more."

Los and Jordan came out from the back, shaking hands and laughing.

"Do I even want to know?"

They both giggled like Beavis and Butthead.

"Uh, see for yourself."

Krish moved to the back of the bus and found Silas covered in condoms. He burst out laughing and fell back against the wall.

"I mean, I'm excited to see you and everything, but don't you think this is a bit excessive?"

Silas tried picking them off of him and putting them in a pile, but the pile kept spilling everywhere until he gave up with a big sigh. "I think they robbed the poor condom guy. Either that, or a local Planned Parenthood."

Krish picked up some of the pillows off the floor and set them back on the bed. "That's all well and good, but you know, I don't fuck on tour, so…."

Silas barked out a laugh, but then his smile faded. "Wait. You're kidding, right?"

Krish worked at neatly folding a blanket and shrugged. "I've got rules. What can I say?" He had to turn his back on Silas to keep from losing it. "I guess these will have to—"

Silas grabbed him from behind and ran his hands up under Krish's shirt, scoring the skin of his chest with his fingernails. He lifted Krish's shirt over his head and pressed a kiss into his back.

"You're right," Silas said, licking his way up Krish's spine, making sure to tease with his piercing. "Rules are important."

Krish's knees buckled when Silas slid his hand under the waistband of his boxers and gripped his cock.

"Rules?" Krish said, quickly losing all coherent thought.

"Hmm. Rules. Like you will be naked in this bed every night—"

"God, Silas," he moaned, turning in his arms. "I missed you. I can't believe how much… how much I feel for you already."

Silas kissed him deeply while guiding him to sit on the bed.

"I know, babe. I feel it too."

Exactly twenty-nine minutes later, Silas and Krish heard the other guys come back onto the bus, and they chuckled.

"We're going to have to work on our stealth game. You were moaning so loud, they probably heard you outside."

Krish nibbled on Silas's shoulder. "Yeah, well you hit quite the high note yourself tonight."

"I can't help it, babe. When you do that thing—"

"I love doing that thing. And you and that piercing.…"

"Which one?" Silas ran his tongue along Krish's ear, and his whole body broke out in goose bumps.

"All of them."

They cuddled and kissed softly for a long time, enjoying the closeness and the fact that they didn't have any time limits. The road ahead would be paved with challenges, but for now they could enjoy the ride.

"I want you to write about us."

Krish pulled back. "What? But Silas—"

"It doesn't have to be the Guru. It can be 'when the rock star met the blogger,' or some shit like that. You're the one with the words. I like the idea of our story in your words, even if you never publish it."

"You do pretty well with the words yourself."

Silas kissed him, and his tongue lingered long enough to make Krish whimper.

"I love you," Silas whispered.

"I love you too. Get some rest."

Krish lay for a long time holding a sleeping Silas, once again astonished by how much Silas truly relaxed in his arms. As he let his eyes drift shut, images, thoughts, feelings from the past few days began to flow through his mind, and he began to see the words come together and how he would write them. His eyes shot open, his body suddenly very awake. He'd decided how to start his book, and he knew better than to let the opportunity pass.

He carefully extricated himself from Silas, who grumbled in his sleep and rolled over, exposing his back and bare ass. Krish smothered a laugh when he saw the teeth marks he'd left there. He pulled on his cargo shorts and his T-shirt, slid his bare feet into his Vans, and quietly crept out of the back lounge.

Los and Jordan were playing cards with Jake and Bowie at the table, and they frowned as he left.

"I need to…. Okay, I dictate my blog posts. I thought I should tell you in case you overhear and—"

"So you talk to yourself," Los said. "Big fucking deal. Your go, Jordan."

"I don't talk to myself. I write this way—"

"Blackjack, motherfuckers," Jordan shouted and stuck his tongue out. "Gimme the cookies."

Krish looked closely at the table and saw that they were playing with the pink-and-white circus animal cookies as money. *Unbelievable.*

"I'll be right back—"

"I'm taking this next one. I can feel it in my fabulous bones." Jake flicked his nonexistent long hair and dealt their next hands.

"Right. You haven't won yet, little brother."

Sure enough, Krish saw Jake didn't have any cookies in his pile.

"I've just been letting you two think you're winning."

Bowie chuckled and took a bite of one of the cookies.

"Uh, Jake? You suck at cards, remember?"

Jake turned and gave Krish an ugly look. "Who asked you? Thought you were going to go talk to yourself."

"I'm not... never mind."

"Hey, Krish?"

He turned around as he got to the door. "Yes?"

"You got a little something on your neck there," Los said, gazing intently at his cards.

Krish looked in the rearview mirror. "Holy shit."

Silas had left a massive hickey on his collarbone. Guess he wouldn't be wearing a tank top the next couple of days.

"And hey, bus is leaving in about fifteen minutes," Lester said from the driver's seat. The guy never said much, so Krish was startled by his presence.

He peered a little closer and noticed Lester was playing a word game on his iPad.

"Gerbil."

Lester frowned up at him.

"That's the word you're missing. I just finished that level a few days ago."

Lester grunted and then swiped his finger on the screen to fill in the word. "I'll be damned. Thank you. I've been staring at that all night."

"No problem. Be right back."

Outside the bus Krish took in a breath of fresh air and smiled. This was going to be his life for the next couple of months. He thought he was ready for the adventure when he arrived at the show in San Diego a week before, but he'd had no idea what one week would do to his life. Everything had changed, nothing was as he'd imagined, and he was perfectly happy. He had a new focus, new friends, a new purpose, and a new love.

He walked and talked, keeping an eye on the time. A few feet away from the bus, Krish ran across Ryan and his acoustic guitar. He was surrounded by a few young-looking boys and girls who'd obviously had a lot to drink. Ryan noticed him and waved him over.

"Hey," he said, offering his hand to shake. Krish took it and smiled.

"You guys sounded great," he said.

Ryan nodded, looking back toward the bus. "Glad you two worked out whatever the fuck you needed to work out."

Krish smiled. "Me too. I'll see you around."

Ryan waved as Krish turned around, but then called to him again.

"Yeah?" Krish asked.

Ryan lifted his chin and looked down at Krish's crotch. "You might want to close the barn door." He winked and went back to playing guitar.

Krish hurriedly zipped his fly and laughed. He obviously didn't have it all together, and that was okay. What mattered was that new focus, new purpose. He dictated a bare-bones outline for the book and started a list of everyone he wanted to talk to. He'd decided to go ahead and announce himself. Too many people knew who he was for him to remain anonymous, and frankly, he'd realized firsthand that anonymity could hurt people, and he never wanted to be in that position again.

"Well… here goes."

Four Months Later…

THE GURU'S Summer of Hush
Blog Post
October 13, 2018

The first day of the rest of your life sometimes hits you like a wall of death at a metal show. There's a scramble to get in position, a moment of breathless anticipation, and then you're assaulted by the force of a thousand bodies hurling themselves at each other in the blistering summer sun. Sometimes there are casualties in the wake of this metal experience, but often there is a moment of clarity upon survival.

When everything comes crashing down, it's time to reevaluate and determine what's most important.

This summer, as I stepped out of my comfort zone after three years of grief, sorrow, recovery, and determination, I found myself facing that figurative wall of death, and I did not make it out of the pit unscathed. I had my head stapled together, I walked away from the job I thought was my destiny, and I fell ridiculously in love with a wonderfully complex man. On a macro scale, I gained a new family and a new focus, along with the new direction my life was fated to take. On a micro scale, I learned all about the joys of living in close quarters on a bus, I met incredible people with fascinating stories to tell, and I watched a beloved metal band rise from the ashes and reclaim their place as the darlings of metalcore.

So what does all of this mean for the Guru?

Oh, well, the Guru is me, Krishnan Guruvayoor. Surprise. I've stood beside you at countless shows. I've spoken to you over teriyaki bowls or ice cream at one of the thirty-eight stops of Warped Tour this summer. And now, after writing as an anonymous blogger for six years, I stand before you as a fledgling author, out to tackle the first of many stories I have to tell. I will be starting with a full-length manuscript on the history of Warpedlandia, which my agent sold at auction this past week. From there, I plan to go deeper into our beloved music genre and tell the stories I've been assured I need to tell.

You see, once I came out as the Guru, people I'd admired for years began talking to me, and from those conversations I learned so much. There are endless stories of strength, hope, and love that I plan to share. I'm not exactly sure how, as of yet.... I'm not convinced that traditional journalism is the route I want to go. After the events that led to this post, I'm finding I much prefer telling my stories to you directly. The book will be my first attempt, and then we'll see.

The blog will still be around, however. I have to have someplace to rant and rave to you, and I've been informed that I should tell you my love story. I might. Then again, Silas can be incredibly insistent and stubborn, so he usually gets his way. What I can tell you is that the man who has swept me off my feet has also been incredibly patient, supportive, and loving as I faced many obstacles, and with him by my side, I have found my voice growing stronger with each word I write to you.

So, thank you, dear readers, for remaining loyal to the blog, for reaching out a hand during my chaotic summer, and for continuing to support the music that brings us all together. May our common language of rock 'n' roll, and its many subgenres, help us find our way during this dark time, and give us the hope we need to keep fighting the good fight.

With you, as always, the Guru....

Epilogue

The Guru
Blog Post
November 22, 2018
When the Rock Star Meets the Blogger's Parents

This is the continuing story of the gangly music-journalist-in-the-making and the rambunctious and ridiculously sexy rock 'n' roller who captured his heart.

Meeting the Parents
Once the final Warped Tour ended, Hush took only a brief time to rehearse before starting their world tour. The blogger returned to San Diego to work on subsequent drafts of his first book, so it was Thanksgiving before the rock star was able to finally meet the blogger's parents. The rock star was

nervous. He'd never done the whole parent-meeting part of a relationship and knew he had to make a great impression. He insisted on wearing the suit he bought when he and the blogger spent their first night alone together in San Francisco. He even brought flowers for the blogger's enchanting mother.

She answered the door and immediately gushed over how handsome he was and how beautiful the flowers were.

"But if you think I can be buttered up with beautiful flowers and a nice suit, you've got another thing coming, young man. This is my son we're talking about here, and it's going to take more than being all that and a bag of chips to win my approval."

Luckily for the rock star, the blogger's father was much more welcoming and engaged him in a discussion about travel, the health of his bandmate who spent most of the summer laid up with a broken leg, and that time he hung out with Ozzy.

"Hanging around with crazy people who bite the heads off of live animals is no place for my son to be. I hope you won't be bringing him around such nonsense."

The blogger tried to plead with his mother to be reasonable.

"The next thing you know, you'll be having your head stapled together—oh wait. You already have. What's next? A tattoo?"

Some things the blogger insisted on keeping from his mother, including the matching tattoos he and the rock star got, and the piercing....

"Mrs. Guruvayoor, I promise, your son—"

"You had better promise my son will not come home with any more injuries."

The injury and ensuing haircut would be brought up several more times in the evening. It wasn't until the rock star presented the blogger's mother with a gift he'd been holding on to that she was finally impressed.

"A very special friend of mine painted this from a photo of your son."

The rock star had commissioned a portrait of the blogger's brother, who passed a year before the rock star's bandmate. It seemed fitting that since the brother brought the blogger into the rock star's sphere of influence, that he do something to honor his memory, and what better way to win over the blogger's mother?

His mother was speechless, a state the blogger assured him was rare indeed.

"You have made my wife incredibly happy," the blogger's father assured the rock star. "You have given her a priceless gift she will always treasure."

"And you both have done the same for me. I love your son very much."

The blogger's father stared at him intently for several beats, and then a smile graced his lips.

"I'm glad to hear it."

The night ended after many stories of life on the road and what the future might hold for the rock star and the blogger. They said good night and retired to separate bedrooms after a quick kiss in the hallway.

"Well? You think they'll give me their blessing when I ask for your hand in marriage?"

The blogger nearly gave himself another head injury when he stumbled over his own feet.

"My hand.... What?"

"You know that's where this is headed. This time next year I'll be back asking them for their blessing."

The blogger felt as though he were on a moving sidewalk that had suddenly halted. His life flashed before his eyes, slowing down for the past five months of complete bliss they'd shared. He was grateful and didn't take for granted that this state of bliss could continue and that they lived in a place where two men could, indeed, marry and spend their lives together. The idea becoming reality was something very different altogether.

"This time next year, huh. Let's see what this year brings for us, and if you can somehow convince my parents that you're a worthy husband, they might just give you their blessing."

The rock star smirked. "I'm so ready."

Little did he know that tonight, the blogger's parents had gone easy on him. The blogger gave his beloved one last kiss and then retreated to his bedroom. "Get some sleep. You've got a lot of work to do, rock star."

The End.

Stay Tuned for more from the Summer of Hush…

KEEP READING FOR AN EXCERPT FROM

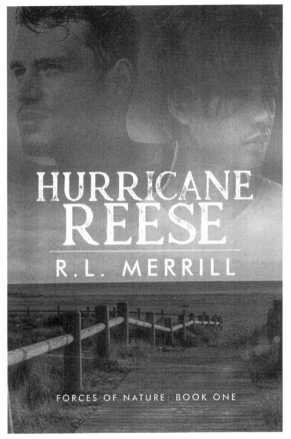

www.dreamspinnerpress.com

Forces of Nature: Book One

The life of Tony-winning musician Reese Matheson resembles a natural disaster, and caregiver Jude De La Torre is caught in the eye of the storm. But can the love of two opposites survive caring for an ornery octogenarian with wayward balls and a meddling family insistent upon tradition?

Fresh off the successful London run of his musical, the last thing Reese expects when he comes home is a house surrounded by paparazzi and his girlfriend throwing his stuff into the pool. All he wants to do is spend time with his beloved grandfather and musical mentor who suffers from Alzheimer's. Reese knows he doesn't have much time left before the elder Matheson forgets who he is. In classic "Hurricane Reese" form, he moves into the cottage by the sea and displaces Jude, the intriguing caregiver he hired two years before. When Grandpa proves too much for Reese to handle on his own, Jude comes to his rescue, taming Grandpa… and the Hurricane as well. Soon all Reese can think about is how to get Jude out of his scrubs and into his bed—permanently. Will Hurricane Reese destroy everything in his path, or will this odd couple learn to harmonize together?

www.dreamspinnerpress.com

Chapter One

"JADA, HONEY, can we please just—"
SPLASH!

Reese Matheson had been arguing with his girl and banging on the front door of his condo for twenty minutes, and it seemed she'd finally gone ahead with her threats.

"Shit."

Reese flew down the steps and around their unit to the pool in time to see his photo album plummet over the railing of their balcony and into the deep end to join his surfboard.

Reese focused on his family pictures, quickly sinking to the bottom. He climbed over the iron fence that surrounded the pool, dove in fully clothed, and swam frantically to collect his precious photos. As he surfaced he could practically see the fire in Jada's eyes as she hurled a stack of his songbooks over the rail.

"You love those books more than anything! Now you can swim with them."

On and on it went. She continued to clear the bookshelves of his irreplaceable music collection. He halfheartedly begged her to stop. She tossed them over into the pool. He rescued them. A crowd formed. Paparazzi snapped pictures…. Suddenly Reese knew exactly why this was happening.

The London photos.

"Jada, please. Can we—"

"We most certainly can*not*! We're through! You can pick up your shit and get out! You want to go traipsing around the world, having fun without me, hanging all over people? I'm too young to be sitting here cooped up!"

Reese snorted. The drama was too much. "Oh, please. You're older than me."

That did it. She squealed and disappeared from his sight only long enough to run back in and grab the pièce de résistance—his Tony.

"No, Jada. Please!"

The hunk of matter of which he was the most proud sailed effortlessly through the air. It landed in the water a foot out of Reese's long reach. He dove after the heavy statue and surfaced in time to see his ex-girlfriend's sorrow-filled gaze. She slammed the sliding door shut so hard that he was shocked the sound of breaking glass didn't echo through the complex.

"Señor Matheson. Oh, I'll help you."

The little old man who tended the grounds took the statue from Reese and held out a hand to help him out of the water. A pile of soggy books lay at his feet—books that chronicled his brief but unbelievably successful music career. He'd gone from jam-band singer, to songwriter for a pop princess, to her tour mate, to singing a pair of smash-hit singles, to landing a movie soundtrack, and finally, co-writing a Broadway musical with his longtime friend and collaborator, Toby Griffiths. It was that last endeavor that earned them the coveted award.

Reese should be celebrating the end of their London run, not rescuing his memories from a saltwater pool. But if he stopped to really think about it, all the warning signs of impending disaster were there—no cute selfie texts recently and complete radio silence over the past week. Apparently she'd been building up to a blowout for seven whole days, during which every television, tabloid, and internet service had plastered his face and that of the lead in his show, Ethan Bradley, all over the planet. He couldn't totally blame her. She was concerned with appearances, and appearing to be someone's beard didn't appeal to her, even if *she* knew it wasn't true.

Reese slowly gathered up his belongings and, with the help of Enrique, loaded them all into his Tesla Model X. He tried to give the man soggy money from his wallet to say thank you, but the sweet guy refused it.

So now what? The condo was leased in his name, and he'd been paying all of their bills for the last two years, but he didn't have it in him to fight anymore. He'd rushed home to drop off his stuff as soon as his flight landed and then planned to go directly to see his beloved grandfather, with or without Jada. Now he needed a new plan, one that involved dry clothes. He turned on the car and pointed it in the direction of the cottage he'd bought for Grandpa on the beach in the gorgeous Southern California town of Malibu. The little two-bedroom house had beach access and was perfect for Reese's passion for surfing. The thought of working off his frustrations by riding some choice waves appealed to him. The whole setup appealed to him.

That was it. Since Jada had made the decision for him, he would move in with Grandpa. He'd already taken an indefinite hiatus to spend time with the old man. Now he'd be right across the hall.

The catch was that the place had only two bedrooms, and the other room was currently occupied by the caregiver Reese had hired for Grandpa, Jude De La Torre. The old man had suffered a series of minor strokes and then was diagnosed with Alzheimer's just over two years prior. He was sure Jude would understand. Reese was determined to have quality time with his grandfather before he'd have to make some difficult decisions. No time like the present. His heart felt considerably lighter as he drove toward his next adventure.

Once upon a time... a teacher, tattoo collector, mom, and rock 'n' roll kinda gal opened up a doc and started purging her demons. R.L. MERRILL is still striving to find that perfect balance between real life and happily ever after, and she'll keep writing love stories until she does. Both self-published and traditionally published with Dreamspinner Press, Ro writes romance in contemporary, paranormal, and horror settings inspired by love, hope, and rock 'n' roll. Ro also loves connecting with other authors online, at conventions, and chapter meetings for the Romance Writers of America, of which she's been a member since 2014.

A sucker for underdogs, Ro has adopted a wide variety of pets including cats, dogs, rats, snakes, a chameleon, and some fish. Her love of horror is evident the moment you walk in her door and find yourself surrounded by decorative skulls and quirky artwork from around the world. You can find her lurking on social media where she loves connecting with readers, or else find her educating America's youth, being a mom taxi to two busy kids, in the tattoo chair trying desperately to get that back piece finished, or head-banging at a rock show near her home in the San Francisco Bay Area.

Connect with Ro:
Website: www.rlmerrillauthor.com
Twitter: @rlmerrillauthor
Facebook: www.facebook.com/rlmerrillauthor.com
Instagram: www.instagram.com/rlmerrillauthor
Stay Tuned for more Rock 'n' Romance.

TYPHOON TOBY

R.L. MERRILL

FORCES OF NATURE: BOOK TWO

Forces of Nature: Book Two

On the surface, Toby Griffiths appears to have it all—talent, money, a brilliant mind, and model good looks. With his best friend, Reese, he's built an empire as a singer/songwriter.

But beneath that glittering exterior, Toby suffers the lasting effects of abuse. To keep his tempestuous past where it belongs, he insists on anonymity with lovers—no names, no personal information. But a vacation fling in Bali changes all that, and he can't get his recent playmate out of his mind.

Therapist Spencer Hart left Bali with a bad case of pneumonia and a broken heart. Although he's recovering, he's shocked to find his secretive partner on TV, and he's determined to see him again. Spencer arranges to attend one of Toby's fundraising galas, and their reunion is tense.

Toby tries to stick to his rules… until a New Year's kiss with Spencer washes away the last of his resistance. But Toby is a man with secrets, and when the storm comes ashore, it could devastate not just his professional life but his fledgling love affair and his longtime partnership with his best friend.

Will Spencer stand by his side and help him weather the storm as Toby faces his worst fears?

www.dreamspinnerpress.com